Till We Meet Again...

Gladys Burchell

Till We Meet Again...

Published by The Conrad Press in the United Kingdom 2020

Tel: +44(0)1227 472 874
www.theconradpress.com
info@theconradpress.com

ISBN 978-1-913567-18-7

Typesetting and Cover Design by:
Charlotte Mouncey, www.bookstyle.co.uk

The Conrad Press logo was designed by Maria Priestley.

Printed and bound in Great Britain by Clays Ltd, Elcograf S.p.A.

To Ken

For decades we clung together enjoying the closeness of our bodies. The touch, the looks, the nearness of ourselves. How we enjoyed the feel of skin upon skin and the warmth that breathed between us.

Now I have to realise that has all gone, for now your skin is cold to my touch and your face is pale like marble.

I bend to kiss you again, this time on the forehead. It will be the last, for now I know you are at peace...

Inspired bt Rodin's statue, The Kiss.

Chapter 1

Gran blinked at the lorry that had drawn up outside next door. Two men in overalls jumped out from the front, also a man wearing glasses. He looked towards the house and beamed, 'OK chaps, we'd better get started otherwise it'll be raining before we're done.'

He looked around as if searching for something or someone, then muttered to himself, 'Damn! Now where have they got to? I thought she'd be here before us.'

Gran inched her body forward so she could hear better, careful to pull her overall down further, she didn't want her bloomers on show.

Voices were heard coming along the end of the road, and a woman and three young people seemed to be making for the empty house. Just then the man with the glasses turned and saw Gran sitting in the porch, and smiled as he indicated towards the noise from the group. Removing his cap in a polite way, he said, 'Good morning, love, I'm George and it looks as if my family are almost here... we're moving in next door. I'm pleased to meet you.'

He walked towards the gate and pointed to the group approaching them. 'Come on you lot.' Then he turned back to Gran, saying, 'This is Vera, my wife, and young Terry... then there's Phyl and Marjie.'

Vera looked very nervous and smiled giving a brief hello, The two young ones just giggled, while the elder girl, who looked about sixteen, gave a brief glance in Gran's direction, before setting her eyes on the men waiting by the lorry. The men eyed her up and down before passing a saucy comment between them, which Gran couldn't hear.

'Where have you lot been? Thought you'd be here before me,' said George. Then his wife tried to explain that they'd missed the earlier tram going up New North Road, and had to wait nearly half an hour for another one. 'Still, anyway we're here now.'

Gran nodded and smiled at each of them. 'Nice to see you... hope you get sorted out afore it rains.' She pushed the chair a bit further back and made out she was snoozing, but she was eager to see what was going in and out of the house.

Jane would be home soon and Gran wanted to be the one to let her know all the news first hand. She knew Jane would call it being 'nosey'. As if it was!

By the afternoon the lorry had gone, and all seemed quiet from next door. Jane did suggest that she took a tray of tea in to the new people and introduce herself, but then the girls came in from school, and knowing that Norm would be home early that day, she decided to give it a miss.

It was two days later, when she heard Vera out in the back garden trying to get to the washing line, that Janie was prompted to make her overtures. 'Hello, you must be Vera. How are you managing? If there's anything I can give you a hand with, please say.'

Vera smiled, and looked slightly embarrassed, 'No I'm OK... it's just that the copper took so long to get the water hot for the washing.'

Jane smiled back. 'I know what you mean... I hated having

to light the fire underneath our one, but now my Norm's got it fitted with gas to heat up. It's such a job having to light the fire under it each time you need hot water.'

'Oh you are lucky. I shall have to let George know… that is, if you don't mind. I don't want to be seen copying you.'

Janie laughed, 'Of course not, now when you've got a few minutes perhaps you'd like to come in and meet Gran and have a cup of tea with us. Getting all the wash done is tiring, so it'll make a break.'

'Please do,' she added, as she saw Vera mumbling to herself for an excuse. 'Alright then, thanks I will.'

Jane left her to it and carried on with her clearing up. She thought to herself that Vera seemed a nice enough person, a little on the nervous side, but then they were all new to each other.

It didn't take long for her and Gran to get to know Vera, who seemed very glad of the company, and when the children came home from school, they were chatting nineteen to the dozen as well. Jane's Helen seemed to get on well with Terry; they were both about the same age.

It was only Marjie who wasn't around very much, she'd apparently found herself a job at the local hairdressers/barbers up by the Angel, and was keen to learn the trade from the boss himself.

In no time at all the two families were well acquainted with each other. Jane was very easy going, and the two girls soon hit it off with Terry. Vera found it difficult to deal with Phyl, who always seemed to be in a mood. Gran said she shouldn't worry about it as the girl was at 'that age', whatever that meant. Being thirteen was neither child nor adult according to Gran, and she should know.

George was a likeable chap, prone to a lot of dyspepsia, for no reason whatsoever. But he did idolise his Marjie, who could do no wrong in his eyes. Only Gran could sense the difficulties between Phyl and the elder sister, and the way Vera was nervous about it, but she knew it wasn't up to her to say anything.

The days drifted into weeks, and the two families soon became the best of friends. It was only Norman and George who realised the situation of the imminent war just around the corner. They both feared that all their lives would soon be disrupted in a very hard way.

Chapter 2

A sudden noise from downstairs told Janie that Norm was home. She rushed into their bedroom and with a quick glance at her reflection in the dressing table mirror she smoothed her dress and ran downstairs.

Norm was slumped in the fireside chair listening to the wireless. His face looked very worried and deep lines of tiredness were etched around his eyes. He looked up as she walked in.

'I don't like the look of it Janie, there's a lot of trouble brewing and there's a lot that Mr Chamberlain ain't telling us.' He stopped talking and cocked his ear closer to the wireless set then shook his head slowly. 'Tut tut tut, it don't look too good... it really don't.' Jane walked over and turned the set off. As she turned to walk past, Norm caught hold of her and pulled her down onto his lap. Janie smiled with pleasure.

'Come here Janie... what are we gonna do if this lot develops into war? It's a good thing we have each other... you... me... the kids and ma... Oh Christ! War... do we need it?'

His face looked so thoughtful and lost. She leaned over and kissed him lightly on the forehead. 'Don't worry Norm... it may not come to anything.'

He looked at her, confused. 'You say that... all I ever hoped was that it wouldn't come to war... but it will Janie... I know it will. I'll be called up and I don't think I can bear to leave you all. Janie, I don't want to... '

Suddenly he pulled her down and kissed her hard on the

mouth. Eventually she had to pull herself away from him... trembling with emotion, every nerve in her body was vibrating. Norm had been so impulsive before, ever, but she had to confess that she liked it. Dear Norm... dear unadventurous Norm.

She rushed into the kitchen where she tried hard to compose herself while preparing his meal. As she pushed strips of bacon around in the frying pan her mind went back to what he had been saying about the war. Surely it wasn't that serious... it couldn't really happen. Or could it?

After he had eaten, they sat talking for quite a while, with Norm relating how the senior fire officer had information that had set them all thinking. 'You know the girls will have to go away somewhere safe, and I want you and Ma to go as well before anything happens.' She looked at him, her eyes widening. He really was being an old fusspot.

He stood up and placed his hands on her shoulders, looking deep into her eyes. 'It isn't as if anything has happened yet... but it can, and it will... it worries me sick.'

He drew away from her and walked out of the room. Without hesitation she followed him upstairs. As she entered their bedroom he was sitting on the side of the bed, his clothes dropping to the floor by his side. She went to him and placed her hand against his cheek. 'Norm, I love you dearly... I always will... no matter what comes.'

He pulled her down to him and in the shade of the curtained room they made love, there on the counterpane... so spontaneous, yet with so much feeling. He was so desperate to show his love for her, and she so eager to please. This was like nothing that had happened for years and years, when they were so inhibited by moral conventions. She was shy because it was daylight outside, also fearful that Gran might call out for her at any minute. But for a short time they loved each other as if there was no tomorrow to worry about.

Chapter 3

Vera patted a dry powder puff over her cheeks and with her little finger smoothed a dab of Tangee lipstick around her pale lips. She made all sorts of facial grimaces as she did so, and was thankful that she was on her own. If Marjie had been there, she would have taken the 'mickey' out of her right enough.

Vera had long since accepted the fact that she had no reign over her eldest daughter, and she more than once blamed George's sister Pearl for Marjie's strong wilfulness.

He was used to being told that 'she', meaning Marjie, was a throwback from his side of the family. '...from your sister Pearl... and we all know what a madam she is, don't we?'

Poor George had given up trying to understand the women in his family. He supposed Vera was right really... Marjie was headstrong. He smiled to himself. But then young Marjie was a very attractive girl in more ways than one.

As time went by, he got into the habit of taking himself off to work extra early to escape the continuous affray between the two women.

Each morning, Vera sighed with relief as the front door slammed, and Marjie took herself off to work. She could then relax, and go about her duties almost cheerfully, whilst mumbling under her breath, 'That girl will drive me to drink one of these days!'

Satisfying herself that she looked presentable, Vera grabbed her handbag and went out. As she glanced over at the other side she noticed that Gran wasn't in her usual place in the porch. That was strange, because in the hot weather Gran was like one of the fixtures and fittings, almost as good as a doorstop.

She closed her gate and thought no more about it, as she made off to the shops in Essex Road.

Looking at the beautiful selection of pianos in Venables, her eyes passed longingly over the shiny black pieces of furniture. Oh, she would give her right arm for one of those in her front room – that would be really something! Her gaze went from one baby grand to another as she gazed dreamily in the shop window. She was lost in a world of her own, until she caught the reflection of the public house on the opposite corner. It was mere curiosity that made her stare at the familiar figure coming out of the swing doors of the public bar. Vera smiled to herself. So that was where the old dear got to was it… and on her own too.

As Gran made her way back along the main road in the direction of the Express Dairy, Vera ducked inside the shop entrance out of sight. She couldn't contain herself. 'I wonder if her Janie knows where she gets to? Hmm…' she smiled to herself, smugly.

By the time she had crossed the junction and reached the front gate Gran was coming from the dairy carrying a quart bottle of milk in her hands. She looked up surprised as Vera approached her. She smiled at Vera, who was staring at her in an old fashioned manner.

'Hello Vera luv, just rushed out for some more milk for our Janie; she's making the kids a blancmange for tea. You can never have enough milk in the house can you?'

Innocently humming to herself, Gran shuffled past Vera as

she made her way through the open doorway and through to the kitchen where Jane was busy.

Vera shrugged off what she had seen – after all it was nothing to her! 'Hmph... milk be blowed... milk stout she means more likely!' The more she thought about it, the more she wondered if she ought to have a word in Jane's ear about the old girl. Drink could lead to all sorts of problems, although to be fair she had never seen the old lady worse for drink... ever.

Perhaps when Norman went off to the station that evening, she would pop in for a chat with Jane, she knew that Gran went up to her room early and listened to her wireless set. Perhaps Vera could enlighten Jane with all she had seen that day.

Vera did like to indulge in a good bit of gossip, especially when George wasn't around to contradict everything she said.

For two people with such contrasting natures, Jane and Vera got on surprisingly well. Jane was passive and easy going, channelling all her energies into the care and welfare of her family. And she knew without a doubt she had their love as well as respect. Vera was secretly a little envious of her contented nature. However, Jane suffered her own personal frustrations, but kept these solely to herself. To all and sundry she was a happy-go-lucky woman. Her personal sexual problems were her own affair!

Chapter 4

The bubble burst that early autumn day, when news of war came over the wireless for all to hear. Vera and Jane's lives were visibly shaken, and dormant emotions came rushing to the surface.

Norm had just come home from the fire station and was in the act of washing himself at the butler sink. His body stopped mid motion, the towel dropping to the floor, as he rushed over to the set and turned it up louder, his face white and drawn as the message came across. Britain was at war with Germany!

'I guessed it, I bloody well knew it ... my Lord, Janie, we've got to get the kids away soon... we must... Oh Christ! We should have seen to it weeks ago.'

Jane had never seen him so upset, so keyed up, so worried. So it had come after all, they were at WAR .

Gran came downstairs on hearing the hubbub. Coming into the living room as the message was relayed, she went to Norm's side and gripped his arm, her face, for once, looking tense. Then she sank down in the fireside chair opposite him, her mind in turmoil, emotions unsteady. She had seen her Albert go in the First World War, like a lamb to the slaughter with all the other virile young men of his time. He came home just a shell, and remained so until the day he died. So she really could understand her Norm and his deep concern for all of them.

Suddenly she came to her senses and with an air of authority thumped her fists down on the table as if she was giving an order. 'Now Janie, best put the kettle on and make us a cuppa, and don't you go getting all steamed up Norm. Everyone's in the same boat, so it's best to wait and see what happens next.'

Norman looked at her, exasperated. Oh Ma! It was alright for her to talk... she hadn't got a young family to think of. And what about his Janie! He was such a pillar of strength through most of life's upsets, but this had got him worried for ages, and now the lid had been taken off the works he didn't know what to do for the best.

It was George who first heard that the schools were to be evacuating all the children, with many of their mothers too. It seemed an awful wrench to split families apart like this, taking the young lives away, and hiding them far away in the country.

Vera had to agree with him for once, and admit he was right of course. In late August it was made public that all the children in London were to be evacuated to a safer place. When the time arrived they went by train, charabanc, and even by car. The young were leaving the nest.

Jane and Vera stood solemnly watching, side by side, in the school playground, as the lines of children were led out to the waiting coaches, hustled and urged by worried teachers and helpers.

Neither woman spoke, they felt as if they were witnessing a mass exodus of the country's future being taken to the far-reaching edges of the countryside.

Gran insisted on coming, even a little late. She stood next to Jane and hugged them all in turn, as they ran to board their respective coaches.

The sad army of women watched their families leave, all smiling bravely, trying not to cry although their hearts were breaking. It wouldn't do to break down in front of the children.

Vera hoped they would all go to the same place. She did so worry about her Phyl, her being on the brink of womanhood too.

The coaches slowly turned away from the school and made for Kings Cross. Jane could see Helen and Cassie sitting near the front, and she ran along the side of the vehicle shouting her goodbyes to them. She was near to breaking down as she fought back the flow of tears that burned her eyes.

Several moments later a smaller coach appeared. The women could see the mournful faces of Phyl and Terry as they sat peering through a window. It passed within inches of Vera as she stood with Gran and Jane, all waving like mad, as if their very lives depended on it. The children seemed bewildered by the whole turn out, each of them wearing their brown identity label, each of them to start a new life in a strange land, in 'the country'.

Chapter 5

Jane had to admit it had been a very trying morning. And like all other life and death situations in the family, it always revolved around endless cups of tea.

Gran had been very quiet, and now busied herself in the scullery finding things to do, while the two younger women sat around the table making small talk, neither of them making reference to what they really felt in their hearts.

If Gran had been truthful, she would have preferred a drop of milk stout instead of tea. That would have been more to her liking. Still she had her time to come. She would pop over the 'Three Crowns' later on while Jane was busy doing Norm's supper. Her eyes sparkled at the thought of it as she poured out three large cups of strong tea.

Vera stayed with Jane for a while longer, she felt much calmer now. The only worry she had now was hoping that her George wasn't called up for the army too soon!

However much she moaned about him, he was a good man to her and the kids, especially Marjie. Vera had always felt that he needed to be 'got at' in order to push himself along in the world, and in her heart she knew that she had really grown to love him deeply as the years went by. She took the cup from Gran and sipped the scalding liquid more than gratefully.

'Surely,' she argued with Jane... 'If they call the men up for fighting, they would take the single men first? If it comes to it, they might not even want George with all his upsets and his ulcer?'

Gran looked sideways and said nothing. She was thinking to herself that George's digestive system was an art form of its own! He was a nervous man, all too chatty, and that just an exterior for people he didn't know. Oh yes, he really did live on his nerves did that one.

After Vera left, Jane continued to stare into space. She was very near to tears thinking about her two girls. She bit her lip to try and stop herself from trembling then sighed deeply, 'Oh God, please look after them. Please...'

Now alone, she sank her face into her cupped hands, and released all the pent up tears that had waited there for so long.

Norman found her still sitting and gazing into space on his return home from the station. He looked at her apprehensively wondering how she would take the news he had to tell her.

Jane looked up at him with reddened eyes. She felt calmer now, and able to talk about things. Norman planted a kiss on her cheek and without hesitation went over to the sideboard. From its depths he withdrew a small bottle of brandy and two glasses. The spirit was kept in its place of reverence for those 'life or death' occasions only. Norm decided this was one of them.

He poured a little into each of the small glasses and handed one to Jane. 'Here you are gel, this'll help.'

Taking it from him she gulped it down in one go, half choking as she handed him back the glass. He smiled in an enquiring fashion. 'That's better, isn't it? You looked like you needed something strong, something to put the wind back into your sails.'

She smiled up at him and laid her head against his body while he stroked her head gently. She felt so much better now.

He grabbed at the glasses and returned them to the place on the sideboard, next to the brandy. The thought went through his mind whether to have another one or not. He glanced over to Janie for an answer.

Neither of them heard Gran shuffle in from the hall or saw the delighted look that swept over her face as she spied the brandy bottle in Norm's hand. She sidled over and stood behind him for several moments, looking at him while he daydreamed. He jumped as she spoke suddenly... 'Are we having a drop of something then Norm? Ooh! I'm just in time then...'

Norman's look of concern gave way to a broad smile as he looked down at Gran, who was positively grinning from ear to ear.

Jane came to her senses too, and smiled. Then they both looked at Gran, who was drooling for a tot of brandy. 'Ooh you are crafty Gran,' thought Jane to herself, '...trust the old'n not to miss a treat.'

Norm continued to tease her for a while longer, pretending that the brandy bottle was now empty, then he looked at her sorrowful face and throwing his head back, he roared with laughter, while the two women giggled at him for being such a tease.

'You cheeky bugger Norm, you know I like a drop... just for medicinal purposes? In fact, I should have an extra one to make up for lost time!'

'Yes Gran, you shall have an extra tot. You deserve it for making us feel our old selves again. Yes, I suppose there's no sense in worrying about this war. It's here and we have got to get on with it. As long as we keep our sense of humour, we'll be alright won't we?'

Jane took the news of Norman's transfer to the docks better than he'd anticipated. When first informed about the impending change, which would occur in about a month's time, he found himself more worried about telling Jane, than the actual move itself.

They both knew that the docks would hardly be a safe area, but Norm told himself it was better than being called up. At least he could get home regularly, and keep an eye on his family.

Poor old George next door was the one he felt sorry for. It was only a question of time before his call-up would arrive, and if SHE thought that a bout of dyspepsia was going to keep him at home, instead of fighting with the others, then she had better think on! Mates of his were already being called up, some with much worse conditions than George. Some of his mates were actually signing themselves up to 'King and country'. Full of spirit they all were – decent fellers with smashing wives and families.

He felt too much responsibility for Janie and the family to do a thing like that. After all, Gran was getting on, with most likely not many years ahead of her now. That in itself made him feel duty bound to do all he could for his own kith and kin.

At least the girls were out of the firing line, in the wilds of the country… at least that's what Cassie described it as on the card that arrived a few days after they had all left.

Janie read and re-read the card over and over again. She must have known every word of it by heart, before finally putting it on the mantelpiece behind a small shell ornament, telling herself she would go and visit them as soon as possible. It was this thought in mind that kept her cheerful through the coming weeks of uncertainty.

She really needn't have worried, for the big onslaught never materialised. There were no raids, no bombing.... in fact, nothing any different from peacetime, so gradually all the children returned slightly bewildered, as if it had been one big new game.

Meanwhile, Gran decided that unless she could lay her hands on a few bottles of port, then Christmas was going to be a bit on the dry side! The two families had agreed to have a party together in Janie's, and share all that was going. After all, there really would be something special to celebrate now that the kids were all back home again. Not forgetting that Norm was due to start at the docks in the New Year!

Cassie and Helen had returned to No 34 just three weeks after going away. After the mass exodus to the country, many London children soon tired of the novelty, and wrote home pleading to come back again. Jane, agreeing that as there had been no bombings nor the likelihood that there would be, wrote to say that they could come home as soon as possible.

Vera was more than happy to do the same. Her Terry and Phyl were far from content, and she knew from the very angry letter from the woman who looked after them both, that Terry had started wetting his bed again. It made Vera very upset to think of them all being miles away when there was no need... what with the added worry of George, making himself so depressed at the thought of his call-up coming at any day.

Although Vera hated to admit it, young Marjie was the one bright spark at home. Marjie knew she would be losing her Alec any day to fight for his country, so she enjoyed each day to the full... and each night. The pair of them were company for Vera most evenings.

Young Alec was making the most of the time he had left, then just a few days away from Christmas Eve he had to go!

Marjie went to see him off, and came back from the station more than a bit depressed. She had to leave her job in the New Year, together with a lot of her friends. A few were going into the services, but Marjie opted for the munitions factory, which she thought was the better of two worlds.

So Christmas came and went. The two families made it a joyous union and spent it under the doting eye of Gran and the ever-looming call-up of George.

Vera thought it was strange that they had only been living in Islington for a matter of months and yet it seemed as if they had known each other all their lives. She had been more than happy of late, even with George. She assumed it must be the war that had drawn them all together so tightly.

After the huge Christmas meal, which the two women had prepared together, Cassie and Phyl did the mountains of washing up. Norman poured everyone a drink and they settled down for a singsong in the parlour. Gran dozed in her chair by the fire in between songs and jokes, while the youngest two sat hugging their knees in front of the fire and enjoying all the grown up conversation.

Norman was a bit of a comedian, and now with his tongue loosened by too many drinks, he came out with a few ripe jokes he should have reserved for the boys at the station only. Janie flushed to the roots of her hair when she heard him stringing them out!

'Norman, Norm ... watch your mouth in front of the kids,' she whispered loudly across to him, as she cast a furtive look in the direction of Cassie and Helen. At this Norman laughed even more. Peals of laughter shook through him as he grabbed the side of the table to stop himself from toppling over. 'Don't worry about the kids, they told me them in the first place!' He fell about laughing all the more. 'Saucy little buggers ... that's what they get up to in the country!'

Vera and Janie had to laugh with him, and at him. Only Gran missed out as she sat snoring by the fire, her mouth drooping open and a yard of dribble hanging out. And for once George didn't complain about his digestion either. They all had to agree... it was a smashing Christmas. Smashing!

Chapter 6

It was one of the coldest February mornings Vera could remember. She didn't know what had woken her so early, but once awake she pushed George in the middle of the back. 'Get up George, time for work love.'

She heard him grunt and then with a swoop he was padding across the ice cold lino to the dressing table, where he picked up his watch and tried to make out the time by the small lamp. He cursed, throwing the watch back on the table again and mumbling to Vera who tried to cover her ears. 'It's only half past six... what do you want me to get up so early for Vera?'

Vera stirred and turned over. She had heard a noise and assumed it was time to get up. 'Sorry George, go back to sleep for an hour... don't know what made me think it was that early.'

Vera lay half dozing, when again she heard a noise, coming from downstairs. Someone was up already! So she wasn't dreaming or going mad.

Gingerly she slipped her dressing gown and slippers on, pushed open the door and made her way down the stairs. She was right, there was a noise coming from the kitchen - a chink of warm light showed across the two bottom stairs.

Vera tiptoed quietly down and pushed the door open wide. 'Good heavens,' she said to the young woman sitting by the table, her head resting in her cupped hand, and a glass of water nearby. 'What are you up so early for Marjie?'

Marjie looked up as Vera walked in, her face ashen and

drawn, 'Hello Mum, I couldn't sleep, I've been so sick and bad… think that shepherd's pie was a bit off last night.' Vera looked at Marjie intently. She was so washed out – perhaps she has a chill on her, she thought to herself.

'Tell you what… have a cup of tea and an Aspro, then go back to bed for an hour. Bet you'll be alright then Marjie.'

Marjie raised her head and nodded, although the thought of taking anything by mouth made her feel even more nauseous.

Vera busied herself making the tea, and they both went back upstairs. Vera placed a cup next to George in case he was still awake, then before returning to bed she went over and looked out of the curtained window into the cold black world outside. She shivered as the icy temperature struck home to her. Hope she isn't going down with her bronchitis, Vera thought to herself… she always did have chest problems!

By the time the sun was up and the household awake again, Marjie looked and felt a lot better. She rushed out of the house just as the two younger ones left to go to school. 'Ta ta Mum,' echoed though the house as the street door swung to.

The postman came just as George was leaving to go to work. He only had two letters in his hand, which George took from him. The two men looked at each other in a strange way, each one knowing the other's thoughts.

George stepped back inside the hall, closing the door quietly. One of the letters was addressed to Marjie. The writing was very familiar and George knew at once it was from Alec. He placed it on the hall table for her to see the minute she came in. The other envelope he treated more cautiously. It was addressed to George B. Baxter, looked very official, and bore a government stamp of authority in the corner.

George felt his very insides churning. 'Oh Christ... this is it. Oh Vera!' He stood immobilised for several seconds, not knowing what to do, but knowing he had to do something. He was looking at his reflection in the hall mirror, trying to find words to tell Vera the news, when she came down the stairs to see where he was. His expression told her all she needed to know.

George's call up was for the following Monday morning. It was decided by both George and Norman to take the two wives and Gran to 'The Spaniards' for a last drink before the big off! It was not a happy celebration, but Norm thought a drink with a few friends might be better than moping around indoors.

Gran kept the conversation going with a few of her own yarns of bygone days, and after several 'port and lemons' her stories were most enlightening to say the least. Even Janie started to look at her sideways at some of the things she was revealing. Quite a gay old thing in her youth was Gran!

They all left the pub at the end of the evening, still trying hard to make light of the situation... George, with Vera on his arm, Norm supporting Gran and Janie. They all said their goodbyes before going into their houses. Norm shook George's hand and wished him luck, while Vera looked as if she was about to fetch her supper up.

The doors slammed and the two families retreated until the morning.

A light shone under Marjie's bedroom, and Vera called out to her. A muffled answer and the dowsing of the light meant that Marjie was now going to sleep. 'Good night Luvvy,' said George.

Vera was undressed and in bed by the time George came quietly up. He was unnaturally subdued, and Vera guessed how he was feeling without asking. He sat on the side of the bed and took her hand, 'You know Vera, for all our ups and downs, we get on pretty well don't we? I'm gonna miss you… oh Jesus, I'm going to miss you all.'

Sitting there in his striped pyjamas he looked so lost and vulnerable. Vera smiled at him, put her arms around him and hugged him to her, whereupon he buried himself in her and let out a deep sob.

Next morning he was up and ready for when his family came downstairs. He bade his goodbyes – then he was gone!

Chapter 7

It was only when Gran, after pushing her way to the counter of the saloon bar of The Three Crowns, turned to see about her, that she noticed young Marjie hovering in the doorway of the four-ale bar.

She seemed to be looking for someone and clung onto the door as her eyes skimmed over the heads of the regulars. Gran tried to catch her eye. What on earth was a young girl like Marjie doing here on a Saturday dinnertime? As Gran tried to attract her attention, Marjie suddenly saw her there by the counter, and a look of relief swept over her. Her face had looked very pale and worried, but when she saw Gran she relaxed and beckoned for Gran to come outside.

Gran made her way over to the door and half dragged Marjie back to where she had left her precious port and lemon. Clutching it in her fist she asked Marjie what she'd like to drink.

'Nothing Gran, nothing really... I wanted to see you and I guessed you would be in here.'

Gran gulped down the crimson liquid and stared at Marjie's face, waiting for an explanation. Marjie fiddled with her purse and blew her nose several times over, while Gran looked at her... waiting.

'What's up gel? You don't look too happy... you ain't heard bad news or something?' Gran leaned across and took Marjie's hand. 'Come on Marjie, you know you can tell me. What's the trouble gel?'

For all her usual flamboyance, Marjie, never normally at a loss for words, hesitated before starting to tell Gran that she was in a spot of bother. Not knowing who else to tell, she thought Gran would be the best one to help her out.

'Course gel, get us a couple of drinks in first though, and then tell me all your troubles.' Gran felt in her purse and passed over half a crown. Marjie declined the drink and said she would rather talk about it at home. She knew Vera was out for the morning... that's why she had come to find Gran to ask for her help.

Gran could see how upset Marjie was, so she downed the rest of her drink, grabbed the girl's arm, and they both left in haste.

Marjie led the way into the small sitting room, Gran shuffling close on her heels, and sinking with a sigh into the first easy chair that she clapped sight on. Marjie stood at the side of the table, her fingers nervously pulling at the curls under her ears.

Gran gave an exasperated sigh, 'Oh do sit down Marjie, you're making me feel nervous. What's up with you? Come on, out with it – I ain't got all bleeding day.'

'Gran... how do you get rid of a baby?'

She was prepared for Marjie to surprise her in some way or another, but her words made Gran speechless for a moment, then she gave a deep sigh. 'So that's what it's all about, I see. Hmph, I suppose you and that boyfriend of yours have been up to some tricks, without being too careful. What made you do it you silly girl? You knew he was going in the army before long.'

She frowned as she drummed her fingers on the table, while Marjie just paced backwards and forwards biting her fingernails.

'It was because he was going away that we did it... I didn't know this would happen.' Marjie choked back a sob, almost on the verge of tears, and she looked across at Gran with a pleading look in her eyes.

'Happen, happen? Of course it happens gel. You don't know much about life and men do you?' said Gran in exasperation.

Gran looked her up and down and sighed. In spite of her saucy ways and her looks, she was quite green for a girl of her age. 'What does your Ma say about it? I suppose you have told her haven't you?' Marjie shook her head dumbly. 'I couldn't tell Ma... she'd go mad. That's why I came to you. I thought you might know of something that I could take... some sort of medicine or something.' Then she stood directly in front of Gran and implored, 'You must have done it before Gran? You must know what I can do?'

It was here that Gran interrupted her in a very raised voice. 'If you think that she won't go mad at what you've done or intend doing, then you must be simple minded gel! Alright... I'll do my best to help you young Marjie, but not without your Ma knowing all about it first.' So saying, Gran fell heavily back into her chair again, pulling her hairnet straight around the side of her ears.

By now Marjie had started to cry, and that didn't help Gran's thinking what to do for the best. She needed time to sort things out, but they must tell Vera for a start. Then, if she was willing to agree, Gran knew that Lulu would come up with some good advice, she was a clever girl that Lulu.

With a smile Gran told her that they must tell her Ma first and foremost, 'Then I will go and see my friend who might be able to help out. It would be best if we left things til tomorrow night... give your ma a chance to get over the shock of it.'

'How far gone are you gel?' Gran asked as an afterthought.

Marjie counted under her breath and mumbled, '… five weeks.'

'Well that's alright then, I'll see what can be done.'

Marjie leaned across and gave her a big hug, 'Thanks Gran, thanks a lot. I knew that I could rely on you.'

As Gran made it to the door, Marjie turned round and thanked her again, smiling as she did so. 'You're a sport Gran, thanks ever so much for helping me out like this.'

'A sport am I? A ninny more like it,' she mumbled to herself, angry because now she had also been allotted the job of telling Vera.

It wasn't long before Vera came tapping along the front path. Gran, who had been gazing out through the front room lace curtains, saw her as she stopped to get her door key out. Quick as a flash she banged hard on the window and beckoned Vera to come in.

Vera was more than mystified and thought at first that the old dear had been taken ill, it was blatantly obvious that Gran had something she wanted to get off her chest. She followed Gran into the kitchen, who then looked across at Vera, trying to sum up the right way to go about it while Vera sat tutting, obviously edging to leave.

Vera spoke first. 'What is it Gran? Is there any trouble… can I help you in any way?'

Gran cleared her throat. 'Trouble's the word, Vera, but it's not me who's in it. It's your Marjie – she's been a naughty girl… she's in the pudd'n club and she wants to get rid of it.'

Vera stared at Gran, her mouth open, her eyes blinking, as if what she had been told hadn't sunk in.

When she did come too, she moistened her mouth and gulped, 'You're telling me that my Marjie is having a baby... but she can't be, she can't ... why didn't she come and tell me? I'm her mother!'

'Sure you are, but the girl's scared. Any old road... the point is she wants to get shot of it!'

Vera's mind was spinning around. Of course, when she thought about it, all the tell-tale signs were there – all those sickly turnouts, and now it wouldn't be long before it began to show. What would the neighbours think of them? Oh, it was all too much.

Rubbing her hands across her temples, Vera sighed deeply. She felt the blood rush to her face... Oh the embarrassment of it all.

'Oh Gran what are we going to do?' she implored to the old lady.

Gran gave a sigh. 'Don't worry, I've got an idea. Leave it with me gel and I'll sort summat out.'

Vera let herself out, and scurried off to confront young Marjie, while Gran got on with the job of contacting her friend, who she knew she could rely on to help them all out. She would go and see Lulu, her old mate from Hoxton, she was only a tram ride away.

Gran was as good as her word, for the following evening after tea, she left Janie doing the ironing, and on the pretence of seeing Vera about some knitting she was doing for the Red Cross, Gran dashed out. Janie gave a sigh and carried on with what she was doing.

Vera was sitting listening to the wireless, and Marjie had just washed her hair when Gran pushed open the door and called through, 'It's only me Vera, alright?'

On seeing Gran Vera beamed with relief. 'Come in Gran … come over to the fire where it's nice and warm. I'll tell Marjie you're here.' She went into the hall and yelled down to the scullery, where Marjie was kneeling in front of the oven drying her hair.

Vera had been worried and apprehensive ever since she had been told the news. She knew Gran had offered to help, but the more she thought about it the more she worried. 'It will be alright Gran won't it?' she asked anxiously.

Gran gave a sigh. 'Now, do you want my help, or don't ya?'

Vera and Marjie both nodded. Gran smiled again, and delving into the small bag she carried everywhere with her, took out a couple of small packets.

When Gran leaned forward and gave Marjie the brown packet, Vera panicked and held onto Gran's wrist before the girl could take it from her. 'Gran… you do think it's going to be safe don't you, there won't be any complications will there?'

Gran tutted in annoyance then turned to face the worried Vera. 'Look my love, what Lulu uses is as safe as houses. It's been used for more accidents, by more women, than my Norm has had hot dinners. And Lulu should know if it works… she's accident prone, and she's alright.'

'Now gel,' Gran turned to Marjie and held out the packet again. Leaning forward she spoke softly to her… 'You have a hot bath, as hot as you can stand it, with these crystals in the water. After that you have a glass of hot port and take these with it.' Smiling reassuringly, she held out the second packet, an envelope containing six white tablets. 'Now, that's all you do… nature will do the rest, we hope!'

Marjie smiled shakily and looked from Gran to her mother. 'You see, I told you Gran would know what to do. I knew you would help me out... thanks Gran, thanks!'

'Don't thank me yet, nothing's happened, but I would make a start as soon as possible if I was you. Take her out to get the bath ready Vera. Now I must get back to our Janie – she won't take too kindly to what we're doing, so keep Mum about it, alright?'

As she reached the door, she turned to Vera... 'I'll see you tomorrow Vera about the five bob I had to give Lulu. OK?'

She made her way back home again, leaving the two women to sort themselves out. Janie was writing a letter to the two girls, and looked up as Gran entered.

'You've been gone a long time Gran, do you want to put a note in this for Cassie?' She held the paper out to Gran who was more than willing to oblige. At least while she was letter writing she wouldn't get pestered with questions about Vera.

I'm not saying anything, thought Gran to herself ...best let Vera tell her about it when it's all over and done with. Gran knew what Janie's ideas were about babies and suchlike – you couldn't convince her it was right to do away with it. No, Janie wouldn't agree to something like that in a million years, not her. No, she had more morals than sense at times!

Later on that evening, Gran thought she heard shouting coming from next door. She rushed to the wall and leaned against it, listening, wondering how it was all going... but there was no more noise of any sort, so she assumed that everything was underway.

Vera helped Marjie fill the bath in the scullery, then while the girl prepared herself for the steaming soak, Vera took herself into the living room, leaving the door ajar.

'Yell out if you want me for anything Marjie... ANYTHING mind!'

She was all on edge, what would her George have done if he'd been at home? It didn't bear thinking about. She was worried sick for both of them. Even a week late was enough to send Vera round the bend, gulping down as many 'Carter's little liver pills' as she dared. Mind you, it was true... they were worth a guinea a box! What a thing, though, to happen to Marjie, and that Alec... and them not even near getting married yet. Stupid girl! Why, oh why did this have to happen! Still, this would be the first and last time... until they tied the knot at any rate. Vera defiantly pulled in her chin as she thought about it.

After what seemed an eternity, the door opened and Marjie appeared draped in a towel, looking very hot and exhausted. She placed the tablets on the table and asked Vera to pour her a glass of port.

Rushing into the scullery, Vera put the kettle on, after which she poured a generous measure of port before topping it up with hot water. Marjie drank it down and swallowed the tablets, although in her agitated state she dropped one in the fireplace, where it fell into the hot ashes. She looked up at her mother, not knowing what she should do. Vera poked it to the back of the fireplace... 'It surely can't make any difference, not that one?'

For a long time afterwards Vera sat with her and waited. She kept looking and wondering what, and when, things would start to get moving. Marjie stood up and walked about, then looked out the window, and walked around again.

Vera suddenly exploded, 'For Christ's sake Marjie, don't keep pacing about the room, you... ' She never finished for Marjie gave her one long look and then stormed out of the room. Vera heard her stomping all the way upstairs to her bedroom, then the door slammed loudly.

Vera jumped up and ran after her, 'Marjie, Marjieeeee...' she called desperately up the staircase. But it was obvious Marjie had gone to bed.

Chapter 8

The next morning a very soulful-looking Marjie came down as Vera was making up the fire. Vera looked up at her eagerly, wanting to know if anything had started.

Marjie avoided her gaze and walked over to the teapot where she poured herself a huge cup of tea. Bringing it over to the table she sat down and sighed deeply, while Vera searched the girl's face for some comment or sign of relief.

After stirring her tea with slow deliberation, Marjie finally spoke. 'It looks like I'm stuck with it! You can tell Gran that her Lulu's lost her magic touch.'

Vera rushed to her side. 'Are you sure Marjie? Perhaps it's too early to know yet? Oh dear, I didn't want this to happen… What are we going to say to your father. And as for Alec… well, he's got to marry you now, you know that don't you … he's got to! Just shows how you can't trust people … I always thought he was a nice boy too. He's good to his mum… just goes to show! What are people going to say? Oh, the shame of it!'

Before she could say any more, Marjie stopped her abruptly. Turning to Vera, she screamed at her like a banshee, giving vent to all her own pent up feelings.

'I don't give a monkey's what people are going to say. I'm fed up! I've half scalded myself, I've been as sick as a dog half the night, I've had no sleep at all, and all you're worried about is what 'people' will have to say. Aren't you worried about me at all Mum? …and this kid I'm carrying? Your grandchild!'

Vera was shattered. She put her arms around Marjie's shoulders and the two of them clung together and shed more than a few tears.

So, what was to be was to be. Alec must be notified as soon as possible, and the two of them must get wed.

Marjie dragged herself back to bed and stayed there for the day, sleeping and dreaming fitfully.

Vera called in at the factory to say that Marjie had been taken ill during the night with a bilious attack. The story did sound a bit feeble and far from convincing the way Vera put it, but it got her the day off, and that's what mattered most to Vera.

The next thing was to tell George the news, and also Alec. She hoped Marjie would tell him that it he had to apply for urgent emergency leave to come home, so they could be married.

Vera worked it out quickly in her head, they'd be lucky if they could be married within the next month or six weeks, after that it would begin to be obvious. Mustn't think about it too much, thought Vera to herself, as she felt the heat rising in her face. Old memories reared again in her mind as she remembered walking to the altar, all those years ago, carrying a twelve-week old Marjie in her womb.

Chapter 9

Gran had spent the last hour propping up the front gate, enjoying the spring sunshine and having a natter to all who dared to speak to her as they rushed on their way. The trouble was, once Gran got started on something, it was the devil's own job to get away from her again. Still, she told herself she was relaxing... and that it must be good for her. The last few weeks had been bedlam, she had been fetching and carrying for all and sundry, what with young Marjie having a rushed wedding. When Alec managed to get a 48-hour leave, Vera had asked her desperately to do her best and get a few extras for the wedding.

It was well known that Gran had a few friends who could come up with almost anything you liked to ask for, at a price! The trouble was tracking them down. The war was disrupting all the known addresses that she had... now it was all done by word of mouth, in the private bar over a couple of milk stouts. As long as Gran had her contacts she could be sure to work a few deals under the counter.

So, on the last Saturday in March 1940, young Marjie became Alec's wife. George, who was stationed in Oxfordshire, managed to get home for the weekend, and stood quite proudly next to his daughter in Islington registry office. Then, after the short and simple service, the happy crowd went back to Vera's for a bit of a celebration. After a few port and lemons Vera started to shed tears, and confided in Gran that she had always dreamed of a proper wedding for Marjie, with a church and a white satin dress, and everything. It was all she had hoped for all her life, not this!

When the photographer finished taking all his shots, Vera started worrying all over again, hoping that Marjie didn't 'show' when the pictures were passed around all their friends and neighbours. Perhaps they'd guessed already, the way the whole affair had been rushed along like it was. The mere thought of it made Vera feel quite ill, and she had been thinking about it for weeks now.

The big day came and went all too quickly, Vera thought unhappily to herself. Alec had returned to his unit, leaving a tearful but happy bride and mother-to- be; George had returned to his camp, and all that remained was for Vera to see Phyl packed off back to the foster farm where she now worked for her keep.

Phyl was the next one she had to worry about - a strange girl, tall for her age, hard to understand, and very prone to moods. She hardly ever spoke to any of them, her or George, and she seemed to have an inbuilt resentment to Marjie. Vera had no idea why.

Gran had given Vera some scented soaps and bath salts for her birthday. Vera had put them away in a drawer thinking they were too nice for everyday use. When she saw Phyl packing her few things in the attache case, Vera retrieved them from the back of the dressing table drawer and held them out to Phyl. 'Here Phyl, you take these … go on love, I shan't use them.'

Phyl glared back at her and carried on with her packing, leaving Vera standing awkwardly still holding them out. 'What's up Phyl? I'm only giving you a little present, come on, here you are.' She smiled as she tried to catch Phyl's attention again.

The girl turned around sulkily, 'You don't have to bribe me Mum, I'm not a kid any more … you don't have to give me toffee bars like you do our Terry.'

Vera, taken aback, felt the heat rush to her face. 'Phyl, I don't want to bribe you. I just thought it would be nice for you to have something special. You're a big girl now... a young woman almost.'

'That's right Mum, I'm a BIG girl now!' Phyllis angrily turned and slammed the lid down on her case. Walking over and dragging her coat off the back of the door, she slipped her arms into it, her face expressionless. 'I'm ready to go Mum, if you are.' She stood looking at Vera, almost insolently.

Vera was speechless. She darted back into her own bedroom, returning after a minute or two with her navy coat and hat on. She bent to take Phyl's case from her, but the girl turned and strutted off downstairs, Vera following quickly behind her.

At the station they had only about ten minutes before the train went. After making sure Phyl had her ticket, and a book to read, Vera stood awkwardly gazing up at the timetable, at the other people, in fact anywhere, except at her daughter.

The announcement blared out and a small crowd made towards platform 7. 'This is it,' said Vera cheerfully, running behind Phyl until she found a carriage she wanted. Without hesitation the girl pulled open the carriage door and leapt in. She threw her case on the seat nearest the window and turned to face her mother. 'Ta ta then, I'll write sometime soon.'

Vera was near to tears in bewilderment, and so puzzled as to why Phyl was so angry. She didn't want her to go back like this, all upset.

'Phyl...' she smiled in an embarrassed way. 'Phyl... step down a minute please.' The girl tutted in annoyance, her face flushed, insisting that the whistle would be going soon. Her

'Just for a second,' pleaded Vera, looking each way along the platform to see if she could see the station master.

Phyllis stepped down again very gingerly. 'Well what do you want?'

Vera didn't want anything, except to fold her arms around her daughter and give her a warm hug to send her on her way. She stood looking at Phyl nervously, then the whistle rang out and doors started slamming. It was too late. Phyl jumped back in the carriage, pulling the door behind her. Vera caught the girl's arm, giving it a resolute squeeze, 'Look after yourself Phyl. Write to us soon... Ta ta love... '

It felt so inadequate; Vera could have cried with the hurt that she felt. As the steam cleared, the train had gone!

As she walked back along the now empty platform, Vera made up her mind to do so much more for Phyl, take more interest for a start off. She would go and visit her as soon as possible. After all, those foster people had said more than once that she could go and visit Phyl whenever she liked. Yes, she would make the effort for the girl's sake. She also knew it would act as a salve for her own conscience.

It had never occurred to Vera before, that Phyl might object to being sent away from her home and friends. Even if there was a war on, there had been little bombing and disruption so far. Perhaps the girl thought she had been conned into it with all the rest when it came down to evacuation.

Vera had thought, like everybody else, that it was all for the best, but now she was having a few doubts.

42

She never had understood politics, but now with her family falling apart at the seams, she felt cheated by it all.

With young Terry being taken into the wilds of Hertfordshire, and George having to go into the army, with his digestive problems too, Vera felt lonely and more than sorry for herself. It was now just her and Marjie and the coming baby! It was so daft having a baby with a war on too. In fact, war was daft... stupid and daft!

All the way home her thoughts were in turmoil. She knew that her attention must focus on Marjie in her delicate state, but at the same time she must try to fathom out where she had gone wrong with young Phyl.

In spite of Vera's hard looking exterior, she was quite vulnerable and helpless underneath it all. It was a good thing she had a seat on the bus to herself as she journeyed back from Kings Cross. At least no-one saw the forlorn woman with the wet cheeks as she sat alone immersed in her own thoughts, her mind still drifting back to the sad parting on Platform 7.

Chapter 10

During the summer months, Marjie positively bloomed with good health. She had now settled down to her grass widow state, and wrote long and loving letters to her Alec. He did manage to come home for a weekend at the end of the summer, but he had a notion they were being set up to go abroad when he returned. Marjie cooed and fussed over him, as if it was he who was carrying, not her.

They took a picnic and went over to Hampstead Heath, like two young lovebirds, holding hands and smiling at each other. He was so obviously proud of his married status. And she so pleased to have her soldier husband back again. Vera went into the garden on Sunday afternoon, in the pretence of tidying up the weeds. It was Alec's last few hours before catching the seven o'clock train. They had both gone upstairs to Marjie's room as Vera washed up the dinner things. She knew they wanted to be on their own, and felt awkward in their company anyway.

As she pottered around she couldn't help but notice the curtains were now drawn in the back bedroom. She felt herself flush as she suspected what they were up to. Marjie's voice came across low and urgent, 'Oh Alec, oh... Alec.' Vera could hear the thumping from where she stood at the back door, the squeaking of the mattress seemed to be blotting out all other sounds. The rhythmic noise went on, until Marjie let out a final shuddering sigh, 'Oh Alec love, oh... oh!'

Vera dropped a flowerpot and bent to scoop up the earth

that had gone everywhere. She was humming loudly to herself, trying to distract her mind and thoughts from what was happening upstairs in the house. Then after what seemed an eternity the curtains swished back and Alec stuck his head out of the window. Vera could see him from her crouching position at the end of the flowerbed, and looked up, feigning surprise. 'I've just about finished out here… had a good nap? I'll put the kettle on and make us a cup of tea.' She bent her head low again in case he saw her blushing. Oh well, he was going soon!

In the weeks that followed, Vera toyed with the idea of letting Phyl come home again for a brief spell before the winter set in. After all there were no raids or anything. In fact the perishing great Anderson shelter that stood in next door's garden was the only constant reminder that there was a war on. It had been put there for the benefit of the two families. At least that's what they had been told, when the men from the council had come down one day in late summer and dug the garden up. After the first heavy downpour, it had filled up, and smelt stagnant. Not one of the four women felt any desire to go and camp out in it, should the need arise.

However with the coming of the autumn mists, the bombing and the air raids appeared as if overnight… in fact, more prolific than anyone had ever anticipated. The 'bog', as Gran named it, would come into its own it seemed.

During September London started having a bout of air raids which went on for days and days. The two families converged in the garden shelter, and spent many bewildered hours, wondering what exactly was going on 'up there'.

Gran moaned about the dampness, and young Marjie kept getting cramp. The local wardens had warned them what to expect, and there were posters everywhere telling them to keep off the streets when the siren went, and to make for the shelters quickly. It was a lifestyle that they all found very hard to get used to.

Spasmodically Vera would hear from George. When she did she always breathed a sigh of relief that he was alright. She kept in touch with the other two as much as possible, content that Terry was loving it on the farm, but annoyed that Phyl still resented it all.

Vera tried to blot it all from her mind, she had her work cut out with Marjie and the air raids. Then as if in answer to her prayers, Phyl wrote with the news that she was going to work on the land, helping the land girls. She sounded quite happy and contented with her new vocation – she would even get a small payment for her efforts. Vera read the letter through twice, and at long last cast all thoughts of Phyl being homesick from her mind.

Gran thought it was a good thing too, as Vera showed her the letter while chatting in the shelter. 'All that fresh air, it must toughen you up, get you fit and strong... lovely.'

They spent hours musing over these problems while sitting in the shelter waiting for the all-clear. Gran put the world to rights over and over again, but then she did have a soft spot for, 'That nice Anthony Eden' … such a well-turned out man, so 'andsome.' Gran cooed.

Janie looked across at Gran as she sat huddled on the bench seat. Gran always set such store by appearances. She had a nephew who was an absolute horror to his wife. Gave her a belting every Saturday when he came home from the pub, why she put up with it no one knew. But Gran would never hear a bad word against him, just because he was so good looking. Jane never interfered and kept him at arm's length when she had to. She felt quite relieved for his poor wife when he got himself called up in the Navy, on the destroyers.

The hours spent in the shelter brought them all closer together, in more than one sense. Problems were shared, secrets told, and mountains of knitting were produced.

Norm was the only one they could cling onto now, his work at the docks was tiring, the hours long. Nobody stuck to shifts any more, when you were there and a raid started you stayed until you dropped. Norman was a bit of a pessimist, he tried to organise his own, and everybody else's family; urging them to follow the code and get to safety. Gran tutted and got most upset when he was home and the sirens went. He would shunt her out of the house and down that shelter before she could argue. 'Come on Gran, it's all for the best.'

'Norm's right you know.' Jane tried to act as peacemaker, but even she knew he was getting neurotic about things.

Janie hummed softly to herself as she prepared Norm's supper, he always took a couple of sandwiches to nibble on between 'shouts'. Seems it tided him over when he missed so many meals because of raids.

As he entered the scullery carrying two buckets of coal, she offered him the sandwiches, wrapped in greaseproof paper.

Norm set the heavy buckets down and washed his hands under the tap. 'Well Janie, I want you and Gran to get down that shelter the very second that siren goes. To tell the truth I don't like it gel... I've got a feeling we're in for a bad night.'

Finishing wiping his hands, he took the package from her, his face worried and concerned. Janie smiled to herself as she watched him get dressed to go to the fire station. He was an old fusspot, without a doubt.

Norman glanced in the small mirror that hung over the sink and fixed a small piece of paper on the cut on his chin to stop it from bleeding onto his clean collar. When he was quite satisfied with his appearance he turned and gave Janie a peck on the cheek, picked up his supper, and went through to the front room, where Gran was busy darning socks by the window.

She looked up and smiled in that lopsided fashion of hers. 'Ta ta Norm, we'll be alright... don't you worry. Ta ta.'

She carried on with her darning in deep concentration. Norman turned to Janie and gave her a chuck under the chin. 'See you love, take care. And look after Gran won't you.'

'Of course I will Norm, go on with you.' He turned to plant a moist kiss on her cheek. He looked so strange thought Janie, so concerned, that she put her arms around his neck and pulled him to her. 'You take care too Norm, for my sake.' She kissed him hard and firm, he trembled slightly as he moved away. 'God bless.' Then he was gone from sight.

Janie felt odd and churned up inside. He was a strange man, she let him take the responsibility for everything all these years, and he never made a fuss.

As usual, once the light faded and darkness fell, so the air-raid sirens started. Janie knew what she had to do and urged Gran to get to her feet and follow her to the shelter. She could hear Vera next door banging on the wall to let her know that they were going down. 'Come on Gran... come on,' she yelled in exasperation as the old dear made no attempt to put her shoes on. Gran sat in the middle of the scullery, legs apart, her feet soaking in the zinc bath. On her face was a look of complete joy as the soapy water bubbled around her legs. 'You go on Janie, I'll come down a bit later, when I've soaked me corns.'

'Oh no Gran, you heard the way Norman carried on before he went. He would never forgive me for leaving you here. I know it's rotten, but we must all look after each other. Oh come on, please!'

Dragging the old lady to her feet, Vera rammed the slippers on over the wetness. Pushing the bath of grey water to one side, she pulled Gran along after her as she dived through the back door. Gran was muttering all the way, '…just a soak for ten minutes more, then I could have got me corn plasters on.'

'Yes, yes I know Gran, I know, but we must get down to the shelter. Come on love, come on...'

Janie found the opening of the shelter and pushed Gran forward, 'Mind the step.' They both climbed down to where Vera and Marjie were already sitting. Marjie was huddled under a blanket, looking very frightened.

'Can't do that baby any good, all this bleeding hassle.' Gran looked across at Marjie and gave a wry smile. 'Don't care what anyone says, this dampness can't be good for us. Like a bleeding tomb it is – if anything fell over the opening, how would we all get out?'

Marjie looked white faced in the flickering candlelight; and wrapped her arms around her huge belly in a protective fashion. 'Shut up Gran, you're a great one for cheering people up.'

Silence fell, and luckily for them the raid was short and sweet. When the all- clear went they cheered. But not everyone was as lucky.

Chapter 11

During that air raid the docks were set alight, and Norman and his mates were among the first to arrive on the scene. It was an inferno; the entire sky was lit with an orange glow. As the appliances neared the site, Norm looked out, almost speechless. Then, through the half-light, he heard his orders coming through... 'For Christ's sake men, get in there and get moving.'

Norman was not the only one staring open mouthed at the spectacle. His mate was a young Scot, nicknamed Jock by the men. He was a likeable lad – never shirked, made a fuss or moaned about a thing. He kept at Norm's side as they ran forward, struggling under the weight of the hose.

They had been on the job for almost an hour and a half, sweating and choking, but it was all getting out of hand. Incendiaries were dropping like fireworks all around them. Above the men's shouts the flames roared on. It seemed hopeless – they were fighting a losing battle with this one alright.

More explosions, more heat. Norm hadn't seen Jock for a while and presumed he must be round the other side. There was so much black smoke – the whole of the docks seemed to be alight. Norm sweated and choked, his lungs filling with the acrid smoke. As he looked up, he saw Jock, high up on a load of packaging. He seemed to be trying to unhitch a load of smouldering canvas, the load moving about as Jock pitched himself precariously on the tiny ledge. He must be mad, thought Norm. That lot could flare up at any moment… we'll never get it clear. He shouted at Jock to get back and let it go. He couldn't save the packaging, but Jock could get himself really burnt.

Norm dragged the hose to where Jock was, and leaving the hose to the other three firemen, he ran forward waving both arms frantically like a lunatic, shouting for Jock to come down. The lad, sweating and smoke-blackened, ignored him… he almost had the packaging untied and pushed free. Norm stared incredulously as another incendiary flashed, and he watched in horror as everything exploded… with Jock in the centre of it, like a living core. He stared as the body swelled with the heat, burning viciously, the limbs distended like swollen sausages, till the skin eventually split and broke away in segments.

Norman stared, in shock, before lowering his sweating face into the palms of his hands. A moment later, he staggered several yards, yelling and shouting, not making any sense, before retching his very heart up.

He would never forget what he had seen, never. 'This bloody war!' He shouted and ranted until it was out of his system. Then with grim defiance, he carried on with the job, all the while muttering every obscenity he knew, his mates turning a blind eye, and a deaf ear, to the behaviour of their normally subservient friend.

Almost thirty hours later Norm made his weary way home. Janie noticed immediately how quiet he was, and told herself that sleep was what he needed more than anything.

It was quite normal for Jane not to see Norm for several days at a stretch. When they were on long calls, he would snatch what rest he could at the fire station. It was at these times Janie worried the most.

Since the end of the summer, they had to endure almost non-stop bombing and night raids, and the fires at the docks had been long and arduous.

Wearied by all of this, Norm became more introverted and depressed than Janie had ever known, in all the years they had been married. When she did get to see him face to face, he was a strained and tired individual. All his old humour and bravado seemed to have gone.

Jane stared at his tired face as he slumped in the armchair. She went to him and gently stroked his head. 'What is it Norm?' She knelt at the side of the chair, holding his hand between her own. 'Can you talk about it? It might help you know, if you get it off your chest.'

Raising his eyes to look at her, Norm mumbled something.

'Did you say something Norm… what is it, Norm?' He continued to look at her with a blank stare, his mouth trying to form the words. Moistening his lips, he tried again… 'I don't understand it gel, why do we have wars? It does such damage, and such a waste of life.'

Smoothing his hair across his forehead, Janie kissed him gently. Norm had always worried about them all so much; she knew that. But what could any of them do to change things? She crooned to him like she would a sick child, stroking his hand with her own. 'Don't let it get you down Norm. The war must be over soon… it can't go on forever, can it?'

It was all such a worry, what with Norm, the girls, and Gran. They all seemed to be pulling her in different directions. Gran had the hump if she couldn't get to the 'Three Crowns' as often as she would have liked. The girls were worrying to come home to London again. It was only Norm that she felt she could cling to for support, for keeping her sane. Oh God, this rotten war! When would it all come to an end!

All around them the bombing had left its mark. Shops were smashed to the ground, and nearly all had their windows blown out. Some shops still standing had notices scrawled out, saying 'Business as usual', in an act of defiance.

Jane thought they were lucky having their own shelter. Some of her friends had to use the 'Underground'. She'd seen them some mornings on her way to work, all bleary eyed as they staggered out of the entrances, clutching their bundles of bedding and other personal belongings.

It had been very quiet when Jane was detailed for work at the munitions factory early in the year, but then the air-raids started and she constantly worried about leaving Gran on her own, although Vera was next door. Once, when they had a really bad raid during the day, she had raced home from the factory after the all-clear, on tenterhooks, to see if Gran was alright and the home still standing.

Some days, it was difficult to pick your way through the rubble and debris from homes smashed to the ground... they'd been standing in the morning, and were now no more! Jane often thought that so far, they could consider themselves very lucky. Of course both houses had lost several windows, and the blast from a landmine had shattered the dividing wall beside the coal bunker. But this was nothing compared to some of their friends and neighbours, who had lost everything and been made homeless.

Jane confided to Vera one Monday morning as she hung the washing out on the line. 'I must be getting old Vera, I'm so tired I could sleep for a month of Sundays.'

Vera, who had been trying to salvage a scuttle of coal from the heap of coal dust, had to agree with her. 'We never get a night's unbroken sleep now do we? Even when there're no air raids I can hear my Marjie mooching about half the night. Says she has cramp, poor kid. I'll be glad when this lots over and done with. She went to the hospital on Thursday and they wanted to keep her in!'

Jane took the peg from her mouth, 'So it's as near as that then, be a blessing when it's all over Vera.'

'Near, I'll say it's near! According to Marjie it's three weeks overdue.' Rubbing her stiff back, Vera straightened up, satisfied that she had enough coal to build a fire. 'That will have to do. Christ knows what we'll burn if the coalman doesn't come soon!' She set off with the coal bucket... 'Anyway, come in later with Gran ... save you lighting your fire tonight.'

Sighing deeply, Janie finished hanging out the washing. Fat chance she had of getting it dry, the October mists and damp fog would ruin that little lot. Wiping her hands on her apron, she hurried indoors – she had to race off to do her shift in a moment.

The place felt chilly and dank. Her poor home seemed to be falling apart around her, in spite of all her cleaning and mending. After a snatched meal and a precious cup of tea, she went off to the factory to do her six hours.

'Yours, till we meet again... till the end of...' Jane sang out to the melody on the wireless, harmonizing with the crooner, as she scrubbed the scullery floor. She had almost finished and was lost in the words of the love song, when her dream was shattered by the drone of the siren blaring out.

'Oh Jesus, here we go again… what a thankless job I've got.'

She opened the back door and threw the soapy water into the back yard. At all costs she must get Gran organised. It was becoming more of a problem than ever lately, getting Gran down into the shelter.

'Gran, Gran… as quickly as you can, come on…' Jane called up the stairs, hoping that Gran wasn't going to be difficult. Jane had her emergency bag for the shelter just inside the larder door. It hung there with the gas masks and old coats. She grabbed the bag and checked that everything was in order - rent books, identity cards, knitting, a photo of Norm, and a small bottle of gin… for medicinal reasons. It was a good thing Gran never looked in the bag otherwise the gin would have been long gone. She was a tartar when it came to a drop of 'tiddly'!

Slippers in her hand, Gran came down from the bedroom, moaning about her bunions. 'Oh Gran, I thought you'd be ready. Come on dear, come on.'

'That bleeding shelter is playing old Harry with my screws, Jane… I don't want to go out in all that dampness tonight.'

Janie grabbed hold of Gran, almost bundling her out of the door, as the first crash of the evening echoed in the distance.

'Come on, you know what Norm says,' pleaded Jane. 'That one sounded close… it could be us next.'

Gran tutted to herself… 'I know what Norm says, but he's not me. That shelter is damp and full of insects. I'm telling you Janie, I'm not going down there again after this. If I'm going to die, then it's gonna be in my own bed, and that's that!'

'Yes alright Gran, alright.' As Jane propelled the old lady along, she continued, 'We none of us like going in there, but at least it's safe.'

In the shelter, Vera sat next to a white faced Marjie. Janie and Gran almost fell through the opening to get into the Anderson, where Gran struggled to her seat in the corner and sat down heavily, moaning all the time at Janie. Eventually, after Gran regained her breath she started chatting to Vera, even though the noise above them was almost deafening.

A shrill scream cut through the air, and the four of them held their breath and looked up, waiting for the explosion. But before it came, Marjie let out another scream and slumped forward holding her arms protectively around her belly. There was a series of crashes and as Marjie lurched forward, two of the candles were knocked over as well. In the half-light, panic set in as Vera realised what was happening.

'Oh my God Gran, I think it's starting.' The three women looked at Marjie then back at each other, while Marjie screwed up her face in another contortion of pain. Vera jumped up and sat by her side rubbing her back til the spasm had passed. Terrified, she looked across at Gran, 'It's the baby... what are we going to do... she can't have it down here.'

Jane looked worried too, and hoped that the air raid would abate soon. Of course, it would be hours before Marjie gave birth, but Vera was panicking and shouting more than anybody. Only Gran stayed cool, she needed no second bidding. 'Have your waters broke?' She demanded of the frightened girl. 'My what...?' puffed Marjie.

'Oh never mind,' said Gran as she dragged herself up and out of the shelter, telling the others to follow her. Vera helped Marjie, and the trio made their way indoors. Gran instructed Vera to phone the hospital, from the call-box just outside the pub. At the same time Janie put the kettle on and made tea for them. Fortunately the all-clear went as the kettle boiled.

In no time at all Marjie was taken off to hospital, with Vera in a near state of collapse. Jane watched the ambulance pull away from next door, Gran at her elbow, peering down the street checking what was happening.

Jane felt dreadfully tired – it had been quite a long day, what with one thing and another. Still Marjie would be alright once she got to the hospital. Praying there would be no more air raids that night, she glanced up at the dark skies, and really wondered if she would ever get Gran to go down the shelter again, after tonight.

Gran noted that it was still early enough to have a night-cap. She donned her hat and coat, and still wearing her carpet slippers, shuffled off down the hall. Without looking back, she called out to Janie, 'I'm just going to the corner to have one drink, Janie. I shan't be long, Ta ta...'

The door slammed and Janie settled down to write to the girls. She didn't mind being on her own now, she'd got acclimatized to it over the last few years. There must be hundreds and hundreds of wives, all sitting by the wireless, writing to their loved ones, like she was.

Drawing the blackout curtains, Janie poked at the small fire. She was almost dozing while the music played softly, but woke with a start when there was a shout and banging on the back door. An excited Vera came rushing in, her face aglow. 'Oh Janie... it's a girl, a little girl!'

Janie leapt up from her chair and flung her arms around her, such good news. She fired question after question at poor Vera. 'When was it born... who is she like... what does she weigh?' So much chatter, that neither of them heard Gran let herself in.

They turned to see her grinning in the half-light of the hallway, clutching an armful of bottles. Her eyes were alight and merry as she fell through the door and placed the bottles on the table.

'Gran, whatever have you been up to?' Janie cried.

'Ha, wouldn't you like to know. I just knew it wouldn't be any good coming home empty handed, tonight of all nights. So I managed to lift some milk stout and a drop of port – just to wet the baby's head with.'

'Good for you Gran,' shouted Janie as she ran to fetch three tumblers from the sideboard. Gran poured them each a liberal drink. 'Now,' she beamed, '… cheers, cheers to young?' Here they both looked across at Vera to fill them in on the name of the newcomer. Vera blushed, as the two women looked to her in anticipation, holding their glasses high. 'Well Vera, what's the baby's name then?' Gran gasped, eager to get supping.

'Cynthia, Cynthia Ann,' Vera murmured, blushing even more.

'Christ almighty!' mumbled Gran to herself. 'What a moniker!' They all raised their glasses and looked to Gran… 'Here's to Cyn… to the baby,' she corrected herself. 'CHEERS!'

Cor! She could never bring herself to use a fancy name like that, never!

Chapter 12

During the following spring, much to the delight and excitement of Marjie, her Alec managed to get home twice. He had a 24 and a 36-hour pass, all within a month of each other. After many postponements, he knew that on his next return, he was to be in on a big job – and they all knew that it would be overseas.

Marjie was all excited when he first breezed in late one Thursday evening. Vera was at the Carlton picture house, with a friend. The baby was sound asleep in her tiny cot, so without any more ado Alec chased young Marjie upstairs, two at a time, to make use of what precious little time they had together.

On Vera's return from the pictures, she was surprised to see the bulky army bag in the hallway, and the khaki hat tossed on the hallstand. She guessed immediately that Alec was home on leave, although there seemed to be no sight of either of them.

It was only on hearing the deep, undulating moans coming from Marjie's bedroom that Vera realised where they both were. The cries of sexual enjoyment echoed down through the thin walls, Vera imagined that the whole street must be able to hear them. She felt herself go all hot and sweaty as she stood in the hall tightly clutching the banister.

Her mind was working overtime as their moans of pleasure, and the squeaking of the bedsprings seemed to engulf her, leaving her quite weak. She was sure she never carried on like, that even on her honeymoon. The truth was, she was as green as grass from the word go, having got herself pregnant a couple of months before the wedding! From what she had gleaned about married life from her mother and the girls she worked with, the policy seemed to be, when it came to 'it'... just grit your teeth and get it over with as quickly as possible! No one ever explained that you could actually enjoy the act!

Her early experiences with George were furtive and confusing. She had been taken to a party at one of his friends, a Romeo called Johnny, handsome as you like, and never without a girlfriend.

They had been having a whale of a time, dancing and drinking fruit punch, even smoking. Some of the couples appeared to drift away upstairs, and then more records were played, and more people arrived.

Vera drank her fruit punch very hesitantly, after one of the girls giggled and said she was sure it was 'laced'. What with, Vera had no idea at all.

George was very attentive to her, and she felt pleased. After all, he had only been taking her out for about three months... perhaps he regarded her as 'his girl' now? After several more drinks, George must have felt that he had to prove his masculinity, for he steered her from the dancers, to a room at the back of the house. It was quite dark and smelt musty. He pushed the door open and poked his head around the corner... 'No one at home, but us chickens,' he giggled, and drew her in, closing the door behind them.

Clinging to his arm, Vera followed him. There were a lot of books in a glass-fronted case, and an old leather-topped desk, on which stood an Imperial typewriter, and a mass of papers. The only light was from outside, shining through the fanlight over the door.

George pulled her down into the space behind the desk. There on the threadbare carpet, he caressed her and told her he liked her a lot. Vera was very conscious of his wanting her to 'be nice'... which she thought she was. So, afraid of losing him, she would be as 'nice' as he wanted her to be.

His fumbling suddenly became more intimate. He grew very insistent, while she struggled to keep her wits about her. Suddenly, without hesitation, her skirt was pulled up as around her waist, and he was tugging at her new cami-knicks. Panic swept over Vera. She had no idea what was happening to her, but all of a sudden she let out a yell, as George forced himself into her. Even with all the hurt and soreness, her only thought was that her new skirt and camis would be ruined!

At last George let her go and she sat up in tears. His face alight and smiling he turned and offered her his handkerchief to clean herself with. Then he planted a wet kiss on the side of her cheek. 'Thanks darlin' ...you're a little bit of alright, do you know that?'

Vera smiled back at him. He was really pleased with her ... he was her fella now without a doubt. That thought seemed to ease the pain of the ruined skirt and camis that she had bought on 'the never never' and weren't even paid for yet.

But George wasn't quite as pleased with her six weeks later, when Vera broke the news of her condition. She shed a few tears, and they decided to get married as soon as possible. After all, she thought to herself, he wasn't a bad catch. And George soon easily adapted to the idea of being a married man.

Vera chose her wedding dress and bought it one Thursday. The bouquet she got cheap, but it contained the largest looking lilies ever seen. If she held it in front of her navel all the time, no one would ever guess. George's mother did pass some comment at the time, but Vera kept mum about the rushed arrangements, and why.

Her train of thoughtful memories snapped, as the bedroom door burst open, and an excited Marjie came trailing downstairs in her best black nightie. She reddened when she saw Vera, 'Oh Mum, I didn't know you were back... Al's home, upstairs,' she added with a giggle.

As she pushed her way past Vera, the intimate smell of their bodies wafted under Vera's nose. She found herself feeling a little envious. In her middle age the need for satisfaction was stronger than ever.

One thing about Alec... he idolised his young wife, and adored his new daughter. He hadn't the same fear that George and the others had, about the war and its outcome. Being young gave him added assurance. What would be, would be! He was more than confidant that they would all get though this alright, and that the war would be over by this Christmas anyway.

As for Marjie, she seemed to have grown up overnight. She was a devoted mother, and could not be faulted for the way she ran the home and looked after things. The authorities had pressed her to take the baby and evacuate to the country. But to Vera's relief Marjie refused, stating firmly that she would rather stay put.

Gran had taken a shine to young Cynthia, as much as she had done to Marjie. Oh, Gran knew that Marjie was still a bit of a girl with the fellas, she had seen her walking down the street pushing the pram, her blouse still deliberately half undone, as she was still feeding Cynth.

Gran saw the looks from the older men as they gazed appreciatively at her slim, young body. The cluster of ARP wardens always made a comment from their post outside the shelter. Marjie remained as seemingly innocent as always, smiling sweetly as she passed them by. Given the chance, if she was fifty years younger Gran would have been the same... if she was about fifty years younger. She thought Marjie was a real morale booster.

'Good job your Alec's away fighting for his country, my girl,' Gran said good-humouredly to Marjie, '... otherwise you'd be having a permanent green book.'

Marjie shrieked with laughter, 'Oh Gran, I don't know what you mean?'

'You know all bleeding right... can't get enough of him when he's at home. Go on... tell the truth.' Marjie grabbed her shopping and ran indoors, actually blushing.

Chapter 13

Cassie and Helen had been home for a month during the summer break, now that they had returned to their foster home, Janie walked around the house in a most despondent fashion.

She knew she shouldn't have let th

em come home in the first instance, but they had written and asked so many times, so now that the raids were almost non-existent she had relented, and agreed to their pleas.

Not seeing them for such a long time, she had quite a shock at the changes she saw. Not so much in Helen, but Cassie seemed to have grown up and developed overnight.

Gran noticed it too. 'Getting like a young woman, you are, shall have to put you in some corsets my girl, keep that fat bum in trim.'

Jane laughed and told her to stop being so silly. 'Come off it Gran, it's only puppy fat, she is only thirteen after all.'

But Gran knew that it wouldn't be long before Cassie would be leaving childhood well behind her, in more ways than one. She was more knowledgeable and developed than Janie realised.

After the girls had packed their things, Gran called Cassie to one side, and taking hold of her hand, pressed a ten bob note into it. 'A treat for the two of you, don't forget. And don't get into any trouble... stay well away from the boys.' She wagged her finger at her in a knowing fashion.

'Oh Gran... don't be so silly, I don't even like boys.'

sighed Cassie.

After the girls left on the midday train, Gran took herself off to The Three Crowns for a drop of stout, and a chat to whoever might be hanging about there.

Gran found consolation for most of her problems at the pub. Her loneliness could be pushed far away with a glass of milk stout in her hand, and one of her old cronies to have a laugh and a chat with. Because she didn't act miserable, it didn't mean she didn't sometimes feel it. Bloody war... bloody Hitler!

Jane missed her Norman, more than she could have ever imagined. When they had all been together before the war broke out, she had a good relationship with him. He was her one and only lover, and she had never wanted or needed anyone else. Now that they were a divided family, she missed him enormously.

Even when he wasn't on duty at the docks, when he was home with just her, there was not the shared intimacy that she had known before. He was a changed man. She felt that he didn't need, or want her, at all anymore. The girls didn't need her either – they were more than independent since they had been evacuated.

Jane felt unwanted, and a little sorry for herself. She was not an old woman; she reckoned she was still attractive. And yet, even in her happy marriage, she felt there was no love for her.

Perhaps she was just in a rut, depression was not in her nature. But the more she thought about her empty life, the more despondent she became. What she needed was some sort of stimulus... something to break the monotony. Sitting darning her stockings as if her very life depended on it, Jane thought she must do something different soon, or she would explode. She was fed up. Fed up with shortages, lack of sleep, being told to fight for her country, and fed up with machining parachutes!

Ten years ago she would never have dreamed of thinking those thoughts, but now, she seemed to be obsessed by the shortage of love in her life … and the lack of a man in her life. She screwed the stockings together, and sobbed softly in her anguish, 'Oh Norm, I want you home with me... now.'

Letting the stockings fall from her lap she placed both her hands over her face and broke into pitiful sobs, deep throated sobs that welled up from her very inside. Then, exhausted, she dozed fitfully in front of the fire.

After a matter of days, the air raids started up again, as if in rebellion to the respite of the previous weeks.

Janie went off to the factory very half-heartedly. She was still worrying about Gran. She knew that Norman worried about the both of them, and would have moved heaven and earth to get Gran shipped out to the West Country with the girls. Gran was obstinate; she would not be moved. Her plea was, 'If I'm going to go, I'd much rather be in my own place than some strange country.' And that was that.

One particularly cold day, Jane had no sooner left for the factory, than the air-raid siren started. The raids went on fast and furious all day. Gran, Vera, together with Marjie with the baby, darted in and out of the shelter like yo-yos, until eventually Gran sprawled herself out in the armchair, and refused to be moved again.

Suddenly the wail of the siren started, 'Oh Christ, not again.' moaned Vera, downing her flat iron and shouting out to Marjie. Pulling on her coat, she tore round to chase Gran out. 'Gran, come on ... quickly. I'm taking a thermos flask this time.'

After several moments Vera realised that Gran was not appearing. 'You go on down, Marjie. Steady, the front's very muddy.' She turned and picked her way through Janie's garden, all the time calling out to Gran. The old girl was getting more obstinate by the hour.

'Come on Gran... come on.' Vera was getting annoyed. This was beyond a joke! She flung open Janie's back door, and saw Gran quite comfortable in the armchair, with her feet up on the fender. She looked up at Vera through half closed eyelids, determination written all over her face. 'No Vera... I'm not going into that bleeding damp tomb again. I'm stiff and tired, there's some stew on the gas for when Janie comes in, and I'm going to make meself a cuppa. So you go on down with Marjie and the baby... I'm going to stay put here, in the warm. Alright?'

Gran waved her hand towards the door, as if to dismiss Vera. Then she leaned forward to turn the wireless on. As the set warmed up and the music drifted across the room, she sank back into her chair, closed her eyes, and hummed to herself in time to the melody.

Vera stood holding onto the door not knowing what to do for the best. The old woman was obstinate. The noise from above was getting worse, and she ran forward to drag the old dear from her chair. But Gran pushed her away, half fighting with her, 'Leave me be Vera. You go and see to Marjie, and the little 'un. Go on, sod off...' she muttered under her breath.

Terrified and panic stricken, Vera ran through the back garden and made for the shelter. Marjie was clasping Cynthia tightly to her, and screaming for her to come at the top of her voice. Vera leapt in and fell onto the bench. Marjie looked at her in horror. 'Where's Gran ... why hasn't she come down with you?'

Before Vera could answer, there was the most deafening noise as an almighty crash sounded all about them. Instinctively they both threw themselves on the floor of the shelter, amongst the old sacks and bits of lino.

Vera was shaking all over when she slowly raised herself back to the bench again. The two of them looked at each other, 'What on earth was that? ...it was damned close.'

Moving to peer out of the entrance, Vera had no idea what she expected to see. 'What's happened Ma, whatever is it?' whispered Marjie, huddled behind her.

At first, as she leaned forward out of the shelter in the hazy light of the late afternoon, Vera could see nothing for the dust from the rubble. She peered still further and made out the outline of the two houses. A deep sigh of relief ran through her. 'Thank God the house is still standing.' She turned and surveyed the area past the houses, where the parade of shops met the corner of the street. With Marjie close behind, she hesitantly climbed out from the shelter.

Vera stood motionless, unable to take it all in. She looked right as far as she could see, then to the left, peering hard through the dust-laden smoke. Everything had gone, nothing left but debris and rubble. She took two steps forward and turned a complete circle, her mouth open in disbelief at the sight before her.

Thank God their homes were still OK, she breathed to herself. At least they were still standing, along with a couple of others along the road. Her heart missed a beat, suddenly she remembered Gran. 'I'd better go and see if she is alright Marjie.'

'Why not wait until the all-clear goes, please mum. Please.'

Vera looked at Marjie clasping the babe to her in sheer terror. She was right, nothing could be gained by rushing back now. So they waited, and after what seemed an eternity the all-clear finally went. They were just about to clamber out when shouts could be heard from two ARP wardens who appeared from the back of the garden. The first one peered into the entrance of the shelter, 'You lot alright down there? Come on out quickly, I've got to get you over to the relief centre. Quickly love.'

Vera climbed out, and two arms came down to help Marjie up. 'What do you mean, get to the relief centre? We haven't been bombed out. Look... we're going back inside...' But before she could finish what she was saying the warden interrupted her. 'Look here lady, we've got to get you all away from this site, there's an unexploded bomb caught up in those trees, in that house over there.' He indicated a garden about a hundred yards away. 'So, come along now, and follow everyone else quickly, while it's dealt with.'

Marjie, clasping her baby and the holdall, ran in the direction the warden pointed to. 'Here you are Jack, another couple for you... and a kiddie.' Vera followed the small crowd as if in a daze. Then she remembered Gran sitting at home. She screamed out to the warden, who then shouted to two of his men. 'Don't you worry love, we'll get her.' By now Vera was near to tears. Oh if anything had happened to Gran, she would never forgive herself. Never!

After what seemed ages, two wardens came into view, holding Gran under the arms. She was ranting and shouting, but they didn't take any notice of her threats or abuse.

Vera ran to her side and together they piled into the van,

which took them off to a rest centre for the remainder of the evening. Much later a very worried looking Jane came in and found them. She had been out of her mind when she returned home to the scene of devastation. The whole area had been cordoned off, and she was told where she could find the others from her street.

After a sleepless night, the WVS doled out breakfast for all of them, and Marjie was able to feed the baby and give her a bit of a wash. Then the order came through that they could go home, at least those who had homes still standing. The bomb had been defused and taken away, and the wardens looked dead tired and weary.

Jane kept telling Gran off, for not going to the shelter in the first place. But it all fell on deaf ears. Gran knew when to listen and when to cock a 'deaf 'un'. At least they were all alive. That was one consolation.

The three of them picked their way through the rubble to the street door. Vera and Marjie were streaked with dust and grime. Janie smiled, 'Let's get the kettle on…' but before she could finish Gran let out an excited yell. They all turned to face her thinking she must have some untold agony upon her. Gran was biting her lip, shaking her head, 'Oh dear, oh dear. Janie, the stew! The stew – I left it on…'

By the time Jane found it, the saucepan was blackened and the charred remains were glued to the bottom of the pot. 'Oh Gran, look at it, just look at it.' Janie wailed, as she looked, horrified, at her saucepan. Gran winced sheepishly, and looked from one to the other… 'It must have been the dumplings, I thought they were a bit too stiff?'

When Norm returned the following night, Jane related

the chain of events. She tried hard to make light of it all, hoping that he would see the funny side of it as they had done. However, in her heart, she knew it could have been deadly serious, had they all not been warned in time.

Norman was so tense, and worried practically all the time these days. Jane felt thwarted and tired, not in the physical sense, but with all the effort to stimulate Norm's interest in anything.

She washed the supper things and Norm made his way up to bed.

Gran had retired ages ago with her little wireless set all charged up, to keep her 'in touch' as she called it.

Jane had taken a lot of time getting bathed and ready for bed. She pampered herself with 'Evening in Paris' bath salts and talcum, they were a present the girls had given her the Christmas that war had started. She had only used them once before. It was sheer luxury, and heaven knew when she would be lucky enough to get any more.

Norm lay in bed watching her as Jane brushed her hair. She caught his eye in the mirror and smiled back at his appreciative look. His glance, reflected in the mirror, sent a tingle through her. She bent her head low so he couldn't see the delight that crept over her face. She found herself trembling, as excitement ran through her body, and she flushed. 'Please don't let there be a raid tonight... please.'

Finishing brushing her hair quickly, Jane peeled off the dressing gown in a flash, and slipped into bed. Snuggling up to Norman, she put her arms around his body, hugging him to her. She lay quiet for a moment, then looked up into his face. He was still handsome... the cleft chin, deep blue eyes, and the smile that had won her over, all those years ago. She loved him tremendously, now more than ever.

Leaning forward, he planted a kiss on her mouth, 'I love you Janie.' She relaxed, the war seemed to be a million miles away, Norm was here beside her, and she was happy and at peace with the world.

She touched his neck with her fingers, hesitantly at first. Then, tracing his hairline, she ran her fingers over his bare chest. She felt exhilarated and happy, so excited that she had taken the initiative - something she had never dared do in all the years they had been wed. This was wartime, she told herself, women were asserting themselves more than ever now, it was nothing to be ashamed off.

But although Norm kept on telling her that he loved her, he still did not respond as she would have liked, she could tell he had something else on his mind, something he was trying hard to tell her.

She stopped caressing him, feeling slightly ashamed of her brazen attitude. She looked at him in the half-light, he was restless and edgy. 'Norm, whatever is it, what's wrong, tell me please?' He stared at her, his eyes so full of trouble and upset. 'Norm, whatever is it, say something... have I upset you so much!'

Putting his arms around her, Norm looked deeply into her eyes, 'I love you Janie, more than anything else in the world. But, but...'

'But what Norm? What's the matter with you.' Now Jane felt so ashamed and embarrassed, she had wanted this evening to be so perfect, the first evening they had been together for such a long time. She took his hand in her own, 'Have I upset you Norm, if so I won't ever be like that again. I'm so sorry, whatever must you think of me.'

Norm grabbed hold of her and kissed her hard on the mouth, 'Oh Janie, it's me, it's me! I'm no good as a husband any more... I don't know what to do.' With a deep sob, he cried, 'I think I'm impotent!' She put her arms around him as he sobbed into her body.

When he did recover, he lifted his tear stained face to hers, and she was still trembling. He continued to stare at her as she dragged her nightdress up to cover her bare shoulders. Jane was shaking all over, bewildered and confused at what he had said. She had heard of this happening to other men, some other women didn't mind at all. But it couldn't be happening to them! Oh God, she had wanted him so much tonight, and now all she felt was quite ill and shaken, emotionally shattered.

After what seemed an eternity, she reached out and touched his cheek, 'Don't worry Norm, it will all come right in the end. You're just tired... we're all tired. It's the fault of this war.' Three years of war was too long for anyone, something must happen soon surely?

Sleep finally took over, after Jane pitched and tossed about almost until break of dawn, before falling into a deep and troubled sleep. It was quite late when she finally went downstairs. Gran was bustling around the scullery and viewed her with suspicion.

'Hello Gran! Didn't know that you were up.'

Gran smiled to herself, 'I didn't have anything to lay in bed for did I, unlike some!' Jane blushed at this and looked away, if only Gran knew the half of it.

As she stirred the tea Gran placed in front of her, her

thoughts were running riot. How long, she wondered, would Norm be like this? How long do these things last? Would he have to have any treatment? Would things eventually change and get back to normal? A thousand questions ran through her mind, she felt tormented, tired, and cheated. This was not her Norman. Oh God, what were they going to do? She could not tell anyone, dare not tell Gran, must keep it all to herself. She stared at the cup of swirling liquid. How was she to carry on, worrying all the time, wondering, hoping! Time would provide a change for the better... they must have time!

The change that came about the following weekend brought all their lives to a climax, all in the cause of war.

Chapter 14

For nearly forty-eight hours, the air-raids had been coming and going. On the wireless the news declared that 'the docks were having the biggest onslaught of all time' – more than anyone thought possible. Janie hadn't seen Norm since Thursday, when he left for his night shift. He'd been so quiet and worried for them all, as usual. She could still see him as he stopped in the hall before going out. 'Take care of yourselves… look after Gran. I love you,' he had whispered after seeing her worried face.

Gran, listening to the wireless, was the first to hear the news about the latest disastrous air-raid, the worst so far. She sat with her ear almost in the fretwork, as the newsreader's voice gave out all the latest air-raid and dock fire news.

Jane prayed that Norm was alright. Unfortunately, it turned out that Norm was one of three men caught up in the worst raid, and it looked bad. When the news was broken to her, she almost collapsed.

Gran played her most supportive role ever, as the pair of them went to the hospital to see him. Gran, renowned for being as 'tough as old boots' in most things, shuddered when she approached the hospital bed and saw the state of her only son. She winced and her heart missed a beat, his burns looked so bad. 'Hello son,' she whispered in her bravest voice.

Janie, standing at her side, felt so sick she thought she would pass out, but she steadied herself and walked towards him smiling. 'Hello my love, what a fine mess you seem to be in.' She gazed at him, her body trembling, as she willed herself not to cry.

Norm smiled, a bit lopsided because of the dressings on his face, and Jane reached forward and touched his fingers as they lay on top of the covers. He looped his fingers through hers and smiled again. Jane couldn't take her eyes off him; he looked so old and strained. It would take weeks to get him on the mend again. Her heart bled as she stared at the state of him. Poor Norm, poor dear Norm...

She sat looking at him as if in a trance. But soon, the Staff Nurse came over to tell them they must go... he was a very sick man, no more visitors for the time being.

Gran touched his hand and bade him a 'Cheerio love,' while Jane bent to kiss him on the forehead. 'See you tonight Norm. I love you.' As she bent over him she inhaled the smell of the antiseptic that surrounded him, a smell that was to linger with her all the way home.

Norman whispered something as she leaned forward, her face near his. 'Look after things Janie, love,' he croaked. 'Take care of...' She nodded, smiling, 'I will, I will.'

As they got to the door, Jane stopped and half-glanced over her shoulder. Norm's eyes had closed and he appeared to be sleeping like a babe. 'That's what he needs,' Jane thought to herself, as she took Gran's arm and they hurried out.

It took them ages to get home from the East End. Two more raids started and stopped, and each time they had to rush down the street shelter with the masses. When the second all-clear went they made a last dash for home. Gran was getting very irritable, thinking she might get her dinner time stout.

At last Jane finally turned the key in the lock, and rushed to fill up the kettle to make a pot of tea. Gran had other ideas, though.

'Tell you what, Janie. Don't bother with that. Come over the road and have a drop of milk stout with me instead... I could do with it gel.'

That was the last thing Jane wanted, but she shook her head and smiled. 'No thanks Gran, but you go and have one love. I'll have a cuppa and a rest in the chair, before I go back to the hospital to see Norm.' She gave Gran some coppers from her purse to treat herself... 'You have one for me, Gran.'

Rubbing her weary forehead, Jane poured herself out a cup of tea, took it over to the armchair, and sank down heavily.

Gran smiled to herself as she buttoned her coat. 'That's right gel, have a bit of a rest, do you good, I shan't be long.' The doorknocker went, repeatedly, as she was shuffling along the hall. 'Who's that, I wonder?' thought Gran. 'Sounds important.' Opening the door, she found a tall policeman looking down at her.

'Mrs Howard?' he enquired. Gran went white, 'Oh my gawd!' She turned and called out urgently, 'Janieeee...'

Rising from her chair, Jane stared at them both at the end of the hallway. A shiver ran through her, she wanted to walk towards him, but her legs wouldn't move – she was frozen in her tracks. She knew what he had come to tell her, even before he stepped inside the doorway. Her stomach knotted up, and sweat stood out on her forehead. 'Please God... no,' she mumbled to herself. 'Please... no!'

This was a duty the policeman hated having to perform. Adjusting his helmet, the policeman lowered his eyes, before telling them gently that Norman had died, only minutes after they had left the hospital.

Gran stood like a mute, unable to take it in.

Reaching out, Jane touched her arm with a reassuring squeeze, then half dragged Gran back into the living room. Shaking like a leaf, Jane put her arms around Gran, and together the two grief stricken women cried on each other's shoulders.

Helping Gran into a chair, Jane then collapsed into the one opposite. After what seemed an eternity, Jane raised her eyes and looked at Gran mistily. 'What are we going to do Gran? What are we going to do?'

The cough of the policeman, still standing in the doorway, brought them back to their senses. He took his leave, and arrangements were made for Jane to return to the hospital to collect Norm's things.

It was an unpleasant task, which only Jane herself could do. She felt she had to push herself all the way, and dared not give in and show how she really felt.

The funeral was arranged, and the girls were told. Jane did not insist that they come home, because of the heavy bombing and air raids. She knew that Norman would not have wished it - he cared too much for them to jeopardize their safety. The day before the funeral, Jane went to see them herself and explained it all... she hoped they were old enough to understand.

Throughout the service, Jane felt as if her heart were breaking. With Gran by her side clinging to her arm, she sniffed and tried to be brave. The two of them stood alone in front of the others, not really hearing what the minister was saying. They were only conscious of their own feelings of loss – a mother without a son, and a wife without her mate.

Then, a siren wailed mournfully, interrupting the brief service. On hearing it Jane looked upwards, her face distorted in misery. In a frenzy, shaking her fists in a wild fashion, she shrieked 'Haven't you had enough from us? Can't you even let him be buried in peace? You... you...' She was lost for the words that would ease her burden, so she screamed out instead.

The minister stood, his eyes downcast, waiting.

Gran took her arm, and gently shushing Janie, as she would a tiny child, she steered her to the edge of the gathering. Janie cried unbearably and without control, her sobs mingling with the screams of the bombers overhead.

Whispering, 'that's it gel, let it out... you'll feel better now,' Gran held onto Janie tightly, and steered her to the edge of the gathering. The minister's voice mixed with her sobbing, as he carried on with the service. And at the graveside, although agitated at the sounds of the impending air raid, the friends and family stood, and felt for Jane, Gran, and their loss.

Throughout the rest of the service, while Janie and Gran stood huddled between the minister and the funeral car, the noise of the planes grew louder, and the minister glanced up several times before closing his book. Going to the two women, he urged them to take cover before the journey home. He led them through to the public shelter where the rest of the mourners were gathering.

Vera, white faced and trembling, went to Jane's side. The three women stood without any need of spoken condolences. Their presence together was enough.

In a very short while the all-clear sounded, and the small party headed back to the waiting cars. The minister blessed each of them, Jane acknowledging him with a faint sob.

During the journey back to the little house they had all shared, Jane's thoughts dwelt on the life she had shared with her Norm. He had been her first boyfriend, the only man she had ever loved. Married at seventeen, and a mother at eighteen, the first few years had been spent planning for the future - for the two baby girls, Norm, herself, and then Gran. Why had this happened to them?

She felt so empty, so hollow. Her one reason for living was her Norman. And now he was gone. The thought of the long and lonely life in front of her, without him at her side, was unbearable. A deep and cutting pain seemed to tear through her, making her double up and wince with its reality.

Oh God, why, when she needed him so much, was he taken from her? Why...!

Chapter 15

It took more than six months for Jane to emerge from the empty vacuum in which she tried to lose herself in the months following Norman's death. Gran stood by her and tried to comfort her, in every way she knew, but it seemed that time, and time alone, would be the healer.

The girls came home for a brief spell and returned once more to their old school. They were very different to when they went away. Cassie seemed to have grown up overnight. Gran thought she was a very sensible girl for her age, the way she took to looking after Jane, and the household in general - like a duck to water.

During a quiet spell without any bombing or air raids, Terry and Phyllis came home as well. Vera couldn't let her two stay away, when all around them clutches of youngsters were trailing back to war-torn London. But she found them so different to when they had left, as if a wide gulf had emerged. It was almost impossible to communicate with Phyl, who seemed very quiet and moody.

Terry was in a different billet to Phyl, who was not an evacuee anymore but working on the farm, helping out in every way possible. Vera thought she almost resented having to come home, as if it were a punishment. They had several heated arguments, ending up with Vera almost in tears. She really began to think she didn't know her daughter, at all! Phyl received several letters which she always hid well away from the others, each bearing an Oxfordshire postmark. Vera wondered how long she would carry on in this secretive fashion.

After almost a month, and completely out of the blue, Phyl asked if she could go back. Vera was flabbergasted when she came out with it one morning. But Phyl waved a letter under her mother's nose, and declared that she was '...needed, it's harvesting time,' and anyway she missed her little payment from the farmer.

On hearing this Vera opened her purse and offered a half crown. 'No Mum, it's not just the money, I really am needed there.'

If Vera felt hurt, she didn't show it. Her and Phyl had never been close, she was her father's daughter, always had been. Promising to write, Phyl left quite calmly, and Vera thought she seemed happier than at any time during the weeks she'd been back home. After watching the trail of steam as the train left the station, Vera turned to head for home again, thinking of what she could get from the shops for Marjie, Terry, and the babe's dinner.

Terry got to calling on Helen at every spare moment. He would be at the door the minute she appeared from school, and clung to her side like a leech, whatever she might be trying to do.

Gran liked them to keep occupied – they were good friends and kept out of harm's way. Terry took Helen over to the bomb-sites with him, collecting shrapnel in a large box. Janie never knew of it, or she would have had a fit. But her head was in the clouds most days, with no thought to what any of them were doing with their lives.

The weeks went into months, and Vera insisted that Terry

must return to his foster home. He was now a tall lad for his age, and prone to daydreaming. He needed constant telling what to do from Vera, but really only listened to Helen and conformed to her thinking in everything.

Helen was 'a smasher', confided Terry to Gran one Saturday as the pair of them raced off to the afternoon pictures, Terry feeling very grown up in his first long trousers. It didn't make a scrap of difference that they were a pair of George's flannels, altered and cut down.

Helen blushed to the tips of her ears when he came knocking after dinner. 'Oh come on round the back Terry, like you usually do,' Helen shouted down the hallway. He blushed, and grabbed her arm. Then the two of them dived out of the house, racing in the direction of the Carlton cinema, only a stone's throw away.

Gran watched them with interest, murmuring to herself, 'Nice boy, that Terry… hmm, I shall have to watch those two.'

It was all rather fortunate that George should have a sudden leave coming up, while the kids were at home. It was Gran who saw him first, striding down the street one sunny afternoon. She had been on her way to Chapel Street Market, to fish for bargains, and had only stopped to chat at a friend's gateway en route. Elsie Brewer was the local gossip, and Gran gleaned much of her best information from her. The two women were laughing their heads off when Gran stopped in her tracks, mouth open, and stared at the soldier who was striding along, grinning from ear to ear. As he neared the gate Gran gave a whoop of delight, dropped her shopping bag and ran to meet him, laughing and shouting to Elsie, who was staring in bewilderment.

'It's Georgie! Hello ducks... when have you got to go back?' She flung her arms around his neck. 'Here, gimme a kiss. Does Vera know you were coming home? I think she's gone out with Marjie, won't be long though.'

George stood at the gate, struggling under the weight of his bag, perched precariously on one shoulder. Gran peered hard at him, not believing how well he looked, and tanned; very different from the lily-livered bloke who joined up two years ago. He had been overseas for almost a year, somewhere in Italy. Vera had missed him dreadfully, shame she wasn't here to meet him.

Gran bade Elsie cheerio, and with all thoughts of shopping gone from her head, she led George back to the house. 'I'll make you a cup of tea, while you wait for Vera.' Gran prattled on, all excited to see a new face.

'How's your stomach these days Georgie? You know... your problem?' George looked surprised, as he downed his strong tea. 'Stomach? Problems? What problems? I ain't got time for stomach problems now gel!'

'I suppose not, it must be different when you're out there George...'

They were interrupted by the excited noise of Vera and Marjie as they came rushing through the back door, Vera screaming with joy, and Marjie clutching the toddler's hand as they both fell into the scullery, into the waiting arms of George.

Vera wiped her eyes and glared at George. 'Why didn't you write and tell me you were coming home... and when are you going back?'

'I didn't know meself I had leave till last night, then I had to travel up from Southampton. Come on gel, don't cry.' He wiped Vera's eyes with the edge of his khaki sleeve, and put his arm round Marjie's shoulders too.

Gran busied herself making another pot of tea, while they enjoyed their embraces. Young Cynth was sat up at the table and given a piece of bread and jam to be getting on with.

Soon regaining her composure, Vera took the tray of teacups from Gran. 'Here we are... Gran has made some tea for us.' She smiled at her family in contentment. Gran sat down heavily, 'Yes, another cup of tea Georgie ... blow the expense, that's what I say!'

Georgie knew all about Norm from Vera's letters. He shook his head slowly when Vera retold how it had affected Janie. 'Although,' she pointed out, '...she's a lot better now than a few months ago.' George looked sad and tutted, 'poor Janie, poor bitch ... what a thing to have happened to a woman.'

George was soon looking relaxed and happy, and Vera was itching for them to get indoors to their own house. Gran said Janie could be quite late coming home, so they shouldn't wait for her, she would see George tomorrow. 'Yes, there's always tomorrow,' echoed George.

In their own home Vera watched George laughing and playing with his grandchild, teasing her as he did all those years ago when Marjie was a toddler. Vera sat in her armchair, quite contented, watching them thoughtfully. She was so lucky to have her family in one piece, so very lucky. She realised then how Janie must be feeling, and her heart went out to her.

George couldn't help but notice the countless changes 'at home', apart from the obvious ones. He reckoned that the Anderson shelter shared by the two families was the safest thing going. He admired the blackout curtains Marjie had machined up, and the brown sticky paper she had plastered all over the windows. But the one thing that sent him into howls of laughter was when the two women mixed up a basin of gravy powder and sponged it all over their legs. He watched with interest, as young Marjie got ready to go to the pictures with her friend, leaving Vera to mind the toddler. She finished browning her legs, then turned to Vera with a brown pencil. That was Vera's cue to get down on her knees behind Marjie, and pencil a line up the back of her legs, while Marjie stood as still as possible holding her skirt up to her thighs.

'Strewth, what a way to carry on...!'

'Oh shut up Dad. You don't know the half of it... does he Ma!'

Vera had to enlighten him on a few other dodges they had been up to. What with hardly any clothes and no coupons to buy new ones, Vera, Marjie and Jane were on a 'lease/ lend' whenever they needed to go somewhere nice. All except Gran, whose clothes dated from the year dot, and were infused through and through with the smell of mothballs!

All too soon George's leave came to an end, he had tried to make the most of every minute during his week at home. On the last day before return to his unit, he felt he should take them all out, for Norm's sake. 'Go and have a quick word with our Janie, Vera. And Vera, make her come won't you?'

Looking up from her mending, Vera smiled wanly as Vera, after banging on the back door, flung it open excitedly. 'George says he's taking me, you and Gran to 'The Spaniards' at Hampstead tonight, and he won't take no for an answer. What time's best for you Janie?'

Jane looked up nervously, and it was obvious she was looking for an excuse not to go. Vera wagged her finger, and looked Jane straight in the eye. 'You know Janie, you must start to go out again, you really must. I know what you're going through, but you must try... please.'

'You're right Vera, I'll come, so will Gran. Thank George for us.' She smiled shakily as Vera looked enquiringly at her. 'See you both about seven thirty then, we'll give you a knock, alright?'

'Yes alright, alright,' smiled Jane. After making the first move it might not seem so bad the next time. At least she hoped it wouldn't.

Gran, as pleased as punch, got out her best hat to wear for the occasion. Then she decided on her best coat too. Later that evening, as Gran walked in, all ready to go out, Jane couldn't help but wrinkle her nose. Gran saw her and said quickly, 'I don't know what's worse, the moths, or the smell of the moth-balls? Still, I tried to kill it with some of my new scent... is it alright Janie?'

Jane had to laugh, she hadn't recognised the mothballs, she was overpowered by the 'Evening in Paris'! Gran saw the look she gave and winced, 'too much is it? I smell like an Arabian brothel don't I?'

'Yes you do Gran... you really do!' said Jane, laughing. Gran's face lit up to see her Janie laughing again. 'Good girl,' she whispered to herself. 'There's a good girl.'

They had a smashing evening, and George was as friendly as he knew how, in an effort to get Jane to relax and enjoy herself. As the evening wore on, the crowd got thicker and George suggested they make a move. He knew a nice pub in Euston Road, it was sure to be a bit less crowded than this one. So they all trooped out after him, and he found them an empty taxi to take them on to Euston.

Vera and Gran kept oohing and aahing, 'Fancy, getting a taxi!' But George insisted it was a special treat for them all, until he came home again. 'And God knows when that will be?' he murmured. Vera felt a cold wind blow round her as he spoke. 'Don't be a pessimist George,' she said, avoiding Jane's eyes. Clasping his arm with both hands, she snuggled against his rough khaki uniform.

Jane saw them and blushed, she didn't know why. She felt herself shaking and looked away out of the window. The dark reflection she saw gazing back at her was lonely, but not unattractive. Her plumpness had gone and left her a very pretty and desirable woman. She looked ready for cheering up, and Gran hoped and prayed every night that something would happen to disperse the cloud of sadness that hung about her.

They reached 'The Orange Tree' and while the women clambered out George gave the taxi driver five bob. He felt quite affluent as he dropped him a bob for a tip too. 'Come on girls, in we go.' They all laughed with him as they made their way inside to the mellow warmth of the bar.

It was very bright and noisy inside. George elbowed his way to the counter, while Gran led the other two over to a corner, where they found a round table to accommodate them all nicely.

Gran ordered her usual port and lemon, and the same for Janie - although Janie insisted that she didn't like it.

'You get it down you gel, make you feel better.' Gran pushed it in front of Jane, daring her to refuse it.

Vera snuggled up to her George and let abandonment take

over. Well, it was wartime and she didn't care what people thought. She only had George home until tomorrow, then God knows where he would be shifted out to. Gran downed her port and looked at them, pleased. It was good to see folks enjoying themselves again. Suddenly she stood up, hands on the table to steady herself, 'This ones on me, and I'm having the same again.' All eyes turned to her, and George leapt up to push her down. 'NO, NO! I insist. Go on, you get 'em in George, and I'll pay for them. I'm just going for a pee.' While Gran made a beeline for the Ladies, George gave in and went to fetch the drinks.

Jane sat nervously on the edge of her seat; her courage beginning to ebb away. It was quite a shock when a tall figure bent down towards her and Vera. The uniformed GI smiled directly at her.

''Scuse me Ma'am, is that seat taken?' He indicated the space left by Gran and George.

Jane blushed, and her mouth went dry. 'Yes I'm afraid it is. Taken I mean!'

Looking disappointed, he shrugged, 'Sorry Ma'am, it's my first time here… I only wanted to hide in that corner until I'd got my bearings.' He touched his cap and smiled.

'That's alright, it's my friend's husband's treat for us. He's going back to his unit on Sunday night … I haven't been here before either.'

Vera watched the two of them from the other side of the table, while half pretending to look across the bar for George. She realised that if she hadn't been there, Janie might have struck up a sort of friendship for herself.

Suddenly George returned with the drinks, at the same time

as Gran. The GI made his exit, but not without first smiling at Janie long and hard, before touching his cap with long fine fingers. 'Hope we'll meet again one day Ma'am! So long.'

Jane found herself staring after him, slightly open-mouthed. Then she saw Gran looking across the table at her, smiling. And because she knew what was going on in the old dear's head, she flushed to the tips of her ears.

'Gran... don't go looking at me like that. It was nothing ... he only asked me if the chair was free.'

'I didn't say a thing, did I Vera?' Gran looked blandly at Vera and George in turn. They both laughed and tutted good-naturedly.

Gran leaned forward to Janie and tapped her on the knee with her gnarled old hand. 'He was nice though! Do you good to meet someone of the opposite sex, just for a bit of companionship, eh?'

Jane had to admit that she felt a warm glow all over. It was the first time another man shown any interest in her, since Norm. All the way home that night she couldn't get him out of her mind. Perhaps she wasn't too old and dull after all to attract a bit of male attention. She was only in her thirties -still young enough to want to be admired and loved... for a bit of fun!

As she got undressed that night, after spending what seemed like hours thinking such thoughts, she felt a sudden stab of guilt as she saw Norm's photograph on the dressing table staring back at her. Her face flushed deep red again, and she shook with emotion. 'Oh Norm, if only you were here, if only we hadn't wasted all those years.' Years when she'd suppressed her feelings and desires, not realising that Norm wouldn't have thought less of her if she had taken the initiative with their love making, as she had sometimes ached to do. All those wasted time when she had felt it would be immoral to have her feelings and demands known. Dear Norm, she had tried to be the perfect wife and partner, without ever realising that she could be a lover as well.

Now it was all too late! Perhaps she would get over it all in time. Although in her heart, she knew she desperately wanted to be loved now... now, more than ever.

Eventually she fell into a long and troubled sleep, waking with a start to hear Gran calling from downstairs.

'George is just going Janie, he called over cheerio, but I guessed you were still asleep and dreaming.' Jane heard Gran chuckling to herself, shuffling along the hall in that slow, heavy, deliberate way of hers.

She knew she should be up by now, but work seemed a meaningless chore, when there was only Gran and herself to appreciate it. Without hesitation, she ran over to the window, pulling the curtains aside. Yes, George was still there, at the gate with Vera. She knew she should have been up to say goodbye to him; he had been a good mate to Norm. She felt the rush of warm tears to her eyes. Oh Norm it had all be so lovely a few years ago.

She continued to stare down at the khaki-clad figure standing at the gate. George looked so loaded up with all that army kit, it was a wonder he could walk with the weight of it.

Standing in her housecoat, white faced and wringing her hands, Vera looked as near to tears as it was possible. Jane saw George smile and mouth words which she could not hear, before Vera flung her arms around him and they merged into one. Riveted to the window, Jane could not bear to turn away, all she could see was the splurge of khaki and pale green from the two people she knew to be her friends.

Suddenly, George drew himself away from his wife. Taking a deep breath, and rubbing his hands together, he lifted his kit bag up and over onto his shoulder. He smiled once more at Vera, then turned and quickly strode off down the road to catch the bus to Euston station.

Vera stood at the gate, watching the slowly disappearing figure, her body shaking with silent sobs, while she dabbed at her cheeks with the cuff of her robe.

Jane let the curtain drop, knowing the other woman's agony. Now Vera was on her own too, for God knows how long!

Chapter 16

During the following months, a strange calm seemed to settle over the two families.

Cassie had at last gone back to her foster home, after putting up quite a fight and declaring she was now old enough to stay put, instead of being farmed off into the country. But Janie's insistence, and knowing what Norm would have said about it all, made Cassie agree in the end, although very reluctantly.

Helen was full of Terry, and promised to write to him every day. He went around looking like a love-sick bull, until Vera was almost at the end of her tether with all of them.

On the day that Terry left to return to the country, Helen sobbed on Gran's shoulder, her young face white and tear-streaked as Gran tried to reassure and comfort her. She sobbed that her heart was now broken and nobody understood her agony, while Gran studied her performance, reckoning it was all a bout of wind, from the excessive amount of plums Helen had been eating.

Janie went to see them the two of them off at the station, both still protesting, even as the train steamed away from the platform. She felt strangely light and buoyant as she walked along Euston Road. The houses were few and far between, and she walked on to the next bus stop, enjoying the last of the winter sunshine.

She had tried to work out what to do with herself, now that she was on her own again. She knew she must get work, having been off sick for too long now. It was all resting on her... she must make a life for herself, Gran, and the girls. Eventually reached home, although very tired, Janie now felt clear-minded and quite calm, and more positive than she had been for a long time.

Gran was nowhere to be seen, so Janie rummaged through the cupboards trying to find something to concoct for their supper. All the tinned goods she had been saving for almost a year had now gone. Since the family had come home, all the rations had gone nowhere, very fast.

Scanning the larder shelves, she tutted, pursing her lips. Perhaps Vera could oblige her with a tin of egg powder, till the new coupons started next week. She took off her check apron and ran out through the back door, calling as she skipped across the broken low wall, and into Vera's back yard. 'Vera, it's only me.'

She pushed the back door gingerly. 'Hmph, no one about,' she thought to herself... not a sign of Marjie or young Cynthia either. About to turn tail and go, wondering what had happened to them all, she heard a low sobbing coming from the back room.

Mumbling to herself, 'That's strange, surely it can't be Vera,' Janie walked quietly through to where the noise was coming from, and stood land listened outside the living room door. Yes, it was Vera alright, and she sounded more than upset.

She knocked gently on the door, 'It's only me Vera... is everything alright? Whatever has happened?' Pushing the door open, she went in. Vera was sitting over by the window, her shoulders hunched as she sat rocking herself to and fro. She held a letter in one hand, and dabbed at her wet cheeks with a screwed up handkerchief. Turning to face Jane, her face looked a picture of misery.

Without hesitation Jane rushed to her side, almost afraid of what Vera was going to tell her. Vera held the letter out. 'Here, read this… read this. It's from Phyl.'

Staring at Vera's face, Jane took the letter. 'Whatever is it? It can't be that bad, can it?'

Vera blabbered on through her tears, 'Oh she's a stupid girl, so stupid. She's got herself pregnant … and her only sixteen. She wants to get married… needs my consent. Oh what's my George gonna say? Oh Jane!'

Young Phyl knew what effect the letter would have at home, as soon as she let it drop from her grasp into the collecting box. It hadn't been in her plans to marry Ben Fox, but now after what had happened it seemed the only thing to do. Ben was a huge man, almost twenty years her senior. His father was a tinker, and his mother was of gypsy origin. It seems she had given birth to Ben when she was well past middle age, and the locals reckoned that was what caused him to be slightly 'simple minded'. Ben was the same age as the farmer and had grown up with him as a boy. He worked on the farm from dawn till dusk – his huge strength outdoing any of the others when it came to hard graft.

He had a way with animals that no vet could equal. But it was his mop of curly black hair, and simple happy nature that appealed to young Phyl. She always chatted to him while they worked on the harvest during the golden months of autumn, teasing him often.

One evening after the daily grind, he had called her to the back barn on the pretence of showing her something special.

She had gone readily, and innocently. Ben held out a tiny glass-like object. It was a ring. He said he had made it for her from the shattered cockpit of a German plane that had been shot down in a local field recently. She took it from him and placed it on her finger, and he laughed at her pleasure.

Then he offered her a drink from the stone bottle he kept with his sandwiches... it tasted strong and not at all palatable. Phyl, determined not to show her innocence, played along with him, as he bragged about one thing and another. He urged her to keep the ring, and kept on saying, 'You're my Phyl now.' She laughed along with him, enjoying the way she thought she could charm him along.

Suddenly, he leaned over and kissed her on the mouth, a hard wet kiss that almost made her heave. Then his hands shot inside her blouse, wrenching the buttons open, and tearing at her skimpy slip in an effort to find the bare flesh. She panicked, realising that she couldn't hold him off. Then his mouth was slobbering all over her breasts. He bit her once, then again. His smiling face was only inches from hers ... he was laughing and making noises in the back of his throat. A quiver ran through her body, she knew then that she couldn't control him.

'Ben! Behave yourself Ben. You mustn't... No! No Ben!' But the more she pushed him back, the more he laughed and thought she was playing. Oh God, how could she make him stop?

He stopped groping around inside her blouse for a moment, to lean back and unbutton his trousers. His face was sweating with excitement as he suddenly lunged forward, pushing her off her guard, and onto the straw. One of his knees pinned her legs open at right angles. She yelled at him furiously, but he kept on smiling at her, saying she was 'his Phyl'… 'his own little girl'.

Desperately hoping that someone, anyone, would hear her, Phyl called out. But by now it was past suppertime, everyone was indoors. She couldn't move for the weight of him on top of her. He was crushing her into the very floor, with that thrusting part of him that was hurting her unbearably.

As quick as he had started, so he stopped… and let her go free for a second. She drew herself up, straightening her mucky clothes. He stared at her, smiling, then tried to kiss her face and neck once more. His smile was like that of a child at Christmas, watching the fairy lights.

As she stopped him from touching her again, he kept insisting she was 'his Phyl'. Nodding at him, she said, 'Yes, I'm your Phyl… yes, yes.'

They would be wondering where she had got to, she knew she must get back inside the farmhouse. Rubbing her mouth with the back of her hand to erase any saliva that might still be lingering, she took faltering steps towards the barn door. She felt tacky and wet, and the hurt inside her was almost unbearable. She was so confused, she still liked Ben, but she must never let him do this again!

When she tiptoed back inside the house, Sally, the farmer's wife was mending by the fireside. She hardly looked up as Phyl took the kettle from the hob, and made her way up towards her own room. 'I'm having a bit of a wash, then turning in… goodnight.'

Holding the kettle carefully Phyl made her way upstairs, where in the privacy of her room she gently bathed herself all over. As she touched herself, the hurt gradually gave way to a feeling of utmost pleasure. She caressed and soothed her sore body, until she felt quite heady, and almost faint. Smiling to herself, she thought that perhaps it wouldn't be such a bad idea to keep on the friendly side of Ben Fox. She knew how persuasive his powerful strength could be – being his friend might be to her advantage!

After that, he was as gentle as a lamb to her, and she derived a lot of love and pleasure from their friendship over the next few weeks. This was a feeling she had never known before, in all her young life.

It was during the frozen mornings in the short month of February, that she realised she was feeling bilious far too often. A quick count up on the calendar assured her that unless something happened in the very next week, she would have a problem on her hands.

She knew that she must tell Ben, for however much he was nicknamed a simpleton by all and sundry, he was the father of her child.

He was out helping with the lambing when she made her way up to the top meadow; and on his own for once. As she explained everything to him his face lit up with joy. He really was like a big kid at heart, but he did agree with her that they must get married – if only to give the child a name.

As she walked back to the farmhouse she felt quite elated at the thought of her, Phylis Baxter, being a married woman. What would 'they', meaning those at home, have to say about that then?

Marrying Ben, and the coming birth of their child, would be the smallest of her problems. The biggest worry was telling her mother, and getting her permission to marry… that was once she had got over the shock. Phyl told Ben to leave it all to her to sort out, knowing that this problem would cause no end of a scandal at home, whichever way she looked at it!

Chapter 17

All the time the train headed out towards the heart of the country Vera sat on the edge of her seat, just staring into space, not seeing the other passengers sharing the carriage with her.

She looked out of the window, then at two soldiers who were obviously returning from leave. She started to bite her nails, then opened her handbag, foraging through it in the pretence of looking for something she needed.

At long last the train pulled into the village station. Vera was the first to leap from her seat, eager to get going on her mission. She had written to Phyl a few days earlier and hoped that the girl would be at the station to meet her.

After giving up her ticket she made her way along the narrow slipway that separated the platform from the outside of the station. She looked about her apprehensively until there, in the distance, she saw Phyl walking down the lane. Vera instinctively raised her hand and waved.

She had to admit to herself that the girl looked different – plumper, and a lot happier. It was such a silly thing to annoy her, but she could not condone the state of her daughter, despite the fact Phyl had never looked better in all her life.

'Hello Mum. I'm glad that you're here early. I want you to see over the farm, and also to meet Sally and Joe... and Ben, of course.'

Vera told herself it was best to play it by ear and see what came to light. She would not rebuke Phyl for what she had done. It was much too late for that. The best thing was to act sensibly, as Janie had advised her, and to meet this Ben character. She was more than prepared to hear his side of the story, and what his intentions were regarding Phyl and the little 'un.

The farmer and his wife made her very welcome, it was obvious they thought a lot of Phyl. Vera beamed with pride and felt quite pleased, hoping that when she met this Ben, she would also find him above criticism.

It was quite late in the afternoon and she still hadn't met this Ben yet. She was getting quite agitated for she knew she must leave to catch the train back to London very shortly. In spite of Phyl's friendly chatter, it was as if she was somehow preventing Vera from seeing the man who was to marry her daughter.

The darkness closed in on the cold and wintry afternoon, and Vera was about to bid her 'goodbyes' to everyone, when Ben stumbled through the back door. Phyl ran to his side and drew him forward to meet her mum.

Vera stood staring at him, almost stunned. He must be as old as her George - he was a huge man, like a bear. He smiled down at Phyl, like a big kid, all eager to please... and when he spoke he sounded as young as Phyl.

Her mind going round in turmoil, Vera stared at his simple face. His bottom lip was trembling in excitement and uncontrolled saliva ran from the edge of his chin. Jesus Christ, was this the man who had forced himself on her girl? Was this the man Phyl wanted to bring into their family? How could she do this to them? How could she let herself be close to this creature...?

Staring at the two of them, Vera was too stunned for words.

'What in God's name has she let herself in for?' she kept asking herself.

Phyl clung to Ben's arm. 'Well, what do you think Mum… shall I get married next month?'

Vera continued to stare at the two of them. What hurt the most was their obvious happiness with each other.

Making the excuse that she had to rush and catch her train, Vera bid hasty goodbyes to all of them, and let Phyl walk with her to the end of the lane. She would get the bus to the station by herself. She must have time to think, to convince herself that this was the right thing for all concerned. Phyl put her hands on her mother's shoulders and bent to kiss her on the cheek. 'Bye Mum, I'll let you know the date. Perhaps you…' Here Vera stopped her, 'No, no! I tell you what, take this fiver and come home next weekend… we can talk about it properly then. I can't discuss it here and now. I can't think straight, I really can't…'

The bus loomed into view, and Vera turned to go. 'Don't forget, next weekend, then we can talk about it, OK? Cheerio.' Before Phyl could object or find an excuse, Vera had leapt aboard the crowded bus and disappeared.

Phyl tucked the note inside the pocket of her mac and walked slowly back to the farm. The more she thought about it, the more she realised it wasn't such a bad idea. She would have the chance to see everyone again at the same time… that is except Dad. She would have to write to him with all the news at some later date. He wouldn't mind what she did. After all, she told herself, it was no different than when Marjie got herself lumbered by Alec.

She would tell Ben her plans when she got back, and they

would make their own arrangements for the coming wedding. Of course they would live in the farmhouse for the time being, that was until Ben organised a home of their own. She hummed to herself as she made her way across the pitch-black field and through the short lane to the back of the farm.

Chapter 18

The weekend promised to be cold and damp, Vera had been in the Anderson shelter with Marjie and the babe for most of Friday night, and the complaining of Gran about her screws did nothing to alleviate the tension she felt building up inside of her, at the thought of Phyl's visit on Saturday.

Her mind was going round in circles. She wished that George was home with her, just to help her decide what to do for the best. She needed to be level-headed and think straight. She yawned. Those blasted air raids did nothing to help things along either.

Should she go along to Kings Cross to meet Phyl off the train, she wondered. No, better let Phyl do it her way. She looked up at the clock on the mantelpiece, if the trains were running alright, Phyl should be home about one o'clock... she must stop herself worrying.

Going to the window she peered down the street for any sign of her coming yet. 'Hmph, only Gran. Making off to 'The Three Crowns' for her usual,' Vera tutted under her breath. 'Funny how her screws kept her immobile all through the night, and yet that didn't stop her going across to the pub during the day!'

At the moment Marjie was up in her room, and the baby was asleep, so she would have Phyl all to herself. Perhaps she could make her see sense. 'Oh God! I hope she isn't going to be too late home, I really want to talk to her before everyone else gets to see her.'

Suddenly the siren started up again, Vera gave a shout to Marjie and they raced down the shelter. Janie had gone to the market. Anyway, she always used the large street shelter when she was caught out.

'When do you expect Phyl home, Mum?' Marjie cuddled the infant to her, while Vera plaited her fine hair for her. Vera's face flushed, and she looked thoughtful. 'Any time now really!' she murmured as something crashed in the distance.

The sound of the ack-ack could be heard very clearly. 'I thought this bloody bombing had finished... seems like it's never ending.'

The barrage died away, but although the peace seemed imminent, the all-clear didn't sound for another hour.

It was raining steadily when they clambered out of the shelter. Vera was careful to secure the waterproof sheet over the opening, fixing it well down with a couple of bricks. She had seen it flooded with ankle deep water more than once before. Now they were very careful on exit.

Back in the house, Vera spread herself across the hearth with a page of the Daily Herald at arm's length, trying to light the feeble looking fire. Suddenly it gave a roar, and taking the paper away just in time, she watched as the flames caught the draught, and away it roared.

She stood up, rubbing her wrinkled kneecaps, and stared at the clock over the mantle-piece. It was almost two-thirty. Surely Phyl should be home by now? Her mouth pursed in annoyance. 'I bet she won't come home, I bet she's staying there and being stubborn. The little bitch ... and I gave her the fare money too.'

An excited voice at the back door, and in came Gran, half

soaked from walking through the rain, but looking as pleased as punch. From underneath her voluminous mac, Gran produced a shopping bag, and grinning from ear to ear, she plonked it down on the table while she hung her wet dripping coat on the back door.

'Here you are gel, have a go at this!' She plunged her hands into the wet shopping bag and drew out tinned butter, tinned peaches, jam, and some white soap. And the best of the lot - so Gran reckoned - was a pack of lipsticks in a variety of pinks and reds, all wrapped in cellophane.

'What do you make of that then?' beamed Gran, as excited as a kid on Christmas morning. 'They're all Tattoo lipsticks, without the hard cases on. Half a crown each, not bad eh! The groceries are a present for Phyl, to start home with.' Gran looked around the room. 'She is home ain't she?'

'She should be soon,' Vera said. 'Where did you get this little lot from Gran?'

Gran touched her nose with her forefinger. 'Tut tut, never you mind. That's my business.   Sort out what lipsticks you want, and then I'll let Janie have a look when she gets in.'

Vera turned the lipsticks over lovingly. She hadn't seen a new lipstick for ages. After carefully looking, she chose the one she wanted. It was a deep plum red, and she smiled in anticipation of using it. Fetching her purse, she counted out the coppers and silver into Gran's hand. 'Here you are Gran, two and six... alright?' Then she stopped, and gave her another half crown. 'Can I take one for Phyl, for when she gets in?'

'Course you can... they won't last long I can tell you!'

Vera picked out another colour and carefully put it away in the sideboard. That would please Phyl, she hoped. When she got in!

Suddenly realising that Gran was dripping water on the floor, Vera insisted, 'Gran, you should dry yourself off. You must be damp and cold.'

'Don't you worry love, I've had something to keep the chill out.' She laughed deep and long, making Vera blush guiltily.

Gran could suss out a drop of gin or port, even if it was hidden under ten counters. She had wily ways of getting people to buy it for her. She had no qualms about talking to strangers, and was well known for her contacts in the black market. Harmless, was what most people thought of her. She could carry goods around and no one would look at her twice. Anything that came along, if she thought she could use it to an advantage, you were on! There was always a willing customer, somewhere!

Gran wasn't very fast on her feet, but she was reliable, and a lot of people knew her.

She pocketed the money and, stuffing the rest of the lipsticks into her bag, she made off for home. 'I bet my Janie will be in and doing her nut, wondering where I am.' She turned and looked, puzzled, at Vera. 'When is young Phyl getting home? Looks like she's had second thoughts to me.'

Vera noted the time... it was getting late. Where on earth could she be?

Chapter 19

It was hardly light when Phyl donned her coat, wrapped a scarf around her neck and, clutching her small hold-all, left the warmth of the farmhouse kitchen to make her way down the lane to catch the eight thirty bus. Sally was in the milking shed, and Ben was nowhere to be found. Still, she had said her goodbyes to them last thing yesterday.

It was difficult to walk in her best and only pair of shoes, with frozen ground and the mud tracks made by the cows. Normally when she wore her wellingtons about the farm she never noticed it, but she had sported her decent set of clothes, knowing that her mum would be casting a very critical eye over her.

The train left about nine-thirty – they were few and far between, as were the buses. To miss one could make an hour's difference, sometimes more.

Standing apart from the small crowd waiting on the platform, stamping her feet together to keep warm, she kept her eyes downcast, hoping no-one would recognise her, or attempt a conversation. At last the train came and she was thankful to get a window seat – not that she could see out much, with all the protective tape across it. Still, she would close her eyes and feign sleep, until they pulled in to London, which shouldn't take too long.

It was the ticket inspector who brought her to her senses. He clipped her ticket and told her that a change had to be made.

'Going through to Liverpool Street Miss... bit of bother on the lines. You'll have to take the bus back to where you want to go.' She thanked him and replaced her ticket inside her bag. It was a nuisance, but well, there was a war on, and it only meant an extra bus to catch.

She settled back down to doze again, thinking of home, and all that she had in her mind to say to her mum. No arguments, just her point of view about matters. She was determined to have her say about her own future, and Ben's... and the baby.

In spite of the cold, it was quite bright and sunny when Phyl walked out of the station, lifting her face to the sky to breathe in the fresh morning air. It really was too nice to line up for a bus. She would walk through the city streets and get one if she felt tired.

Everywhere looked so different. A lot of places had suffered awful bombing, while most buildings had their shattered windows boarded up. She had never really seen London so early in the morning, or on her own before. After half an hour she came to St Pauls, and stood for a moment catching her breath. She would make for Holborn, and then jump on a bus. Tucking her scarf around her neck more tightly, she eased her toes inside her shoes, which were beginning to pinch. Then she sat on the edge of a low wall, thinking over her plans.

The droning wail of the siren made her jump, it must be coming from somewhere quite near. She was near a large building flanked on each side by sandbags, but people were running in all directions, calling out to her as they ran. She stood, as if in a trance, watching them. With no idea where the nearest public shelter was, she ran away from the sandbagged building and out into the middle of the street - searching for somewhere to hide. The noise of the Luftwaffe and the ack-ack together was deafening, making her panic. She was unused to all this, and really frightened.

A warden on the other side of the street yelled out to her, but she just stood staring at him – too terrified to move. Ambulances tore down the road, and smoke filled the air. Suddenly, a man grabbed her, pulling her down against a wall, and flattening himself to her side on the icy pavement. He put his arm over the back of her head and across her ear.

There was a deafening explosion, and she was aware of bricks, glass and rubble falling on top of them. Her back was pinned down by something enormously heavy, and she couldn't breathe for the dust and smoke. All she could see were rivulets of blood coming from the man's forehead, trickling down his face and over his nose. Dust enveloped them and she closed her eyes.

After laying there for what seemed like hours, she came to, hearing shouts from above the pile of bricks. Then two pairs of hands were frenziedly pulling all the debris away from them. She heard the bleeding man beside her say something to their rescuers – he was complaining about his foot. She tried to move and see if she could help him in any way, but realised that her back was numb with the force of whatever it was that was pinning her down.

Voices from above kept drifting down to them, as more people tried to free them from the wreckage. Suddenly, waves of nausea hit her, and she knew no more, except to feel transported high into the air as if she was floating.

When she came too, Phyl was surprised to find herself in bed. She tried to look around, but could not turn her head at all, and her body hurt in a thousand places. Her mind was still not clear as to what had happened. People were leaning over her, their faces bulbous and looming as they stared at her. They were speaking - about her, but she couldn't hear what they were saying. A man wearing a white mask looked deep into her eyes. She blinked as he did so, and she saw him nod. Then a sharp needle was pushed into her arm.

The people in white floated away, to be replaced with others, looking and waiting. She thought she saw her mum, and her eyes filled with tears. She so much wanted to tell her what had happened, how scared she felt. But most of all, tell them how sorry she was for everything. Her body shook with emotion, as she realised that her family were not really against her - they loved her. The faces became a blur... she was so sleepy, so very tired. She wanted to tell them, but she couldn't drag herself from the dark abyss drawing her down. She must sleep... must. Tomorrow, she would tell mum, tell them all, how happy she was, and how she loved them all... tomorrow! When the pain had gone from her head, the terrible pain!

Vera stayed at the hospital throughout the afternoon and evening, while Phyl slept. Several times the nursing staff came to see her, but there was no news.

Then the staff nurse came along to Vera, and took her to one side, gently telling her that Phyl had not regained consciousness, and had died while in a deep coma.

A young nurse brought Vera a cup of tea, asking if there was anyone they should contact for her. Vera took the cup and drank the tea, hoping that it would make her stop shaking. The news still hadn't sunk in! She thought of George - he idolised Phyl. He hadn't known about the baby... Oh God!

It was not until George came home on compassionate leave

the next day, that Vera let go and sobbed herself dry.

Chapter 20

It was almost a year later, to the very day, that Vera and Jane went to a Sunday service in a little church in the City - almost in the shadow of the great St Paul's. This was where Phyl had lost her life during that terrible raid.

Time had taken its toll on Vera, who, almost ten years' Jane's senior, had at one stage looked like an old and grieving woman.

Jane still felt bruised from the loss of her Norman, but her cheery and determined attitude was now rubbing off on Vera, who told herself life had to go on. She had Marjie and young Terry to think about... as well as George, bless him!

For ages she had made herself almost physically ill with remorse and guilt over Phyl's death. All that kept going round in her mind was 'if only she hadn't insisted on Phyl coming home to talk about things, she would be alive today'

Ben had been notified of the tragedy, and had come down for the funeral. But she had heard nothing of his life and where-abouts since then.

After the morning service had finished, the two women walked, slowly and silently, through the small gardens to the main road, both absorbed in their own thoughts and dreams.

Vera stopped to pick a small wild flower from the rubble that edged the roadside. Staring at it hard and long, her eyes misted over with tears, as memories of Phyl came flooding back. Dear Phyl, she would never know just how much she was missed... and loved. Never.

Oh yes, Adolf had a lot to answer for, in more ways than one. It seemed that there was always a woman somewhere, weeping for a loved one. The only consolation being that even the deepest hurt must heal itself someday!

Chapter 21

The pub where Janie worked in the evening was only a bus ride away at Euston. She had been there for almost a year now, egged on by Gran to '…go and meet people.' Under Lulu's influence she had started at 'The Orange Tree' to cover for a barmaid who had gone sick. After only a few weeks, the publican was so pleased with her efforts, and her pleasing nature, that she was asked to stay on.

Gran was proving a great help, and did far more than her fair share of household jobs, only too pleased to see her Janie getting a bit more out of life again. The two of them helped each other, and while there was no fear of air raids, Janie didn't worry.

She had her hair 'Toni' permed, and it suited her admirably. A dab of Miner's make-up, and a touch of lipstick, did wonders. Gran smiled as she watched her get ready to go out at night. 'Who knows,' she thought to herself. 'She might find herself another fella... can't blame her if she does.'

While Janie put the finishing touches to her hair, Gran sat in her usual chair tearing the old newspapers into small squares. It was her job to keep the paper going in the lavvy. She was so proud of her neat squares, which she strung onto a cord, before hanging them in the outside lavatory on the long nail that Norm had put up, after he had done the distempering. She often wondered who would do the distempering now; it was something that had to be renewed over the years.

Gran had a friend in Bloomsbury who had a lavvy in her bathroom. And one indoors too! It sounded nice, she convinced herself it wouldn't be very healthy having one inside the house – far better out in the fresh air.

Janie put her coat on, all ready to out. 'I shan't be late... and I might get a lift home with Del.' Gran smiled, as Janie tried to sound all casual. This Derek was a projectionist in a cinema, and had taken a liking to Janie. He always gave her a lift whenever he could - all in the line of duty, he explained. He had a battered old van which he used to take the reels of film from one cinema to another. That was his story! Gran felt it was put to other uses - such as taking the usherettes home and cadging a spot of supper.

Humming to herself on the bus journey to Euston, Janie made the blonde Clippie smile, as she pushed her way along the centre of the bus. 'How nice to hear someone a bit blooming cheerful – the whole world could do with a bit of cheering up, at times!'

Janie flushed, she felt downright happy and at peace with the world at the moment. Spring would soon be here, the few daffodils in the gardens always cheered her up no end. The raids had eased up, and everyone hoped that it wouldn't be too long to the end of the war. Four years had been a long time. Poor Alec was fighting somewhere in the Middle East, and Marjie worried herself sick over him. Janie often wondered what Norm would have made of all this... all those years that he worried himself silly.

Gran was the one who had surprised them all, she was a real fighter and had been a great comfort to them all, dear old soul that she was.

Skipping lightly off the bus, Janie ran across the road in the darkness to start her evening behind the bar. Her trim figure and smiling face betrayed nothing of the worries of a widow and mother.

Sid, the publican, was cleaning down the tables when she let herself through. 'Hello, my angel,' he called out to her, his face alight and grinning. 'Did you hear on the news? A load more of them GIs have arrived in London. Lil says there are lots of them out in Bushey Park, where her daughter lives.'

Jane started wiping glasses, listening to what he was saying. 'Oh they don't worry me Sid, after all they are customers, all said and done. They're harmless.'

Sid grinned all the more, 'I don't know about harmless, I'm not a nice looking woman like you. But anyway, watch yourself girlie!'

'Don't fuss Sid. They're lonely, like our men are, and anyway, I'm an old married woman, who's...' Sid cut her short, and looking her straight in the eye, said, 'You're not old, and you're a woman... so take care!'

They were exceptionally busy that evening. Poor Lil kept complaining about her aching feet, so Janie did more than her share of running backwards and forwards round the different bars. The regulars were waiting beside the GIs, who were more than courteous and let them be served first.

Jane had noticed an American, who sat propped at the end of the bar for a long time that evening. Every time she looked in his direction, he caught her eye and smiled. It was embarrassing to say the least. She tried to be all efficient when he ordered a drink, but she was a little unnerved by the way he continued to stare at her.

She whispered to Lil to change places with her in the other bar, but Lil knew she was on a cushy thing as far as her poor feet were concerned, and stayed put, next to Sid. 'Why, I do believe he's giving you the eye Janie, you're alright for a lift home in a taxi tonight.'

Jane trembled, hoping the American hadn't heard Lil. But he walked up to her, bending his huge frame over the counter. 'You know Honey, I will give you a lift home tonight. I'd be really pleased if you would accept!' He smiled warmly, as if to confirm his suggestion.

Damn Lil, for putting her in such an awkward situation, thought Jane.

'I don't know... all the same, thank you. I might be getting a lift with a friend... later.'

She served him his drink and placed the change on the counter. He was quick to cover her fingers with his, as he reached out for the coins. His warm touch sent a tremor through Jane's hand, her cheeks flushed and she felt her mouth go dry. For the rest of the evening she kept as far away from him as she could, going out of her way to serve everyone as far from him as possible. His eyes never left her, the whole time. He smiled to himself – she was a real lady, that one! A real honey!

By ten thirty Jane knew that Derek would not be showing up, and she would have to catch the bus home. That is until she saw the GI still leaning on the bar at the far end, looking at her and trying to catch her eye. When Sid sounded last orders, she felt quite pleased to be on the other side of the counter. As soon as the last customer left, Sid let the two women go off at once, holding back the blackout curtain for them to go, and wishing them both 'Good night'. The two women walked down the main road together, and as Lil only lived in a basement flat off Euston Road, she'd be home in next to no time. They parted at the bus stop, and Janie pulled up her collar against the cold night air, and waited for the bus to come.

She had waited for about ten minutes when she was aware of a person walking towards her. Tall, broad and with a squeak to his shoes, it was the GI who had been in the pub all night. She stiffened and tried to remain distant.

He smiled and touched his fingers to his hat. 'Hello Ma'am. Could I offer you a lift home? It doesn't seem like a good night to hang around for a bus, and on your own too.'

Janie was just about to refuse and argue that she was alright, when it started to rain, cold and heavy. Taking her by the arm, the GI steered her towards the corner, where a taxi stood purring by the kerbside. 'By the way, my name is Franklin... you know, after the President. But everyone calls me Frankie. Here we are. Here's the cab.'

As they reached the taxi and he opened the door, her mind was racing. It was all really too much. She didn't know him, how could she let him take her home? Perhaps she could give a false address, lead him away, then she could make her way home afterwards?

After ushering her into the taxi, he slammed the cab door and sat next to her. She was very wet, and as she tried to shake the rain from her hair, he offered her his handkerchief. She smiled at his thoughtfulness. 'Thank you ... I do seem to be rather damp.'

'Hey, why don't we stop for a coffee? I know a place near here. It would warm you up... keep the cold out?' He hesitated, smiling at her... 'Please?'

Why not? She thought. He did seem so very nice, and she could do with a hot drink on such a bleak night. She smiled shyly at him. 'Thank you, I'd love to.'

He leaned forward and gave an address to the cabbie, then, settling himself back next to Jane, he started to tell her all about himself.

By the time they reached the small cafe at Kings Cross, she knew that he was a fighter pilot, and had loathed London on first sight. And back home, he lived in a place called Cleveland… well, at least on the outskirts. Jane listened attentively, he was obviously very homesick, and seemed to enjoy talking about his home and family.

They both sat in the semi darkness sipping their drinks, until the owner started to close up. It was twelve o'clock, and he wanted to go home.

Leaving the warmth of the cafe, they and walked along the wet pavements. Jane didn't want to take him home, at least not now. He was prepared to find another taxi and take her, but she wanted to walk a bit. 'Just as you like, Honey… whatever you want.'

Turning up his coat collar, he put an arm around her waist in a protective fashion. They walked slowly, and for quite a while, just exchanging confidences. She learned that he was to stay in England for another two months at least, but then he wasn't sure what was happening. He had married a long time ago. He showed her a photograph of a pretty looking woman, with dark bubbly curls. 'That's Kitty… she was a great girl. We were married at nineteen.'

Jane looked at him enquiringly, 'But you are still married?' she enquired gingerly. He looked downwards, a wry smile etched across his face. 'No, no. I'm a widower… Kitty was drowned in an accident the year before the war started. I think I was the first one to enlist when it all began. All I wanted was to be in the war, and perhaps get killed! Oh, I'm sorry… I know a lot different now, I've got over it. But I still miss her, you know!'

Squeezing his hand, Janie listened in silence… she knew what he had been through. She looked deeply into his face. He wasn't a handsome man by any stretch of the imagination, but his wide eyes and deep smile gave off a very pleasing picture.

'I must go now… I really must.' She had no idea how she was going to get home other than walking it.

Suddenly, Frankie leapt forward and whistled a taxi as it steamed over the junction. The cab stopped at the side of the pavement, and taking her by the arm, Frankie ushered her inside with him, and waited for her to give the cabbie her address. After a moment's hesitation she gave it, then sat on the edge of the seat wondering what he would do next.

As they slowed down by the shops, she jumped up quickly, thanking him for everything. He opened the cab door, getting out with her, and told the cabbie to wait. Then taking her hand, he thanked her warmly for her company, and with a touch of his cap, he got back in the cab again. She smiled, 'Goodnight… goodnight.'

He waved from the cab window, 'See you on Thursday… yes?'

Janie remained silent for a second, holding back, then… 'Yes, Thursday.'

Then he was gone, into the darkness. She could hear the engine as it roared away. Turning her key in the lock, she was trembling with emotion, and she wondered. Oh, whatever would Gran say if she knew what had been going on tonight.

Still, she might not ever see him again, knowing what soldiers were like... especially those Yankees!

She tiptoed around the kitchen for fear of waking Gran. Her shoes were wet and wrinkled, so she stuffed them with newspaper to dry them out. Her hair looked a bit of a mess, but she was too tired to bother with it now. Turning off the light, she dragged herself upstairs to bed.

He was nice – she couldn't stop thinking about him. She could still smell that spicy smell that came from his wet clothing. Before climbing into bed, she said goodnight to the photo of Norm, as she always did. She put the photo frame down, feeling vaguely excited, as she had done three years ago.

Chapter 22

During the spring of '44, young Terry came home on a short holiday break to see his family again. There had been no air-raids as such for a long while, so Vera had relented to his pleas – written in every letter – suggesting that he came home for Easter, while the village school was shut.

When Vera met him off the train, she was amazed at the change in him. He was tall and broad shouldered, and looked extremely well. Gone was the milky looking lad of a few years ago. Here was a strapping young man, whose chin boasted golden stubble, and promised future handsomeness.

Striding along the platform, Terry waved, grinning broadly. 'Hi mum! Hi!' Vera rushed forward to hug him, as she had when he had left, and then felt all self-conscious as she did so.

All the way back to Essex Road, he chatted about the farm, the sheep, the milking, the dipping – his voice could be heard above everybody else's. She blushed, thinking what the other passengers might be saying amongst themselves, then she looked around and realised that other people weren't really interested in them at all. She felt quite at ease then. He was home again, her Terry was back with them.

He quite openly declared that he still kept in close contact with Helen, they wrote to each other all the time. He only wished they could be nearer to each other to meet occasionally. Vera raised her eyebrows on hearing this. So, it was still going strong, their little relationship. Still, she thought to herself, he could do a lot worse than be friendly with a nice girl like Helen. She wondered if Janie had any notion of what was going on, she would have a word with her later on.

Vera knew that Janie had recently met an American soldier while working at the pub. She hadn't seen him yet, but according to Gran, Janie was quite taken with him. She had taken him home one evening last week, and Gran had been really impressed. 'Such a gentleman, lovely manners, and he don't smell!' Vera laughed when she had heard this. 'Smell Gran... what do you mean?'

'You know... smell! I can't abide smelly socks, and my Norm, bless him, must have had the worst. I know he couldn't help it, getting his feet soaked all the time. But still, it used to rile me to see him sitting in his chair with his socks orf, picking the bits between his toes. Nasty habit it was Vera, he never did get out of it.'

Smiling, Vera poured them both another cup of tea. Terry had gone out for the day, with an old mate of his. She felt that Gran was in a talkative mood so she plied her with cups of tea, to glean what news she could.

Now that Janie worked in the pub, as well as helping out in the re-homing centre, Vera hardly saw her at all. There was a great lull everywhere, and Vera asked Gran if she thought that the end of the war might be soon. Gran's face puckered up thoughtfully. It was true the bombing had slowed right down, although there was still a lot of fighting 'over there'.

'You know Vera, during the last war I thought it was bad. My poor old man used to tell me how the young lads used to cry, who were sent in alongside of him. They were no age at all, but they had to lead the horses in. Bits of kids they were really.' Gran looked all dreamy and distant, as if she was reliving her younger days.

'You've been a widow a long time Gran haven't you?' Vera asked. She had never heard Gran talk so nostalgically before. It was hard to imagine her as a young married woman with a husband by her side. Gran never said much about how she felt over the loss of her husband, and her fatherless son. She was a fighter, who against all odds, had managed to come up smiling and cheerful. She was an independent soul really, but had loved the idea of moving in with her Norman – such a thoughtful girl, his Janie was. Now it seemed like history repeating itself all over again.

Gran wouldn't like to see Janie remaining on her own, like she had done. It wasn't good for a healthy young woman... her Janie deserved a lot more. She deserved a man in her life, someone to fill her needs, to share her love. Gran hoped one day to see it happen... or perhaps it had already?

Chapter 23

Franklin Somers pushed the last of the papers into the file and shoved them into the tall cabinet. At last he was finished, and with any luck he could be cleaned up and out of the camp by nine.

He had not wanted to be put on administrative work for three months – he was not ill, only tired. True, he had done more than his share of sorties since arriving in England, and knew that when his senior officer suggested the alternative post for three months, he was only thinking of his wellbeing. However, that was before, when he had been all uptight and sorry for himself, still grieving over the loss of his darling Kitty.

Helped greatly by the fellas he flew with, it had taken a lot to come out of his shell, get rid of that chip on his shoulder, and come to terms with the world. It had been hard, very hard, but now he had found the answer to his silent prayers. Janie Howard was unlike anyone he knew, let alone an English woman. She had made him look twice where he normally wouldn't have looked at all. So out of character to the usual barmaids, whom he considered to be peroxided vipers, out for all they could get, taking the yanks on rotten when it amounted to buying drinks for them.

He had caught his breath when he first saw Janie standing there at the bar. Just like Kitty, her nature was as genuine and natural as the grass that grew by the waterside. He saw her and knew – she was the one person who could make or break the last five and a half years' state of celibacy. Yep, Janie was the brightest thing on the horizon for him at the moment. He wanted to know more about her, and her thoughts about him.

It was almost ten o'clock when he dashed into the private bar and scanned the sea of faces, looking for her. All at once he grinned widely and his eyes shone! There she was, talking to an elderly couple with interest. Waiting his time till she lifted her eyes, he tilted his head, smiling fully at her.

There was no mistaking the pleasure that shone from her face as she caught sight of him. He was etched in the half-light... smart suit, clean shaven and looking very handsome. The large brown eyes fringed with heavy lashes, the clear skin, made a wonderful compliment to the honest looking smile that played on his firm mouth.

Janie's heart skipped a beat, and she blushed instinctively for behaving so foolishly. You're acting like a schoolgirl, she told herself disapprovingly - after all he was only a man looking at her. But in her heart, she knew it was the look of a person she could feel for, and come to like in a much stronger way if the opportunity arose.

Propping himself up at the end of the bar, and enquiring how she was, Franklin ordered a drink. He watched her intently as she poured it, trying to catch her eye. She placed it on the counter in front of him, but before she could speak he looked straight at her... 'I'll wait for you outside when you finish honey, OK? I have something I want to tell you!'

'Sounds interesting...' Janie, her face aglow, placed the drink down in front of him, and rang the money in the till. Elbowed out by another soldier waiting to be served, Frankie took his drink and sat in the far corner of the bar, where he could observe her while she worked.

It was hard to believe that she was the mother of two girls. She'd told him she had lost her husband at the beginning of the war, and now lived in Islington with her mother-in-law. After meeting the old dame briefly, and knowing Janie, it wasn't hard to see how they all got on amiably together. It was the sort of family relationship he and Kitty had hankered after, before the war had transpired. As he looked across at her, he felt a warm glow from within. She was lovely in every way. He must get to know her better – to know her as a woman.

Sunday was Janie's day off, and Frankie was picking her up at around mid morning. He had organised things so he wasn't needed anywhere near the camp for the whole of Sunday. All he wanted was to share the whole day with his Janie, leaving it up to her to suggest how she would like to spend it. After all, it was her day off!

Janie dressed herself with great care, choosing her almost best dress – the full-skirted, pale green crepe-de-chine that showed her colouring to its best. She brushed her hair till it shone, coaxing it into a pageboy roll around her neck. Standing back from the mirror, she looked at herself in various poses, before smiling with satisfaction. She couldn't do any more to improve matters. She had never been a martyr to a lot of make-up, using only the merest touch of lipstick on her full lips, and a dab of face powder when it was needed. Staring at her reflection, she wondered if she should have used some of the liquid cream-powder that Marjie next door had offered to lend her for the 'big date'. But no, she would have felt too overdone, and quite unused to it.

The doorbell rang, and Gran called out to say that Frankie

was waiting downstairs for her. She could tell that Gran had put her posh voice on by the way she called up the stairs. 'My dear, you have a visitor, a soldier. I'll show him into the front room!' Janie laughed to herself. Gran was trying to be all proper but was really busting at the seams to have a good natter to him... but that could come later. At the moment, all Janie wanted was to go out and enjoy each other's company, and have some time together.

Gran gasped as Janie came down the stairs, her eyes staring appraisingly at the way Janie had 'turned out'. 'You do look nice Gel!' Gran cast an eye in his direction, looking for a word of approval. 'Don't she, Mr Somers?'

'Please call me Frankie... and yes, she does look stunning.' He'd felt himself go all to jelly as she came into sight, and as she walked down the stairs towards him he felt really chuffed. To think she had turned herself out like this for him! She was a honey, a real honey.

'Well where are you taking me to?' Janie smiled at him and drew her gloves on, while Gran looked on admiringly.

'I thought perhaps we might go as far as Windsor Park. Perhaps go on the lake and have a bite to eat somewhere along the riverside?'

Janie's eyes widened as she heard what he had in mind, it all sounded wonderful. She looked at Gran to see what she had to say about it. Gran caught Janie's eye and winked her approval. 'Sounds like a smashing idea to me. You two get along then, afore the weather breaks. We might have some rain later.' She threw her eyes upwards. 'It won't be long orf... not if my screws know anything about it.'

Janie and Frank both laughed, and as they bade their

goodbyes, Gran smiled at Janie in a knowing fashion. 'Enjoy yourself love. I shall be up the corner when you get back, don't worry about me, alright?'

She watched them go down the street, arm in arm. He was so tall and protective at the side of her, while she looked lovely, like a young woman again on a new date. Letting the curtain slip from her hands she smiled to herself. 'Make the most of your opportunities Janie gel... life's too short to cut yourself off in the middle.'

Gran got herself ready to go and see Lulu, who she hadn't seen for ages. Lulu had a boyfriend of a sort herself, some old geyser who worked in the tailoring trade. He was as old as Lulu, a widower, and by what Lulu said, had pots of money, even before the war started.

When she arrived at Lulu's flat, the other side of the Angel, she hammered hard on the door. No response! She banged again and waited, her face puckered, wondering where Lulu could be at this time of the morning. She was not an early bird by a long shot. Lulu believed in late to bed, and late to rise. Her day never began until almost noon, and that was on a good day.

Gran stood awkwardly, wondering what to do if her friend was away for a few days. Lulu trusted her, and left a latchkey so Gran could always let herself in, should the need arise. Pushing over the small flowerpot on the window ledge, Gran took the door key from its hiding place. Looking all around the area outside the flats and scanning the square below, she satisfied herself that Lulu was nowhere to be seen. She would let herself in and wait for her return. Gran tutted at the waste of time, but there was nothing she could do about it. No doubt Lulu had made a new contact in the black market, if she sat and waited for her, she might do herself a bit of good in more ways than one. With a sigh she turned the key in the lock and entered the flat, making up her mind that she would only wait a short while, just in case Lulu had nipped around the corner.

Gran almost thought that she was in the wrong flat, as a man's irate voice shouted from the bedroom at the end of the passage. 'Hurry up ducks! How long are you keeping a guy waiting?' Stopping dead in her tracks, Gran peered along the half-lit passageway to see who was calling, and to whom. She edged her way slowly along to the kitchen, and with some hesitation peered into the familiar room. The wireless was full on, and Lulu was standing in front of the sink, in her peach dressing gown, with one bare leg cocked over the edge of the sink. She was so engrossed with what she was doing, and the noise from the wireless, that she obviously hadn't heard Gran come in. 'Christ Lulu, what's the point of me banging on the door gel?'

Lulu turned, a cigarette hanging out of her lips, and a row of bright henna curls dangling across her forehead. Her face lit up as she saw who it was. 'Ellie, Ellie love, how long you been there?' She lifted her leg out of the sink, and placing the cigarette in a saucer on the draining board, prepared to dry herself. Suddenly the man's voice could be heard bellowing through the flat again. Lulu's face turned red, and throwing down the towel, she rushed from the kitchen. 'Oh Christ! I clean forgot 'im... just a mo Ellie.'

Gran followed her, eager to know what was going on. 'Come on Lulu. You said last night you would... come on...' shouted a man's voice from the bedroom, followed by Lulu's pleading tones, '...please understand Bob, I've got a friend come to call.

She's only in the kitchen. Come on Bob, be a good 'un. I'll see you again tonight? Go on Bob.'

Gran stood in the doorway of the kitchen and watched with interest. An elderly man with a balding head, dressed only in a check shirt and a pair of socks, was battling to stay on with Lulu and finish what she had obviously promised him. He looked so sorry for himself. As he caught sight of Gran staring at him in all his glory, he turned quickly, trying to hide his nakedness as he fumbled around and dragged on his trousers.

Gran turned away and couldn't stop from laughing. Poor old sod! He must have been getting on – the state of him reminded her of Janie's bit of grey crochet work she'd been doing … before she'd unravelled it!

In less than five minutes Lulu had dressed herself and helped the boyfriend on his way. He wasn't too pleased at being ousted, but the promise of 'see you later on' from Lulu must have done the trick.

Gran and Lulu sat draining the pot of tea, and laughing for some time afterwards. Lulu said she felt sorry for the old boy. He was very good to her moneywise, but he really couldn't always 'make it'.

'So I see,' laughed Gran, '…so I see!'

Chapter 24

The afternoon had been wonderful. Together they had walked and chatted, laughed at each other's silly jokes, and now Janie held Frankie's hand and they walked along the riverbank. It was quite warm for May although the threat of rain was imminent. Remembering Gran's last words, Janie suggested they should begin to make their way back home.

Finding a dry patch of grass under a willow tree, Frank sat down quickly, pulling her down beside him. Janie laughed and fell into a heap at his side. They sat there for what seemed an eternity, not making any movement nor saying a word. There was no need, for the feeling of mutual contentment was enough. Janie stared at the movements of the swans and ducks as they stirred the muddy waters.

Frankie was quiet too, she could sense him breathing deeply next to her. Suddenly, his hand found hers, and their fingers intertwined. It was so peaceful just to sit and daydream, without being conscious of the war and the rest of the world about them.

Quite unexpectedly and out of the blue, Frank leaned across and kissed her lightly and without reservation. She felt herself tremble. It was not without reason that it caused a stirring of emotions within her. His face turned to hers, and she looked deeply into his eyes. There was no need for words, no need for any explanation. The feeling for each other was there... deep and throbbing with life itself!

He leaned forward and bent low over her, and as their lips touched a tremor of fire leapt through Janie. She swallowed hard. Their lips touched again, more urgent this time, and the fire that had lain dormant within the two of them for so long, sprung into life with a raging force. He covered her face with his kisses, stroking her neck gently with his hands, and murmured words of love to her. Janie felt as if she was on heat, consumed by the very fire that raged within her. She clung to him as if her very life depended on him for its survival.

As he kissed her he pulled her down to the grass with such gentleness, that she felt she would explode from the very pinnacle that her feelings were rushing to. She knew he was restraining himself, and when he pushed her away and sat up, she suddenly felt embarrassed by her wanton thoughts.

She lay on her back staring up at him, outlined by the sky. He turned his face, smiling down at her. 'I think you are one hell of a gal, Janie. I think... I think I've fallen in love with you.' Sitting up and looking deep into his eyes, she tried to suppress the excitement his kisses had brought on. 'And I think I'm in love with you Frank. I... I think I must be.' She looked away as the colour rose to her cheeks.

All the way back home thoughts ran through her mind. What would Gran think of her, and this new involvement? What would she say to Helen and Cassie about her feelings for Frank? What would her Norm have thought about all this? Should she have rejected this chance of love? Was she doing the right thing to encourage this, or not?

Only one thing she was sure of, that Frank had stirred up feelings that she only knew existed in the latter part of her married life. What had been stifled by convention early on, had come to light all too late for her and Norm. Perhaps this was a second chance for her as a woman. She had so much pent-up love raging within her, bursting to erupt. So much so, that at times in the past without her Norm to be with her, she had felt physically ill with the frustration of it all.

They reached the corner of Essex Road, but she didn't want to go straight home, just in case Gran was out. She knew she couldn't face the responsibility of being alone with him without giving way to her emotions and demands. He understood what she was going through, and tried to bluff it out humorously. 'I think I'd better take you right home Janie. It's all for the best.'

Without warning the rain cloud that had held off for so long burst above them, and they ran down the main street squealing and laughing like children. Her dress was almost soaked through by the time she had the street door unlocked and open. He pulled her into the dry and closed the door with a slam.

'I must get a towel to dry myself off.' Giggling, she ran out to the back scullery, while Frankie pulled off his wet jacket and hung it over the chair to dry. Handing him a towel to dry his hair, Janie went into the front room where she switched on the small fire they used for emergencies.

He warmed his hands and smiled at her, giving her a look that made her shiver in spite of the glowing heat. Taking her wet top from her, he laid it on a chair, then turned back to her. His glance took in the whiteness of her shoulders, the smooth skin that showed through the white lace top of her slip. His eyes were drawn to the tiny pulse he could see racing in her neck. However much he tried, he couldn't distract from it... it was racing like a wild bird.

She shivered again, and he put his arms around her to draw

her to him. He smiled, 'Don't worry Janie, I'll keep the cold out.' Janie still shivered, her eyes huge... 'I'm not cold.' His hands went to the base of her neck and along the silk edge of the slip. She held her breath wondering what he would do next – half expectant, half longing.

Abruptly, he turned away from her, and with a half groan mumbled, 'Please get dressed Janie, please.'

She stood shaking, staring at his broad back. It couldn't be wrong for her to love Frank... it couldn't. 'Frank, I love you. I love you.' Surely he wouldn't walk out and leave her... not now.

Turning quickly, with deft movements he let the straps of her slip fall from her shoulders. His fingers found her bare breast and then his mouth came down - searching, searching, until it found the crest it hungered for. All the time, they were sliding down to the small hearthrug that glowed with warmth from the fire.

His whisperings were taking over her mind and her very soul. She offered no resistance when his mouth edged its way along her neck covering her with kisses. Along her shoulders, her ear tips, and along her bare flesh, until she was a quivering shaking instrument, a toy in his hands. He explored and rekindled parts of herself she never knew existed, causing the flame to go higher and higher until she thought she would burst into fragments.

At first he had also urged her to explore him, and she had experienced an awakening of desires never known before. She murmured incoherent cries of pleasure. For so many years, so long, she had felt like a desert, all dry and arid. She stared at him with eyes full of pleasure, pain and exquisite longing. 'Please love me... please?'

His answer came back as he parted his lips and bent to kiss

her again. 'The drought's over my darling. I'm going to love you for the rest of our lives together.'

Their two bodies merged again and again, amid cries of undulating pleasure from Janie. Then, after what seemed an eternity, the two of them lay quietly before the fire in each other's arms, their energy spent, their thoughts relaxed and happy.

His cigarette lighter broke the silence with its click and hiss. In the red glow of the two cigarettes, their voices murmured soft endearments to each other, as the rain fell steadily against the windows.

It was much later that Frankie washed himself in the small bowl that Janie put out for him in the scullery, while she took herself upstairs, to return clean and glowing in a pale pink housecoat.

The sight of his bare torso made her all shivery again. She walked over to him and kissed the back of his neck, as he finished drying himself and hastily pulled his clothes on. Janie frowned as she felt his damp jacket. 'I shall let it dry on me and blame you if it shrinks,' he laughed. Then taking her face between his palms, he kissed her lightly. 'I'm going now, I'll see you on Monday night. And Janie... I love you.'

A glow enveloping her, she bid him goodnight... 'I love you too.'

The door closed and he was gone, his footsteps echoing down the path and along the pavement. Janie stood as if in a trance. It was the first time in years that she had felt so warm, so happy, and so loved.

Chapter 25

It took Janie a mere three weeks for her to make up her mind and agree to become Mrs Somers. When Frank met her from the bar the following Monday night, he was beside himself with impatience. He let her chat first, then pressed his fingers to her lips to call a halt. She looked so worried... it thrilled him to see the effect he was having on her. He called a cab and they headed for a small cafe they both knew in Gray's Inn Road. Finding a table in the corner he took her hand, staring deeply into her eyes. 'Does the idea of living near to the water appeal to you madam? How does the thought of living in the USA appeal?'

She tried to answer, but he leaned across the table and kissed her mouth shut. All the while the cafe owner watched them from the other side of the counter, beaming as he made the sandwiches.

'Now for heaven's sake Frank, what is it you're telling me?' She hated being teased and kept in the dark. But he was giving no secrets away, continuing to tease her with questions and innuendos.

Old Joe walked slowly over to their table and placed two steaming cups in front of them, looking up, startled as Frank turned and quickly grabbed him by the wrist. 'Hey, how would you like to be the first to congratulate us? Go on, congratulate us then.' The poor man thought Frank was the worse for drink, and Janie looked as if she needed one.

'Stop larking about Frank, what's got into you?' She

reddened and bent her head low, scarcely believing what she thought he was about to say. Frankie laughed like an excited child on Christmas Day. He grabbed the cup and offered it to Joe. 'Drink a toast to the future Mrs Somers.' He looked across at her and blew a kiss. 'I love you, I love you Janie. What's your answer?'

She felt her head reeling, and her eyes smarted with tears. Blinking them away, she held her cup high. 'Here's to us ... here's to my new found love. Here's to our life together.'

Old Joe beamed down on them both, 'Good luck, mate.' These Yanks certainly knew how to do things!

Janie was pleased to see that Gran was still up when they both arrived back at the house in Essex Road. Her mind was still spinning at the thought of the pre-wedding plans, and what everyone would say about her, and the news she was about to impart.

Gran was beside herself with joy, and hugged Frankie like a long-lost son. 'Good luck to you both I say. You know you have a good gel there...' she nodded at Janie who was beaming at them both.

'Gran... what do you think the girls will have to say about me?' The old woman pursed her lips, 'It's hard to say Janie, but I'm sure they will be all for you settling down again, with Frankie.'

Janie thought for a few minutes and decided that after Frankie left that evening, she would write to tell the girls she would be coming down to see them that very weekend. It would be best to discuss it together, and hear their side of the story. After all, they were young women themselves now, not children!

So it was arranged that Frank would see his senior officer and put in his application, while Janie would go off to visit her girls and put them in the picture. She was certain she would have all their support, and never reckoned otherwise. She casually asked Gran if she wanted to go with her, but Gran thought it was the one time in her life that Janie should be alone to deal with the conversation she had to have with her girls.

The days passed quickly, and Saturday arrived in all the heat of early summer. Janie caught the train and was met by the two girls prompt as punch. She caught their arms into hers and the three of them walked happily along the dusty road to the Jackson home where they were both billeted. Mrs Jackson made her very welcome and invited them all to sit down for dinner. She let the girls ramble on and on, it was clear to see they had so much to tell her. She wondered several times when she could broach the subject of her impending marriage.

It was Mrs Jackson who seemed to detect that there was something on Janie's mind other than 'her visit', so she left the table early, on the pretence of gathering up some fruit in the bottom orchard for bottling. The three of them had long finished their meal and were exchanging news and views amid howls of laughter from the two girls. Janie sat awkwardly, not knowing how to begin her news.

She rose and left the table, walking to the back door, where she stared out into the wide open greenery at the range of flowers and vegetables, hedges and brambles. It all looked so peaceful – no wonder the girls loved it here. It crossed her mind that they might not even like the city life back home again. She jumped when a hand touched her arm. Cassie leaned forward and smiled at her inquisitively, 'What is it Ma?... what is it?'

Janie took a deep breath. She must tell them, she must let them know how she felt. If they disapproved, how could she tear herself away from them all and go with Frank? How could she live the life she so badly desired if they didn't approve? Turning, she faced them both. Helen was so young and vulnerable, and so happy with things as they were at that moment. Cassie gave her a cool and lingering look, her obvious maturity and composure making Janie tremble a little.

Taking a deep breath, she lowered her eyes and told them of her deepening friendship with Franklin, and his offer of marriage. Once it was said she waited, not daring to raise her eyes to see the looks on their faces. Her head throbbed a little; her mouth was dry. After what seemed an eternity she looked up hesitantly, not daring to contemplate the reprisals.

Helen was beaming, her face wrinkled with laughter, and Cassie leant towards her mother and kissed her lightly on the cheek. They both clung to her as they shouted their happiness. Cassie said in a very mature fashion that it was the best thing she could do with her life, now that Dad was gone. She knew just how much her mum missed her Norm, and knew that her dad would have approved wholeheartedly.

The tension left Janie, and she wept tears of happiness with her two daughters. The weight was gone from her mind.

Chapter 26

The wedding was to take place on Midsummer's Day in June. Although it was almost a month away, Janie rushed about to get all the last little jobs finalised before the big day. She never stopped for one moment organising her family this way and that, to arrange what was best for them all.

Frankie had said that it could be a long time before she was likely to meet his own family back in Cleveland, and he tried to put her in the picture with the background of his homestead, spending the long summer evenings yarning to all of them. As Janie listened she smiled wistfully, thinking he really did love his American roots.

At one point she had wondered if he would ever contemplate staying put, here in London. It was an awful lot to ask of him, but she knew she would never convert him, not after all the chat about home in Cleveland.

It had played heavily on her mind, the fact that she would eventually have to join him in America, leaving Gran, and perhaps the girls, behind. Helen had ideas of going to Pitmans to study shorthand, so she would want to stay put and get her career going. Oh, of course she would be alright with Gran and Cassie, but then Gran wasn't getting any younger. Janie sighed deeply, hating the wrenching thought of leaving them all, in spite of all Gran's arguments. Of course she had to do it, she was marrying Frankie, and his home was her home. And that was in America.

On a hot afternoon in early June, the postman stopped at the gate and handed a letter to Gran. She beamed as she took it from him. It was from Cassie, no doubt asking what day they would be coming down to London. Janie was out at the market, trying to get herself a dress to get married in. Gran had told her of a stall at the Angel where she should get something she liked without coupons. 'It might be a few quid dearer, but he won't ask you for any coupons.'

Janie laughed. 'Thanks a lot Gran… shan't be long.' Then she was gone, her heels tapping along the pavement as she hurried in excitement to get her purchases.

Gran stood in the afternoon warmth and stared at the letter, trying to imagine all the news that was hidden inside. She stuffed it away in her apron pocket and walked back indoors. Time to put the kettle on, she would have another brew up… and blow the expense!

Humming to herself in happy anticipation, she set the largest cup and saucer on the table. While waiting for the kettle to boil, she ambled out to the back yard and stared up at the sky. There was hardly anything in the garden worth looking at these days - no flowerbeds, no rabbits, only mounds of potatoes growing alongside the greens. And of course that bleedin' monstrosity, the Anderson shelter, stuck in the middle like a corrugated tomb.

She looked up as she heard what sounded like a plane overhead, her forehead puckering as she stared at it. 'That was a strange one alright,' she mused to herself. Then as she stared at it droning away, the noise suddenly stopped. She rubbed her ear thinking she'd gone momentarily deaf – she couldn't hear a thing, not a thing.

Without warning there was the most deafening explosion. Gran felt the ground shake beneath her feet as she flattened herself against the back door, open-mouthed. Dust rained down upon her, all she could see was debris and mortar. She remained immobilised as if in a trance, not seeing or hearing anything. Then came the sound of an air-raid warning and Gran wondered if she was going mad. It didn't make sense – whatever was that thing that dropped? She tried to move and call out to Vera, but her body wouldn't budge. The brick dust was making her eyes smart and water, but she couldn't lift her arm to wipe it away. Something warm was running down her leg, she assumed she must have wet herself in fright. She tried to move again, but couldn't make her body respond, so she leant against the door for support, hoping and praying that Janie would be back home soon to help her. For the first time since the war had started, Gran felt ready to cry... to cry in frustration.

Janie was waiting outside 'Nottages' department store at the Angel, for a bus to take her home. She was well pleased with herself. She had found the stall Gran had mentioned, and had bought herself a lovely polka-dot dress in navy with white spots. It had cost her more than expected, but at least she would save on shoes, by using the black patent pair she had treasured all through the war. And she would borrow a bit of veil to adorn the lovely white hat she already had for a friend's wedding.

As she got on the bus, she felt quite calm and happy for the first time in ages. For the past week she had been waiting to hear when the girls could come home, just for the few days of course. And Gran wanted to take her out to buy a wedding gift for her and Frankie, insisting that Janie should choose something really nice. 'I don't care how much it costs. I want you to have a really good present... spend as much as five pounds on it, please!!' Gran had a twinkle in her eye. She knew that Janie had always wanted a statue of a dancing lady to put on the sideboard. Vera had one in green and gold in her glass cabinet, and Gran knew it was the envy of Janie, every time she saw it.

Just as the bus drew to a halt, the explosion came from somewhere distant, and everyone turned in horror. Then, as the babble of voices became more excited, the sound of a siren split the air. Janie slumped down in the seat, feeling crushed. After such a long spell when they all thought the war was almost over and air raids a thing of the past – now it was all happening again.

She clutched her parcels and jumped off as the bus reached the junction. 'Hold tight there!' shouted the clippie as the bus made off down Essex Road. Janie walked quickly past the Carlton cinema, hoping that Gran would have had the sense to go down into the shelter, and that Vera and Marjie were back from Vera's sister in Highbury. She knew that if they weren't, Gran certainly would not be in the shelter.

'Obstinate old dear,' muttered Janie to herself as she unlocked the front door, then raced through the house, scattering her shopping in a heap on the hall table as she did so. At least there was no sign of Gran. Thank God she'd had the sense to get down the Anderson! Thoughts ran riot in Janie's mind; it was always such a worry with Gran.

Dashing through the house, she reached the back door, which stood wide open. Her mouth dropped open and she shivered with shock and fright. There in a heap was Gran, doubled up in a most awkward fashion. She didn't appear to be hurt or bleeding at all, and she wasn't unconscious.

Janie knelt down at her side and pulled her gently round to face her. 'Gran … Oh Gran, what happened to you?' The old woman looked at her and tried to smile, but it was all lopsided, and as she tried to talk she dribbled. 'Gran! Oh Gran, whatever is it dear?' It was then that Janie lost control and began to cry. Gran looked so stupid sitting there with a half smile on her face.

Almost immediately she heard the voice of Arthur from the other side of the street. He was on Warden duty and had come over to check. He pulled Janie away and gently touched Gran's face. 'She don't appear to be hurt by anything … she isn't bleeding is she? Looks to me gel, like she's suffered a stroke. I think you need to get her to a doctor.' Wrapping his powerful arms round Gran, he lifted her up. 'Come on me darling, I'm going to pick you up and take you indoors.' He carried her inside to the front room, where he set her down on the best sofa.

'Don't give her nuffink to eat or drink, until she's been seen by the doctor.'

Janie stood by wringing her hands, almost in tears, as he let himself out of the house. 'Oh Gran! Oh Gran… please be alright, please.'

All thoughts of weddings were wiped from her mind as she raced down to the corner to phone the doctor. On her way she collided with Vera and spilled the news to her. She felt better knowing that Vera would watch over Gran till she came back.

Much to Janie's relief, the doctor described Gran's stroke as 'only mild', brought on no doubt by the sudden explosion. Janie let him out and felt a great sense of shame, knowing that while Gran had lain in a heap by the back door, her only thoughts had been that her marriage to her beloved Frankie might have to be delayed. She tried to reject any feelings of guilt during the following week, while she waited on Gran hand and foot, hoping and praying that she would be better and on her feet for the wedding.

Frankie came to see them both as often as he could, and instead of going out themselves, as Janie knew Frankie would have liked, they stayed in instead and kept Gran company. It was only when Cassie and Helen came home that Gran really seemed to perk up and get back on her feet again.

Cassie was a right little ministering angel, and knew just how to soft-soap Gran into doing what she wanted. She made her try to use her arm and hand, and attempt to have a conversation. In spite of Gran's funny facial expressions, Cassie never laughed or lost patience with her.

On the eve of the big day, Gran astounded them all by standing up straight and walking very slowly to the door. She turned and asked Cassie to take her arm and lead her out to the lavvy. In a slow and deliberate fashion she announced to all and sundry, 'I'm not going to use that bleedin' chair-pot any more. I'm going to get to the back yard if it kills me! Those bleedin' commodes are for old ladies... not me!!'

It brought a smile to Janie's face, and the girls laughed. Cassie was putting curlers into Helen's hair, and all the pipe cleaners were laid out across the kitchen table. She had only just started when Gran made her announcement, but by the time Gran had finished and come back, Helen was like a porcupine, with little knobs of hair covering her head.

She looked up as the door opened slowly. 'Cor Gran! I thought you'd fell down the hole!' Gran went to clip her one and nearly fell over. 'You little sod...' she giggled.

Janie felt very apprehensive about the wedding tomorrow. She had no qualms about herself and Frankie, it was the thought of the eventual break from the family and going over to America that really gnawed at her. Of course no one knew just how long the war would be on for; and when it was over, how long it would be before all the married servicemen and their wives would be shipped back to the States.

She busied herself in the house and then went to queue for the week's rations. It was as she was making her way down to the Angel that she spotted Gran's friend Lulu, arm in arm with a very attractive blonde wearing a WREN's uniform. Janie's curiosity made her stop and acknowledge them, although she had only met Lulu very briefly before, while out with Gran. 'Morning Lulu, are you popping in to see Gran?'

Lulu looked surprised and arched her heavily pencilled eyebrows.

'Yes duck, I'm on me way to see her now ... have you met me daughter Rosie? She's on leave from HMS Dighton, came home last weekend. Lovely girl ain't she... had her in me change I did!'

Janie and Rosie said hello. Rosie wasn't a bit like her mother. Apparently, she'd been brought up by her father's family in Wimbledon. It had grieved Lulu that she hadn't much to do with her upbringing. But then, having a baby at nearly forty and working as a manageress in a pub, it suited her to let her estranged husband and his lot take over the child's welfare. In spite of past circumstances, there was a deep bond between the two women, and Rosie clung onto her mother's arm as if she was her world.

'Lulu, did you know that Gran had a stroke?' Janie enquired tentatively. Lulu's eyes opened wide and she leaned towards Janie to gather all the information that was going. As Janie related the ins and outs, Lulu shook her head and tutted. 'Well, I thought it strange that she hadn't been around to see me. Still, now we're here, I'll grab a couple of milk stouts and call in. Don't you worry gel.'

Janie bade them both goodbye and went on to the shops, content that Gran would enjoy their company for an hour. She thought about Lulu's daughter. What a nice person she seemed… funny that Lulu had never said anything about her before. The more she thought about it the more she puzzled. It just went to show, you think you know people, then you still get surprises out of the blue.

It was almost afternoon by the time Janie had queued at all the various shops for her rations. The shopkeepers knew she was on the verge of getting married because of Gran's gossip, so they had been more than lenient with her meagre allowances. She was really pleased that Vera had organised a buffet for them and the girls were setting the table in the front parlour later on that afternoon.

Frankie wouldn't be coming round tonight; he was having a few beers with his mates at the camp. Janie had left the evening free to have a bath and wash her hair… there would be no chance of doing that sort of thing tomorrow – not with Gran to help and the girls taking over the bathroom between them.

Tonight she needed to be quiet, to think about what she was doing, and their lives together once the ceremony was over. It had all happened so quickly. She had gone along with the others, but now she had stopped in her tracks, and felt that she must think about her life seriously. Of course, she had no doubts about her love for Frankie, or indeed how he felt about her. But still the thought of Norm kept nagging at the back of her mind. What would he have done if the boot was on the other foot? Would he condemn her for what she was doing, for easing the pain of losing him, and using Frank's love to salve the ache that remained within her? She told herself that Norman would have wanted her to do this, trying to convince herself. But would he?

After a long soak in the shallow water, she donned her dressing gown and came downstairs to sit with Gran for a while before going to bed. Her face was flushed with the steam, her hair clinging to her face in wet tendrils. She looked a very young woman, and Gran smiled as she sat down in the armchair opposite her. Placing her reading glasses on the mantelpiece, Gran leaned forward to talk.

'You look smashing Janie. He's getting a good bargain for his money. I'm sure he will agree with me gel.'

Flushing, Janie rubbed at her wet hair with the towel. She still looked a bit worried and Gran could sense it immediately. 'What's up Janie love? You ain't getting second thoughts are you? You know I think my Norman would have been right proud of you, the way you've coped with everything... and the bloody war.'

Janie stopped and looked Gran in the eye. 'You don't think it's wrong do you Gran... wrong for me to marry again? I've felt so confused, wondering if I'm doing the right thing.' Kneeling in front of Gran, she sobbed tearfully. 'Oh I love Frankie, that's true, but I did love Norm too. Oh Gran...'

Gran stroked Janie's hair, waiting until she lifted her head up.

Staring into Janie's eyes, she held her fingers between her own, and the reflection of the two women close together in the faded light seemed very natural and peaceful. Gran's voice broke the silence even before the clock struck on the mantelpiece. In a very solemn voice, which didn't sound a bit like Gran, she said, 'Janie, my Norm was never a man to carry a grudge. He would not only have admired you for making a new life for yourself and the girls, he would have loved you for doing so. Janie, you are so young still… you must have more life for yourself, and more love in your life. A woman needs that, I know from experience gel… I know. Take what life is offering you and be grateful. Norm would have wished it, I know he would.'

Janie wiped her wet cheeks with the edge of her sleeve and smiled at Gran. 'You're right Gran, you're right!' She stood up and kissed her on the forehead. 'Goodnight Gran… see you tomorrow. God bless you Gran.'

Chapter 27

The sound of the all-clear went and Gran heaved a sigh of relief. 'Thank gawd that's over with. That's all we need... a bloody flying bomb just as our Janie's getting wed.'

She took her place once more in front of the hall mirror, trying to find a satisfactory way to wear her new hat. With a mouthful of hairpins, she pushed it this way and that, grunting and groaning as she tried it at all different angles. Finally, pleased with the end result, she gave it one final pat and smiled. She was pleased with the end result, and stood turning her head in front of the mirror. 'That's all the soddin' about I'm going to do. And that's that!'

Janie came downstairs slowly and caught sight of her in the doorway. 'Oh Gran, you do look nice... I always did like you in pink,' she exclaimed delightedly. 'It's dusty pink,' mumbled Gran in agitation.

'Yes, I know it is Gran, and you look very nice.'

Janie waited for Gran to finish then she went to the mirror to give a final check to her own outfit. The white speckled veil around the dainty hat complemented Janie's smiling face, and the dress and the high-heeled shoes completed the outfit. Gran thought Janie looked as pretty as a picture. She sighed over and over again as she looked longingly at her Janie, who was about to become Mrs Somers.

Smiling, she said, 'Any man would be proud to have you for his wife Janie, and I'm glad that Frankie is the lucky bugger.'

As she said this, she leaned forward and kissed Janie lightly on the cheek. 'You have nothing to worry about, nothing at all.'

Flushed with excitement, Janie turned to call the two girls from their bedroom upstairs, just as the hired car purred to a standstill outside the house. Gran rushed forward and opened the gate, calling to Janie to get the girls moving quickly... 'Oh, we shall all be late, or one of those damn sirens will start again if we're not careful!'

The sight of Janie and the young girls hurrying through the doorway brought a smile of assurance to Gran's face. She turned to beam at Cassie as she brought up the rear. 'Good girl, we don't want to be late for this, do we?'

She rushed forward to drag Cassie into the back of the car, but Cassie leaned forward to whisper in Gran's ear, bringing a look of horror for all to see. Gran clapped her hand over her mouth, turned tail and sloped off back indoors... as fast as she could in her lopsided manner.

'Whatever is it... what's the matter with her?' gasped Janie. Smiling broadly, Gran soon reappeared and clambered into the cab. 'It's me teeth Janie. I was so keen on having 'em clean and bright, they've been soaking all night and morning and then I forgot to put them in!'

Cassie and Helen were giggling like mad as Gran slammed the cab door shut. 'You wouldn't have had much to eat without them Gran... or drink.' Gran laughed as she beamed about her looking like a female Caesar Romero. 'Saucy little beggars!'

As the car neared the registry office, Janie could see Frank talking to two other servicemen. He looked very smart and handsome. She felt a shiver of excitement go through her, and her stomach turned over.

Vera was also there, and Marjie with young Cynth. They were talking to some of their old friends from the factory. As the car stopped, Frank came rushing over to open the door. Smiling at Gran, he gave her a peck on the cheek, making the two girls giggle as he did the same to them too. Then he drew Janie out of the car. Holding her at arm's length he kept on murmuring, 'Wonderful... wonderful!' She smiled shyly up at him and he whispered, 'I love you, my darling.'

His friend and co-pilot Jules ushered them all through the huge doors to the room where they were to wait. Gran looked at Janie, and they smiled at each other. There was no going back now, Janie thought. This was it! For the first time in ages she felt at peace with herself, and her world.

It was early evening before Frank and Janie left the happy crowd, still chattering and laughing in the front parlour. Quite a few friends had arrived later in the afternoon and the spread Vera had organised did them all proud. The wedding cake was a sight for sore eyes; even Cassie gazed at it in wonderment, all three tiers of it. Then as Janie lifted the top two cardboard layers away and placed them on the side table, the girls giggled, realising they had been deceived. Amid a hail of cheers and congratulations, Frankie helped her cut the cake. It was only when Vera pointed out the time that Janie realised she would have to grab her things and go.

Frank had booked them in for a brief weekend at Brighton – it was all the time they would have together for the moment. He had to report for duty on Monday morning, and Janie had the job of seeing the girls off to the country again. Gran had insisted she could take care of things until Monday. 'We'll be fine, you go and enjoy your bit of a honeymoon. And, yes, yes, we shall go down the shelter if we have to!'

When the taxi arrived to take them to the station, the stream of well-wishers tumbled out the front door into the garden. Frankie waved and pushed Janie into the cab, as a hail of coloured paper showered on them. Beaming delightedly out of the window, Janie blew kisses to Gran and the girls who stood waving madly.

The echoes of the well-wishers grew fainter as the cab raced along in the slowly fading light. They reached Victoria in no time, and Frankie ushered Janie along to the first class carriage he'd got tickets for. Janie's eyebrows went up as she saw what he had planned, '…such extravagance… well well!'

Kissing her gently, Frankie smiled and drew her towards him. 'Having just a brief honeymoon, I thought at least we'd do it in style.'

The rest of the train was comparatively crowded, and Janie tried not to feel upset by the hoards of other servicemen and their girlfriends, as well as nurses, mothers and all the other members of the public, who were cramped on their journey south.

Soon, they were walking along the seafront to their hotel, one of the few still available for overnight bookings. The moon was out and it was a clear night. Apart from the lack of lights shining across the seafront, and the mass of barbed wire that seemed to stretch along the beaches as far as the eye could see, it could have been any place on earth – not war-torn Britain. Folding his arms about her, Frank stopped walking, and stroking her face, murmured, 'Let's go back now Janie, back to the hotel.' His smile told her everything she wanted to know, and she trembled as she took his hand and they walked silently back together.

Their night together was like a dream. Gone were the uncertainties of the previous time together on the parlour floor, and the thought of intrusion by Gran at any moment. Gone was the guilt Janie had felt when she thought of Norman. Frankie had awakened in her more desires than she knew she was capable of. She was a different person with Frankie, they shared a different type of love. This was to be her new life, hers and Frankie's. And in time she would share his home in that new land across the wide sea. Tonight was theirs, to love each other.

Early the next morning, the sun was filtering across the floor. Janie had drawn the curtains back before they went to bed. The moonlight had seemed so romantic, although he had laughed at, and with her, for doing so. She had regrets now as the beam of daylight woke her so early. As she stirred, Frankie's arm came down across her waist and he opened his eyes slowly.

'The daylight woke me... I'll close the curtains,' she said, springing out of bed and covering the two windows. As she climbed back into bed, his mouth found hers, and his sensuous fingers once again explored her warm body. Their lovemaking went on and on, until they slept, exhausted.

It was late afternoon when the two of them spent some of their precious time walking through the nearby park. They had eaten a sparse meal in the hotel and had decided in favour of the parkland and the greenery, rather than strolling along the crowded seafront.

Janie's face nestled against her new husband and he felt elated with happiness, more than he'd ever thought could exist, since the death of Kitty.

As they strolled, they planned their life together when the

war was over. He was sure she would love Cleveland and the folk back home. They even talked of the possibility of Cassie and Helen getting jobs out there. Only Gran gave Janie cause for worry, and what she should do for the best... for all of them. It was these damn bombs that had started it all up again, just when they thought the air raids were on the wane. She must be firm with the girls as well; they must go back to their billet in the country, no matter how much they argued with her!

'A penny for them, my darling?' Frank looked deeply into her worried face. Relaxing, she smiled and told him she was only day dreaming about things back home. 'They're alright honey. Don't worry, please! We only have a few hours left... that's if our train goes on time. Tell you what, let's go up on the downs.' Laughing, they ran along the side road that led up to the open downs that seemed to stretch for miles. They found a small teashop open, and sat outside at a round table by the window. The woman behind the counter eyed them both suspiciously, watching Frank as he walked out to the bright sunlight bearing two cups of tea.

They sat with their backs to the shop staring out across the green downs, sipping the almost tasteless liquid. Janie pulled a face, 'Ugh! No sugar!'

After drinking as much as she could manage, they left the half finished tea, and ran off like two youngsters, giggling and laughing as they made off to the very top of the downs.

'Did you see the way that old sourpuss kept looking at us... no doubt she thought we were away on a dirty weekend together, and that I seduced you over and over again,' laughed Frankie.

They stopped giggling and sat down on the warm grass.

There were no other people in sight. Janie thought it was the most heavenly place on earth. All other sights and sounds were blotted out as they nestled together closely in the warm afternoon sun, content to be near each other, fulfilled and happy with the world and themselves.

Janie suddenly came to and sat bolt upright. The sun had left their patch and moved some distance away, and she realised she must have dozed off in the heat of the afternoon. Frank lay on his back smiling up at her, 'Hi darling... do you have a kiss for your old man?' She leaned forward and kissed him lightly. He went to grab her to him, but she pulled away and laughingly stood up. She felt quite calm and serious enough to cope with returning home, but if she let him arouse her with his kisses, she knew it would be all the more difficult to drag themselves away in a civilised fashion.

Frankie stood up and brushed himself down, and they turned to look at each other. After moments of silence, their eyes searching each other's face, he kissed the tip of her nose. 'This is it darling, we're on our way home.'

Janie's footsteps were heavy as she followed him down the slope. It was all over so quickly. Goodbye honeymoon.

Spilling its weary travellers onto the platform, the train pulled into the station. Soldiers, sailors, in fact all servicemen from many nations, intermingled with civilians. Janie was very quiet, and sat in the taxi hardly saying a word. The gentle reassuring pressure of Frankie's warm hand on hers, although bringing a sense of comfort, did little to allay the sting of tears that came to her eyes as they neared the familiar house in Essex Road.

It was all over so quickly, and he had to report back to his camp before midnight. As they alighted from the cab, he kissed her one more time before they went in to meet the others again. Her tears tasted salty and he gripped her arm tightly into his.

Chapter 28

Life's pattern soon took away any despondent blue moods that Janie was feeling, for during the next three months, London was battered constantly. The V2 rockets were the newest of Hitler's weapons and the destruction left in their trail showed itself in every area. For the first time since the war had began, even Gran now trembled at the sound of the siren, and the knowledge of what would follow in due cause. Many homes were blasted and left in a heap of rubble, while scores of families, mostly women and old folk, searched the remains in the cold light of morning, for anything of any use.

Vera was worried sick for her Marjie and the child, her nerves not her strong point at the best of times. She wondered when she would hear from George again. It was ages since his last letter to her and she had no idea how he was, or even where. All strung up like a piece of elastic fit to snap, she suffered a lot with headaches now, which Gran insisted were all to do with having too much worry over the family.

Only Marjie seemed unscathed by all that was going on. She must have felt a sense of loss with her Alec fighting away in Italy, but she never let it get on top of her – true fighting spirit took over if her confidence ebbed. She sensed that after years of war, her mum was beginning to crack up under the strain of things, and knew that she'd promised her dad, as well as Alec, to keep the home front going strong.

One particularly bad night in late September the four women

and young Cyn had crawled from their warm beds to make for the Anderson shelter, Gran huffing and moaning, Janie taut with fright, and Vera urging and half-pushing her Marjie along the pathway through the bit of garden to the shelter entrance. They all fell onto their respective seats on the hard wooden benches. Gran liked to sit near the opening so she could be the first to get out again, her bundle of bedding was always the largest to unwrap. The rest took just a blanket and a candle with them – they didn't want to be too hampered. Once the flap was closed down firmly Janie went to light the candles, to put one in each corner, firmly fixed on the shelves above them. 'If you don't hold the torch still Vera, I'm never going to get these candles lit!' Janie shouted in agitation at Vera, who was shivering with premonition. 'Sorry Janie, but I'm all of a shake tonight, feel as if something is going to happen.' Gran looked across at Marjie, then back to Vera, before raising her eyes to the ceiling. 'You're a bleedin' Jonah tonight, Vera… talk about put the mockers on us!'

The hours went by more slowly than ever before. Gran made all the usual remarks about her screws, and Janie tried to chat about the last film she had seen at the Carlton the previous Saturday. Amid all the chitchat and other items of unwanted gossip, only Vera remained quiet, it seemed as if she knew something was eventually going to happen. Her brows were furrowed in concentration, while her fingers twitched in agitation with the bit of knitting she was doing.

Young Cynthia, clad warmly in her siren suit, was asleep on her mother's lap, Gran was dozing on and off, but Janie sat staring straight ahead of her, trying not to keep looking at Vera's worried face.

They heard the noise, distant at first, then getting louder as it came towards them – then it stopped. Holding their breath, neither Janie nor Vera dared to look in the other's direction for the fear that was written on their faces. Suddenly there was an explosion, almost deafening all other sounds.

Gran shouted out in her half-sleep, and Marjie screamed loudly. Janie threw herself across the front of Gran to protect her from God knows what, and in doing so knocked the remaining two of the candles off the ledge, the other two having spluttered out just before. In the darkness of the shelter the women waited with baited breath, until the noise from the explosion finally stopped, and the sound of falling debris echoed away to nothing in the distance.

Hauling herself back to her seat, Janie felt for Gran's knee. 'Are you all right Gran... are you? And what about you Vera? Oh my God what was that... Oh Vera, whatever was it!'

Mumbled voices of reassurance in the dark were the only noises to be heard above the deep breathing of the child, who still slept on through it all. Vera fumbled in her holdall for the torch, and a beam of light showed them where the candles had fallen in the dirt. 'Best get them lit again Janie. Here you are... have a match gel.'

Once the candles were lit again, the warm flickering glow eased the tension that had mounted in the last few minutes. The fright showed on each of their faces, then suddenly Gran tut-tutted and sat with her finger to her lips, her ear cocked to the opening. Looking puzzled, she inclined her head again. 'Sounds like water... or something running. What do you make of it Vera?' The sound seemed to be coming from all around them, like a rushing stream. But there was no stream, and the canal was miles away.

Vera tried to push the shelter door back, but it was blocked by something outside. She heaved and pushed at it with her shoulder, but it stayed fixed. 'There must be something heavy against it on the other side. Crikey, that's all we do want, to be shut in! Come on Janie… you have a go as well.' Standing up, they both pushed at the improvised door with all their might, but it moved just an inch, letting in dirt and sludge. 'I think we'll have to wait until the all-clear goes… the wardens will be around to help us out by then.'

It was a good thing Vera always wrote the number '5' on the street door in chalk before going down the shelter, thought Janie, at least that way the wardens knew how many were out the back. 'You did remember didn't you Vera?' she asked worriedly. 'Yes, yes of course I did. I do it every time don't I?' 'Then it's just a case of wait and see how long they take… can't be much longer. Although I can't make out what that running water is.'

It seemed hours that they all sat in the semi-darkness. Noises from afar could be heard, and voices shouting to each other in the distance. Gran rubbed her stiff legs, complaining bitterly that she wanted to use the lavvy. Marjie held her child close to her, keeping them both warm with the heat of each other's body. More noise and voices could be heard, but no sign of any help to put them wise to what had happened.

Then, suddenly, the all-clear went. A sigh of relief went up from all of them and the feeling that they would soon be out and on the move again slightly restored their spirits. They waited and waited, calling out as Vera suggested, but to no avail.

At last, at first light, they heard a man's voice in the distance. 'Are you alright in there, are you OK? Hang on, we'll soon have you out. Come on Jacko, there's another lot buried under this one.'

The sound of shovelling and digging went on and on for what seemed like an eternity to the four women, who sat patiently waiting inside the Anderson. Then the tarpaulin was wrenched open and the daylight flooded in. 'Come on out girls ... come on old lady.' A hand was offered to Gran and she grabbed it without wasting time. As she stood up in the garden and looked about her, her mouth dropped open in amazement. 'Oh my gawd, Janie, come and have a look here!'

Vera made her way out next, closely followed by Marjie and her child. They were so traumatised by all that they'd heard in the last few hours, they couldn't get out of the Anderson quick enough to find out just what had been happening. Jack helped them out one at a time, warning them to be careful where they put their feet. 'It's like a swamp in parts,' he commented.

The three women stood in bewildered silence, amid the slimy, ankle deep sludge that now covered what had once been their garden. They were too stunned to realise the horror they had narrowly escaped from, or to grasp the state of demolition around them. The entire row of houses had gone. Everything was reduced to a heap of rubble, with choking dust still clinging to the early morning air.

Vera let out a deep cry as she pressed her fingers to her lips. In the distance they could hear others doing the same – muffled sobs were carried along the stillness, and in the semi-darkness they all stared at the horror and destruction caused by last night's raid. What had, until only twelve hours ago, been a habitable estate, was now just a heap of bricks and mortar.

Janie let out a deep sigh. At least they were safe. It was all so near – it could have been them! She felt herself trembling at the very thought of it.

Gran squelched her way across the yard to the back door, and saw that there seemed to be water everywhere. The smell was awful, enough to take their breath away.

Jack Tunney chatted to Gran in an abstract fashion as he guided her to join the others. Gran really wanted to know all about the raid last night! She was most curious. He urged them all to get themselves in the dry and warm, but Gran was not to be brushed off lightly. She knew there was something more by the way he was acting. He was covering something up, she was sure of it. Gran wasn't going to miss out on this one, not after it had happened almost under her very nose. She fixed him with a knowing look and waited. 'I've seen you, Jack, through times worse than this. I've seen what it's done to you. But this one had you wetting yourself didn't it? What caused that little lot eh?'

Shaking his head, Jack looked at Gran, casting his eyes down before taking a deep breath. 'Yes... it was a bad'n. One of them bloody rockets hit the flats, a direct hit... it went through and struck the main sewers at the corner. No one stood a chance. As the sewers broke up... the nests of rats were disturbed and they ran like quick silver, in all directions.' He stood lost in thought for a moment before going on. 'My old mum was in that lot... she didn't have a chance.'

Gran gasped, not knowing what to say next. Then she put her hand on his arm reassuringly, her lips trembling. 'I'm so sorry Jack, so very, very sorry.' It seemed inadequate to say that to a man like Jack Tunney... so meaningless. Even in the half-light she could see his face quite clearly. He looked so lost, the despair showing under the heavy lines of tiredness. He looked almost crumpled with the effects of the long night.

Gran reached out again, touching his arm gently. 'Are you sure she didn't escape Jack. I mean... really sure?'

He shifted his weight from one foot to the other, sighing deeply. 'No. I know she didn't... you see I was the one who helped to pull her out of the debris. She was right by the exit... she died of fright by the look on her face!'

Gran stood close to him, nodding absentmindedly as he spoke. She was really lost for words.

Thankfully the silence was broken by a grunt from him as he ushered her inside the back door. 'Well, ta ta... I best be getting back to the lads. They'll be wondering what I've been getting up to.'

Gran stood staring after him as he clambered back over the mud and debris to join the small group of ARP wardens. She could just about see them in the distance. She stared into the cold light of day and shivered. What a sod of a war it all was... what a sod!

Janie's voice echoed through to the back yard. 'I've made a drop of tea Gran, come on in and have it while it's hot... and bring Jack in too!'

Brushing the sprinkling of brick dust from her coat, and giving another deep sigh, Gran went inside to join the others. Janie had busied herself getting them all a hot drink, her own exhaustion forgotten. At least they still had a roof over their heads. She looked up as Gran shuffled inside, and smiled enquiringly. 'Has Jack gone then Gran, he could have had a mug of tea to set him up before he does any more.' Gran took the tea and sighed.

Janie stopped what she was doing, the teapot poised in mid air. 'What is it Gran... what happened out there?' Vera was also staring at her, then Marjie looked up. Gran kept them waiting while she savoured the welcome tea, then placing her cup down she sighed again. 'He'll need more than a mug of tea, gel, to set him up after the shock he's had. A tot of brandy is more in keeping for him, poor lad!'

The three women continued to stare at Gran, wondering what exactly had happened. 'Come on Gran. What do you know that we don't?' murmured Vera, as she sat tightly clutching her beaker of tea. Gran looked up from her corner chair, and with an air of authority she related to them all what Jack had told her.

Vera sat motionless with horror, her eyes getting larger and larger as Gran went on about the rats. 'Oh how awful... the poor man.' Janie closed her eyes and tutted silently as the words formed such pictures in her mind. She then urged Gran to go on. 'What a terrible thing to have happened. You knew his mother too, didn't you Gran?'

'Yes, I knew her... seen her at the pub before now. A little woman she was, very polite. Always ready to help someone worse off than herself. She had a lovely smile she did too... what a bleedin' shame. I don't know where it's all going to end, I really don't.'

The four of them sat in silence, each consumed by their own private thoughts.

It was the whimpering of young Cyn from the sofa in the front room that brought them all back to reality again. Marjie pulled her coat on and pulled the sleepy child to her. Dragging herself to her feet, Vera joined her and the pair of them made off to their own house. As the back door slammed Janie bade them goodbye, adding, 'Try and get a few hours sleep in Vera... if you can.'

After pouring another mug of tea, Janie sat down opposite Gran, both of them staring in an abstract fashion into space, neither seeing nor hearing – only conscious of each other's presence.

It was almost twenty minutes later that Janie' eyes flickered open and she sat bolt upright. It was the noise of the postman that brought her to her senses, the clatter he made at the letter-box. He'd gone by the time she reached the street door, but the smile that Gran knew so well had appeared on Janie's face, as she snatched up the beige envelope with Cassie's scrawl all over it. She was smiling broadly when she returned to the kitchen. Her face had shed its worried look and she laughed out loud as she read out all the tit-bits of news the two girls had put in their letter. She read it over once more to herself before handing it to Gran, who took it greedily from her.

'You know Janie, when you hear about all these dreadful things that happen during the air-raids, you realise that we have a lot to be grateful for. Don't we gel?'

Emotional relief seemed to be enveloping Janie, and she dabbed at her eyes with the back of her hand. Gran looked at her in alarm. 'Here, don't take on so Janie, don't let it get you down. This war hasn't beat us yet.' Janie laughed rather shakily, 'I'm not sad Gran, I'm only too happy that we've survived so far... all in one piece.'

It was Vera's reappearance at the back door that took the

smile from her face. Vera stood there all white and confused, clutching a letter in her hand. She never spoke, just handed the letter to Janie. Gran paled as she watched her open it. It was an official letter stating that Corporal G Baxter had been wounded and was now in a hospital somewhere in France. Vera was near to tears, 'I wondered why I hadn't heard. I just knew that something was wrong. I...'

Janie cut her short. 'Vera you don't know how bad things are. He's just wounded... you must take a grip on yourself.'

Poor Vera was not to be comforted. She was so certain that her George was mortally wounded, perhaps limbless for all she knew, lying in some strange foreign hospital - perhaps dying. She screwed up the letter in agitation, before banging her fists down on the table in temper. 'Why, oh why did it have to happen to my George?'

Janie went to her side, placing an arm around her shoulders. She felt quite helpless, and yet she knew what Vera was going through. After Vera had shed more tears than Janie thought her capable of, she quietened down and seemed more relaxed.

Gran looked at her thoughtfully. 'You'll feel a lot better for that Vera, you mark my words!'

Vera did look a sorry sight, not a bit the dragon of a woman that she was made out to be. Janie continued to look at her, now the weeping had subsided – she looked quite vulnerable and sad.

In between deep gulps, Vera kept clasping her stomach. She did it several times, the whites of her knuckles showing as her right arm went back and forth. Janie noticed it and wondered if it was a nervous reaction, or if Vera was in any pain at all. 'What is it Vera, is something else worrying you? You know you can talk to me about it. I'll help if I can... is it Marjie or Terry? What's up Vera? A problem shared is a problem halved, or so they say.'

Shooting a glance at Gran and then back to Janie, Vera took a deep breath, and moistening her mouth slowly, she gave Janie a half-smile. 'Yes... I think I shall have to tell someone Janie, or I shall go potty. You know I haven't felt all that well lately... well I know of course we all haven't. But I've had such a pain that it's got me down. I don't know the last time I slept properly. I feel a bundle of nerves. I just want my George home again with me before it's too late.'

'Too late? Too late for what Vera? What have you been worrying yourself sick over? Oh Vera, you know you really should see the doctor with your nerves.'

Vera cut her short. 'I've seen my doctor, and it's not for my nerves either... I have an appointment to go to the hospital, next Monday in fact. The truth is, I'm scared stiff Janie. I was wondering... I was going to ask you the other day... would you mind coming with me?'

Janie relaxed and smiled. She sat down opposite Vera and looked her straight in the eye. 'Now Vera, if one friend can't help another! Of course I'll come with you, we all need a bit of moral support these days.'

'Thanks Janie, thanks a lot. I know I'm a nuisance but...' Janie cut her short. As Vera made her way back home again she turned at the doorway and smiled, 'Ta ta, Janie... and thanks!'

Gran and Janie were still talking about it later that evening. Janie couldn't understand why she had got herself all worked up over a visit to the hospital. There couldn't be anything seriously wrong with Vera... only her nerves!

'Wonder why she didn't ask Marjie to go along?' Gran asked Janie, who was folding the clean sheets for ironing. 'Oh, you know Vera, she feels she can talk easier to someone her own age,' Janie said. 'After all, I expect it's her age problem that's causing all this. And after all, it's not the same talking to your daughter about 'those sort of problems' is it? It's sort of personal, you know.'

Gran laughed, 'I wouldn't know, I haven't had such problems for quite a long time now. Going from memory I am!'

Janie carried on smoothing and ironing the clean washing, in between changing the hot irons over on the gas ring. 'I think she may be just missing her George you know,' Gran mused. 'He's been away for quite a long time... and now to be injured as well!'

'I don't know... we all have someone to miss. I know I miss Frankie dreadfully now that he can't get home every weekend. Why did he have to be transferred to Lakenheath, just after we were married too... it beats me it really does.' Finishing at last, Janie placed the irons on the quarry stone under the sink to cool off. Then she carried the high pile of clean laundry upstairs to put away later.

Gran was getting herself ready to go to the 'Three Crowns' for a nightcap. 'Come along with me Janie. Haven't you done enough?'

Janie declined, saying she would rather catch up on her mending. A proper little married woman she was becoming, without a doubt. She rummaged in the tin on the high shelf, where she kept the coins for the gas, and gave Gran a shilling to treat herself. Gran's eyes twinkled and she gave Janie a smile that thanked her without the need for words. 'Ta ta gel...'

The door slammed and Janie knew she was by herself. She relished the small amount of time she could be on her own. She always wrote to Frankie at weekends, reading and re-reading his letters to her before she did so, savouring the sweet sentiments over in her mind time and time again, before applying pen to paper. How long, she wondered, would this war carry on? How long would they have to wait before starting their married life? She sat daydreaming for a long time, her mind confused and the paper still blank in front of her. They had been together for such a short time really – it had been an awful wrench when he was drafted to the wilds of East Anglia.

It was almost dark when Janie came to her senses again. She poked at the small fire, sending a myriad of flames upwards in a bright blaze. The writing paper still lay beside her on the floor, and the handful of letters from Frankie nestled in her lap. Pressing them to her cheek, a deep sigh went through her. 'I love you... love you.'

Chapter 29

Janie wriggled her backside in an agitated fashion, trying to find a more comfortable position on the hard wooden bench. Even at this early hour the hospital was very crowded, and as she and Vera came through those swing doors and faced the large sea of people, Janie knew it would be some time before they would be called in.

After what seemed an interminable time, a white capped, starched uniformed nurse called out. 'Vera Baxter... Mrs Vera Baxter!' The nurse looked around enquiringly. 'This is it...' Vera turned her worried face towards Janie with a half-smile. 'Don't worry Vera, it's nothing. I'm sure of it... you'll see.'

Rising shakily from her seat Vera followed the nurse into a small room off the corridor, both of them disappearing out of sight to the smell of antiseptic and the swish of the starched uniform.

Janie looked around at the rest of the waiting crowd – white worried looking faces, jaded glances as each one heard their names called. With hands folded in her lap, she stared into space, daydreaming. She had sat listening to Vera for the past hour, and realised for the first time how very little she knew of the woman, the true Vera.

For weeks, apparently, she had been suffering pains, and thought, innocently enough, that it was nothing but a bout of dyspepsia. She had other worries too, with young Marjie. Worries she had kept to herself for too long. Once Vera started to talk, there was no holding her back. Janie listened, wide-eyed, as Vera nervously related to her a whole side of Marjie's character that she never dreamed existed. Janie didn't stop her talking, for she felt that letting it all out would make Vera feel a bit easier.

Apparently now, for over a year Marjie had been carrying on with an American GI. On the pretence of going to the pictures with a friend, she had been going to the West End looking for male company, which she soon found in the shape of Danny Leach, a GI from Ohio.

Danny worked in the canteen and was introduced to Marjie through a mutual friend called Pearlie. He was a handsome lad. Tall, blonde and what Marjie had described as 'beefcake', whatever that was.

Vera had twisted her hankie nervously as she told Janie all that had gone on during the past twelve months.

All the time Janie listened, she wondered to herself just what had prompted Vera into sharing such confidences. She even found that she was not in the least embarrassed, but eager to hear all the intimate details. As the conversation lulled, she pressed Vera to go on, hoping she didn't sound too eager or excited.

'Poor Vera, whatever happened after that?' she begged. Vera blew her nose noisily and taking another deep breath went on. 'I told her over and over again to stop seeing him... told her she was not being fair to Alec. But you know what it's like for a young married girl being away from her husband... you know Janie. Anyway, she wouldn't stop seeing him. I knew what was happening, but I couldn't do anything about it could I? ...could I Janie?'

Blowing her nose hard, Vera took several deep breaths before going on. Janie sat listening wide-eyed at what she had been told. Who would have guessed it of Marjie? She seemed so content with life, with everything. It just goes to show that you don't know a person, even when you are living in each other's pockets.

Vera went on to tell Janie more, at the same time asking her if she minded listening to all this upset! 'No, no, Vera, of course not, if it helps to talk about it... go on please...' She tried not to sound too urgent, too full of amazement at the workings of one she had thought 'a quiet girl'.

'Anyway,' continued Vera, '...last month he was drafted up to Lincolnshire and I breathed a sigh of relief, thinking it was all finished. Now I find she's carrying on with his mate, who was Pearl's friend. He's a big brute of a bloke - I've seen a photo of him. Oh Janie, why is she like this? I can't understand her at all. It seems she can't leave men alone... it's like a drug to her. I feel so sorry for that poor bleeder Alec – what's he going to say when he comes back from the front? What's she going to say to him? Oh, I don't know Janie. I don't know which way to turn or what to do about it... I just wish that George was home. He would know how to deal with it all!'

'Try not to worry too much Vera – you have nothing to condemn yourself over. You've been a good mother to all of the kids... anyway, it's about time you looked after your own health now.'

Nodding in agreement, Vera raised her tear-stained face to Janie. 'Oh I know you're right of course, and my George would side with you... he would know what to do. I feel so... at a loss... so inadequate. What with not feeling well myself, I think it's all become too much, and got on top of me.'

Janie patted her friend's arm. 'Look Vera, what about a cup of tea, I can see the lady with the trolley just down the corridor. Don't know how long we have to wait still, but I'll go and fetch us back a cuppa to be going on with.' She rushed off before Vera could object, searching her pockets for a few coppers, soon to return with two thick white cups of scalding liquid, which Vera gratefully took from her.

'Ta… you are a good'n Janie. I feel a lot better having got some of that worry off my chest. You know my Marjie isn't a bad lot… it's just that she always has been one for the boys.'

'Please don't say any more Vera. I do understand, really I do… such a lot of things happen in wartime. It makes it hard for all of us. I don't profess to…'

Janie had never finished what she was saying, for the formidable looking nurse had then come out with a list in her hands. The next thing they knew Vera had been taken in to see the doctor. She had left her holdall and topcoat for Janie to look after while she was examined.

Janie had watched her following the nurse into the small room. She hoped they would sort out Vera's medical problem for her, although in her heart, she knew the biggest of the problems came from Vera's family itself. Her mind went back over the past months and she recalled that Vera hadn't seemed well since the shock of losing Phyl in that awful air raid in the City.

The moments dragged by. Janie stared at the cream walls, then the floor… in fact, anything to distract her attention from the tedious waiting. She read the notices on the walls over and over again, and counted the people waiting on the long benches. Her mind was reeling with what she had been told, and what she was reading... 'Careless talk costs lives', 'Your country needs you', 'Eat more potatoes...' All the words whirled together. Then she became aware of Vera, standing in the doorway in a white gown, limply holding a bundle of clothing.

She smiled at her. 'What's happening now Vera? Are they all your clothes?' Vera explained that she had to have an X-ray, and passed her clothing over to Janie until she came back.

Sitting down again, with the clothes in a pile on her lap, Janie noted with a smile that Vera had worn her best slip, the one with the coffee coloured lace around the bottom. It hadn't come out for George's benefit, only the Doctor's. Hope he appreciates it, Janie thought to herself. Vera was like that – if she had anything new or especially nice she would put it away for an occasion such as this. She was terrified of not having clean underwear on if she had to see the doctor – it could be her morals, but that was the way she was, and nothing would change her now.

When Vera came back, she was very quiet. Taking her clothes from Janie without a word, she disappeared into a cubicle and deftly pulled the curtain across.

Janie waited outside and did not intrude on her privacy. At last the curtain went back, and Vera came out, a little white-faced. 'I have to make an appointment... at the desk.'

They walked slowly back along the corridor, Vera wrapped in her own thoughts and remaining silent, Janie waiting for the first move to be made before asking any questions. While Vera had a word with the nurse behind the desk, she stood to one side.

Still without speaking, Vera placed the appointment card

inside her handbag. She turned to smile at Janie, who was waiting for the big finale, but it never came. Instead, Vera buttoned up her coat, and with a slight shake to her old matter of fact voice she said, 'Let's hurry home Janie... hope we don't have to wait too long for a bus, eh?'

As she followed her out Janie wondered about the last few hours. Had she dreamt it all, or was Vera acting her best role to date? No more reference to Marjie was made on the long bus ride home. In fact, Janie couldn't believe the change in Vera. What had the doctor told her? Was Vera regretting all she had confided to Janie earlier on in the waiting room? Perhaps Vera was playing it all down, after having bared her soul to Janie with all her personal problems. Perhaps she may have a few regrets now? Janie couldn't make it out at all – but she would remain silent about it unless Vera indicated otherwise. After all, it was Vera's business, not hers!

Janie didn't tell Gran all that Vera had divulged to her, but she still knew that something was radically wrong beneath that cool exterior that Vera portrayed so well. She made up her mind to wait for Vera to open up her heart and share the problems that waylaid her, making her almost ill with worry.

The chink in Vera's armour showed itself again less than two weeks after her hospital visit. It was almost midday, and a cold, damp, late October drizzle hung over the cluster of houses. Everywhere had that grey, lifeless look. Gran had popped down to see Lulu, and Janie had mustered a little enthusiasm to do some window cleaning in the front room. She saw Vera in the distance long before she spied her. Vera's stoop and worried frown told Janie that all was not well.

Janie waved from the side window, beckoning her in. Leaving

the duster and the cleaning gear on the small table, she fled into the scullery and filled the kettle, before letting Vera in. One look at her friend's face told her all was not well, not at all well!

'Everything all right Vera? Come and sit over here near the fire.' She tried to sound as bright as possible as she pushed all the newspapers off the easy chair, pulling it up close for Vera to take the chill out of herself. Trying to sound all casual, Janie knew in her heart something was seriously wrong for Vera, or her family.

Vera sat down heavily in the fireside chair. Her face looked the picture of misery, and her bottom lip quivered as if she was about to burst into tears.

Janie bustled in with the tray of tea, stopping dead in her tracks at the state of Vera's unhappy face. 'Vera, whatever is it? What's happened... is it Marjie... have you had bad news about George? Oh Vera...' She stopped, as Vera, sobbing, buried her face in her hands.

After a few moments Vera looked up at Janie, her cheeks wet with tears, her face distorted with anguish. She took a deep breath and moistened her lips. 'I've got to go into hospital Janie... an operation. I've just come from the doctor. He had the hospital report come through. He didn't tell me what it was all about, but I think I can guess. They're trying to get George home on compassionate grounds, that is, if his leg is better. Oh Janie... what am I going to do!'

Placing the tray on the stool, Janie handed her a cup of tea. 'Here, you drink this Vera... don't say any more until you've had a drink. I think you're a bit stewed up. Are you sure the doctor said 'an operation'? I thought they could cure ulcers with tablets or something.'

Vera looked up at her and smiled, 'Oh Janie, I hope you're right, I hope it is 'only an ulcer'.'

'Why Vera... you don't think it could be anything else, do you?' The realisation suddenly hit Janie and she almost dropped her teacup. 'Oh Vera! Oh no...!'

The tea had calmed Vera down instantly. Her reactions now were more resolute and matter of fact. It was Janie who was stunned. Everything seemed so unreal – she was sure that she would wake up shortly and find she was dreaming.

She sat on the edge of the chair opposite Vera, staring into her face, waiting for her to make the first move. It couldn't be anything that bad, like a growth... could it? Oh God! Not poor Vera... oh no!

When Vera did speak again, she was unusually composed, and even managed to smile at Janie. 'I don't seem to be having much luck do I Janie? I hope the army can get George home for a while, I would like to have him home again... and Marjie needs taking in hand. She misses her Alec she does... a lot. Perhaps it will all be over soon, bloody war!' As she spoke, she stared blankly ahead, her eyes misting over with tears.

Chapter 30

Gran thought Christmas 1944 was one of the worst she could remember. It was true that the air raids were now almost a thing of the past, in fact they hardly ever had occasion to use the 'tomb in the garden'. Poor Vera had been admitted into hospital for a big operation, and then after three weeks she had been sent home again, not looking at all well, so Gran reckoned. Her George had come home on leave, his leg still bandaged up, and he now had a limp to contend with. The two girls had written and begged to come home for Christmas, but even they had sensed the dulled atmosphere that prevailed everywhere. In spite of them all 'trying to get into the spirit of things', poor Vera's illness was laid heavily on all their hearts.

Terry returned home, looking almost as grown up as his father. He and Helen still clung to each other, and seemed even closer than ever. It pleased Vera to see the way that their lives had grown together. She had always liked young Helen and thought as much of her as she had young Phyl.

Frankie managed to get back to Janie and they spent a delirious three days together before he had to rush back to camp. She was very worried; he told her that they were sending a lot of his men back to America. She wondered how long it would be before he would be posted back with them. He was trying every trick in the trade to either keep himself in England, or to get Janie back with him as well.

On Christmas morning Gran was the first one up... she

couldn't sleep. The cold damp scullery, with the remains of last night's supper, greeted her as she padded down in her slippers. Gran sighed, it seemed Janie had other things to occupy her last night! Still, she would surprise them all with early morning tea. As she ambled round the familiar surroundings her thoughts were going over Christmases past. The parties they had enjoyed, the upsets and the laughter, the men going off to fight for King and Country, the kids growing up. She sighed and bit hard on her bottom lip. The only good thing about this bleedin' year was the extra ounce of tea they had doled out for the likes of her and the other old'ns.

Vera declined Janie's offer to join them for dinner, she wanted to spend it quietly, with her own family. She had just about come to terms with her illness, and knew what the future had in store for them all. Together with Marjie they prepared the Christmas fayre. The girl watched her mother constantly, and Vera knew it. It was so hard for all of them, George especially. He put his arm around Vera's shoulder and helped her get thought the meal. Young Terry felt so out of place, knowing it was a sad time. He knew that his Ma would get worse, but his ignorance of the situation made him more embarrassed than helpful.

Eventually George told him good-naturedly to, 'Bugger off! Go next door and see Helen!' The relief was immense and showed itself immediately as he grabbed his coat and fled. 'Shan't be long... see you Ma...' The back door slammed and he was gone.

Marjie, thinking that her parents might have things to discuss between themselves, took young Cyn upstairs for a lay down. The pair of them curled up together under the eiderdown, the small wireless playing on the dressing table. Marjie lay on her back, day dreaming of Alec and Danny... and others, a smile on her face as she relived the last few months, those ecstatic, wonderful times. Then she found out the awful truth about her Ma. She shivered, her head ached and her arm was dead where Cyn was lying across it. The melody on the wireless cut into her deeply... 'You'll never know, just how much, I love you. You'll never know...' She started sobbing... for her mother, for Alec, and lately herself. Then, exhausted, curled up with the child in the crook of her arm, she slept.

Chapter 31

Terry faced the prospect of attending agricultural college with relish. It had been decided over the Christmas holiday, that he would not be returning to the country but would attend a two-year course on farming etc at a small place in Hertfordshire.

George was very pleased at the way his son had adapted and taken to farm life in general, and when Terry showed an abundance of interest in sheep farming, George was more than keen for him to take it further. What Terry hadn't told his dad, was that in due course he hoped to make it out to the new world in Australia. He had a good friend, an Australian lad called Barry, who Terry had taken more than a liking too. He helped on the Johns' farm and never for one second stopped talking about the wonderful land 'back there'. As soon as the war was over Barry would be returning home, where he lived with his grandparents. Terry was several years his junior and regarded everything he said as the gospel truth.

In order to gear himself up for the prospect of sheep farming, Terry signed himself in at the 'Bush Farm Institute', his only regret being that he would not see enough of Helen. Still, they would write as often as possible, and he would get home at every opportunity.

A smile curled about his lips when he thought of Helen, she had been his friend ever since they had moved to Essex Road. Time had matured their relationship - from giggling friends, to young lovebirds, who could not bear to be away from each other longer than was absolutely necessary. Helen knew that his ambitions soared way up high and she went along with him. She would wait for him as long as time dictated, although in her heart she was not sure of this talk of Australia he daydreamed about. Still, she said nothing to deter his plans. After all, two years was a long time, and anything could happen between now and then.

Helen had left school at the Christmas term, and found herself a job for a local photographer as a receptionist, and general help. The wages of 25 shillings a week, more than softened the blow of working from nine till six o'clock every day. She loved meeting the customers, and helping Mr Brook, the senior photographer, with his studio sittings. It was a regular thing for the forces to be photographed with their wives and families when home on leave.

Many a shy girl sat with her soldier boyfriend for ages, while Mr Brook fiddled about with the lighting trying to get a good effect. Sometimes it took forever, and Helen felt quite sorry for the clients sitting under the hot arc lamps. She watched him as he ducked back and forth under the black-cloth... over to his sitter, then back again to his tripod. But after waiting a week for their photographs, when the smiling customers left the shop with their treasured mementoes, they all knew it was well worth the effort, every time.

Cassie had taken to nursing, and had started her probation at the beginning of the winter. She was very down to earth, and so full of duty and obligation to her course. She worried a lot about poor Vera next door, and wished that she was attending 'her' hospital, so she could keep an eye on her, for the sake of her family. They all knew that Vera kept a lot to herself. She attended hospital regularly and dutifully swallowed her pills, but all the family could see her slow deterioration. It was George who seemed so strong and able to keep a sense of proportion about everything.

Without much success, Marjie had tried to adapt to being a grass widow. Vera knew she still saw her Yankee boyfriend, but never let on to George. When Marjie went off to the cinema with 'Pearlie' she avoided her mother's eyes, both of them knowing what the other was thinking. Just before the middle of April, a sad George had to take Vera into hospital. He knew it would be the last time.

Cassie was very upset, wishing it could have been the same hospital that she was in. She could have taken a personal care over her, but it wasn't to be.

By the last day of April Vera was at peace, and with her maker. Janie had gone with Gran to see Vera that very afternoon, and Janie noticed for the first time how peaceful she looked. Gone were the lines that had been etched for months around Vera's face. Gone was the pain that showed when Vera talked to them. Janie had filled her vase with daffodils and placed them on the side locker so Vera could see them as she turned her head.

She had even remarked to George on her return that Vera had looked so very much better, almost as if she was at last making a sudden recovery. She had sat holding Vera's hand while Gran chatted on about the day's happenings. All too soon the bell rang, and Janie looked pleadingly at the nurse bustling through the ward, who whispered, 'Alright then, just a few minutes more.'

Vera had smiled at Janie, before closing her eyes. When she opened them she mumbled something about Phyl and George. 'George is coming a little later on dear.' Janie looked away as tears filled her eyes. Why, she wondered, was Vera talking about Phyl? It was such a long time ago. She saw the nurse looking pointedly at them and they stood up to go. Gran gave Vera a hug, and started to shuffle away down the ward. Janie bent to kiss her forehead and felt a shiver go through her, which went as quickly as it came. She smiled at Vera. 'See you tomorrow Vera... have a rest now.' Vera smiled and seemed content with her world. 'Ask Marjie to come tonight with George... Please.' She whispered. 'I will... I will. So long Vera.'

Janie and Gran left the hospital in silence, both lost in their own thoughts. At the bus stop Gran turned and looked at Janie morosely. 'I hope George makes it in time tonight.'

When he returned later, George told them that Vera had died in his arms. Janie had sat with little Cynthia while George went to the hospital; she wasn't surprised when he told her what had happened. He seemed quite in charge of his feelings, and in no way emotional. It was Marjie's lack of thought that angered him the most. Why did she have to go out to meet a 'friend', this night of all nights. Janie kept very quiet, it was not her place to dictate where the young woman should be, or not be. Although she knew in her heart just where and who she was with, the bitch!

Just before midnight the key was turned in the lock and in flounced Marjie. George had dozed off in the armchair; the child was sound asleep upstairs in bed. When Janie heard the front door open she was out of the room like a shot, so as not to waken poor George. She faced Marjie as she turned the hall light on.

'Where the hell have you been?' she demanded as Marjie stood half smiling, her hair all disarranged and her lipstick smeared around her lips.

'What's it to you Janie... Mrs Noseybody.' Janie knew that Marjie had been drinking too, by the smell on her breath. Trying to keep calm, and fearing she might wake up George and the child, she whispered, 'Where have you been Marjie, where?'

'None of your business. You're jealous of me, 'cos I've got a man, and yours is far away... you're jealous.' She leaned against the wall swaying, her eyes as bright as the varnish on her long nails. 'Don't tell me what to do Janie. I can do what I like...'

Janie was near to tears in anger and frustration. She put her arm on the girl's shoulder, 'Listen Marjie... listen. Your ma...' Before she could finish, the door at the end of the hall swung open and George stood there shaking with anger. At first Janie thought he was going to strike Marjie as he lunged forward. Instead he gripped her by the shoulders with both his hands, his eyes full and glowing.

'Now look here my girl! Why didn't you come to the hospital with me tonight? Why?'

Marjie flinched as her father shouted at her, and squirmed as she tried in vain to free herself from his grip. 'Stop it... you're hurting me Dad. I'll go tomorrow, I will. I met a friend...'

George's eyes were blazing with anger and pain. 'A friend, a friend? A fella most likely! Oh no, your mother didn't have to tell me – she knew alright, but kept it to herself all these years. A bloody fella, and you a married woman with a husband out there fighting for you, poor sod!'

Suddenly George let out a deep sob and started screaming at

Marjie all over again, his face only inches away from hers. 'Your mother's dead... you bitch. Do you hear me... DEAD. Even tonight of all nights while your ma was taking her last breath, you were out with your fancy man. Even tonight you couldn't keep your bleedin' legs crossed.' Suddenly, as if to give vent to his feelings, his hand went up and caught her right across the side of the face. Again and again he did it, knocking her from side to side. Marjie screamed over and over, while Janie tried to intercept and separate them.

Eventually Marjie broke free and ran upstairs, blood streaming from the side of her mouth and onto her white silk blouse. Her sobs could be heard even through the closed bedroom door.

Shaking from head to foot, George turned to Janie and apologised profusely. 'I should have done that years ago... many years ago. And to think I idolised that girl... worshiped the ground she walked on.'

Janie stood awkwardly, not knowing what to do for the best, then she steered him into the kitchen and set about making a cup of tea. It gave her something to do while George carried on making apologies.

He seemed as if he wanted to talk, to get everything out of his system. Janie made a pot of tea and poured him a large cup, setting it down in front of him as he rambled on and on.

After a while she felt much calmer and had stopped shaking. She toyed with the idea of going upstairs to see if Marjie was alright, but the look on George's face decided her against it.

Finishing her tea, she stood up to leave, turning at the back door to say softly, 'I'll look in sometime in the morning George, just to see if you need anything. Don't worry!'

Although she felt quite guilty at leaving him alone with all his sorrows, she felt the need to be free of the atmosphere and tension that hung around the house like a grey cloud.

She let herself in as quietly as she could and switched on the light. Walking over to the mantelpiece she came face to face with a photograph of all of them, taken on a day trip to Margate just a month or so before war began. There was Vera smiling broadly, her arm around young Terry. George stood at her other side wearing one of those silly hats. The only person missing from the group was Norman, who had to do an extra shift at the last moment. The girls were happy and smiling, and Gran was looking at Phyl who was scowling somewhat at the bright sunlight. Janie gave a deep sigh. Such a long time ago... such a lot had happened to all of them. She replaced the photo frame and turned in surprise as Gran entered the room.

'Why Gran, what's the matter? I thought you'd be sound asleep by now?'

'What's the matter? Why, that's what I've come down for. I did drift off to sleep, but hearing all that shouting and screaming I thought that summat was up. So what's happened then?'

Gran's eyes opened wide when Janie related all that had transpired between the three of them next door. All the time Janie chatted on, Gran sat gnawing at her gums, and spasmodically 'tutting' as if to prove a point.

At last she sighed, and with her brow furrowed with thought and a look of agitation on her face, she mumbled to Janie that she would go back to bed again. Janie wished her goodnight and watched her make her way slowly upstairs.

Gran's thoughts were going round and round in turmoil. She sat on the side of the bed, her head too full of poor Vera and her Marjie for sleep to come just yet. What a terrible thing to have happened. Poor George... he's had his share of bad luck. As for Marjie... well, time would tell what would happen to her now. It wasn't as if she was a bad girl really, she was just too stupid for her own good.

Deep in thought, Gran wondered if she should have told Janie all that she herself knew about Marjie, and what had happened over the last year. It wouldn't do to let her know how Marjie had carried on, Janie had her own worries with her two girls and Frankie. In a way she was glad she had kept it to herself, it wasn't the sort of thing to go shouting around to all and sundry. But the memory of it came back to her quite clearly as if it was only yesterday... that awful night when Vera had come in screaming for her to help, when those V2 rockets were falling thick and fast. Janie was doing her night shift, consoling herself that Gran was being looked after by Vera. Oh dear, Janie should really know what happened on that dreadful September night!

The sirens had started quite early in the evening, and true to custom Vera had come screaming at the back door for Gran. But this time it wasn't for the usual rush to the Anderson shelter, it seemed that this was the last thing Vera had to think about. She'd looked half out of her mind as she came tearing through the back door, sobbing for Gran to come and give her a hand.

Gran had been making herself a cup of tea when the siren had started wailing. Not wishing to waste it, she was sipping it from the saucer as quick as she could, knowing that Vera would be rounding them all together in next to no time. She wasn't at all surprised when the excited voice of Vera could be heard yelling for her, minutes later. 'OK gel, just coming. You go on down Vera… shan't be a mo…'

Vera never heeded what Gran was saying, she just came running through the back yard and into the small living room, where she grabbed Gran's arm in a right state of panic. 'Oh Gran… come and help us please! Oh God… it's Marjie! Oh Gran, I just don't know what to do for the little fool…'

'Hang on Vera, what's the matter with Marjie? Has she turned Charley about going down the shelter?'

'No, no Gran… it's… it's nothing to do with the shelter. She's in bed Gran, and she's very bad. Oh, what a thing to be happening!' While Gran stared at her trying to get the gist of what was going on, Vera dabbed at the tears that were now streaming down her face.

Gran placed the cup back into the saucer and returned it to the draining board. She was getting nowhere fast with Vera, so she ambled after her as she rushed back out of the door again. Perhaps Marjie would be able to shine some light on the situation. Gran made her way through their back kitchen to the bottom of the staircase where Marjie could be heard yelling from her bedroom.

'Gawd help us Vera… whatever is it? What's wrong gel eh?' Vera led the way up the stairs with Gran closely at her heels. She made her way into Marjie's room, where from the double bed Marjie could be seen writhing and rolling about in a terrible state. There was a kettle on the floor, and a large enamel bowl at the side of it. A bottle of doubtful looking liquid stood in the bowl, and bits of old sheeting were scattered all around the floor. But the most horrific sight that met Gran's eyes, was the bundle of blood-soaked rags on a pile of newspapers, stuffed under a wooden chair at the bedside.

When Marjie caught sight of Gran she moaned loudly and tearfully, 'I'm sorry Gran... I'm sorry! But I didn't know what else to do.'

Vera stood wringing her hands and crying loudly, which only served to unnerve Gran even more. She took in at a glance all that had taken place, nodding her head as she summed up the situation. 'Silly girl... silly girl...' she muttered to herself, '... tch tch!'

Realising they were both looking towards her for the next move, Gran wondered if Marjie was as bad as she was making out to be. And was it was a case for the Doctor or not? She asked Marjie how far gone she had been when this little predicament had happened. By the way Marjie flushed in guilt, Gran had no need to enquire whether Alec was the father or not.

Pulling back the sheets she saw that Marjie was clean and fairly well organised. She had got rid of the main problem... that was very obvious. Gran had a quick look at the blood-soaked rags and told Vera to remove it out of sight. Vera looked at it distastefully as she bent to retrieve it, wrapping it all well in newspaper, before holding it at arm's length and taking it away.

When Vera was out of earshot, Gran was able to have a quick word with Marjie, who had calmed down a lot by now. She confessed that she had been 'lumbered' by Leroy, and knew that she would have to tackle the problem on her own. A girl at the factory had told her what to do, and had offered to have young Cyn for the night while she got on with the job.

'Mum would never have understood, not in a thousand years... and how could I explain it all to Alec after three years in Italy? Oh Gran, I didn't know it would be this bad... I was so scared once it got going. Oh Gran... it was so tiny, like a doll...

and Gran... it was a boy.' She shook as she spoke and started crying again, while Gran placed an arm around her shoulders.

'It's not for me to say that it's alright, 'cos it's not. But you're a lucky girl that it all came away, otherwise you would have to get the Doctor in. You know that don't you? Even so, it remains to be seen whether or not you will have to, even now.' Marjie nodded, sobbing. 'I know Gran, I know.'

The all-clear sounded loud and strong, and Vera went downstairs to make them all a cup of tea. She was not at her best under these conditions, and the worry of what could have gone wrong played heavily on her mind.

Gran gave Marjie a drop of brandy and told her to wash it all down with the tea. The girl was still in a great deal of pain, and Gran didn't like the look of things at all. Of course she had been through the same mill in her own young life, but she had the constitution of an ox, or so she reckoned, and was back on her feet the next day. But she had a feeling there was something amiss with young Marjie, and Gran knew that before very long she would have to seek medical advice.

It was almost three hours later that the doorbell rang, and the tall figure of Doctor Carey made his way upstairs. Vera trembled as she let him in, mumbling silly apologies as she led the way to the bedroom.

Placing his bag on the small table, the doctor asked to wash his hands. Marjie was shaking like a leaf under the clean bed sheets, and Vera was so nervous she couldn't keep still. She felt more than put out when she was asked to leave the room while he examined his patient. Gran was downstairs waiting as Vera tore into the living room, all her bristles up and very annoyed. 'After all, I am her mother,' she expostulated angrily.

After what seemed an eternity the doctor came slowly down the stairs. He hesitated before addressing Vera. 'I hope you still have the... partial foetus... Mrs Baxter? I would like to see it if you don't mind.'

Vera looked shocked, feeling her face go hot and red, as if it was her guilt she was trying to cover up. 'I'll go and get it doctor, it's outside near the dustbin out the back...' She looked flushed as she ran out to the back, returning moments later holding the newspaper package at arm's length.

The doctor did his investigating and waved it aside again, his raised eyebrows giving no indication of what he was really thinking. After washing his hands again, he proceeded to write on a prescription note pad. 'Please see that the patient gets this as soon as possible, I have already informed her that I shall want to see her again at the surgery, in a couple of days. If she is no better in twenty four hours, call for me to come and see her again.'

Vera, still trembling, took in all that he said. As he buttoned up his coat and made to leave, he turned in the doorway and addressed her quite sharply, making Vera shake all the more. 'That young woman is very to have got off so lightly. She could have lost HER life as well. Good evening.'

Gran heard the street door slam as he left, and Vera came back nearly in tears. 'Whatever would George have said about it? Oh Gran, what a terrible shock I've had without a doubt. What a thing to have happened.'

The older woman sat in the fireside chair looking very quiet and thoughtful. She sniffed, and then smiled wryly. 'Shock indeed... not like the bleedin' shock poor Alec would have had on his homecoming...!'

As things worked out, Marjie improved and was soon back to her usual fighting form. She never divulged to Vera what the doctor had said to her, or if he had reprimanded her in any way.

As the weeks passed into months, even Marjie herself appeared to have obliterated the whole episode, almost as if it hadn't happened. Vera still found herself watching her from time to time, always waiting for the big let-down, as if it was her guilt that she was covering up. She wondered if, when Alec returned home, he would ever know about that dreadful night or the consequences resulting from it. She hoped in her heart that Marjie would not confess, as there were some things that did not improve with age, and soul searching was one of them. She comforted herself that only time would tell in the long run, and Marjie had a long time to go yet.

Vera was laid to rest on the last day of April. The small crowd in the graveyard braved the showers to pay their last respects.

Janie felt very sorry for George who seemed to be so lost and bewildered. Gran stood next to Marjie, who cried almost non-stop, sporting a bruised cheek, which she never bothered to hide with face powder. That in itself was most unusual for a person like Marjie. Terry held onto his father's arm and supported him throughout the entire service. He was now towering above his dad, and George looked up at him for comfort.

It was quite a relief when the minister led the small group from the sodden graveside and away to the office. George had a couple of duties to attend to, while the women walked out to the main gate.

The drive back to the house was still tense and awkward, but once home, and after the downing of several 'tots', the red faced undertaker and his companion left the family to their own. The women were chatting and Vera's relatives, such as they were, were caught up in the main stream. They eventually left together and wished George all the best… all promising to do 'something' for him, but each of them knowing that they would most likely never set eyes on each other again.

With a sigh, George closed the door as the last one left. He was glad to see the back of them really, a lot of parasites who only got together at either weddings or funerals. Still, he had got them all here for Vera's sake, knowing how she set great stock by things like that. Poor Vera, she was now at peace… she needed it.

Two days later he had a letter from Canada. He looked at it quizzically, as he studied the handwriting, and stared at the postmark. Then his face broke into a slow smile. 'It couldn't be…' he murmured to himself as he tore open the envelope and drew out the thin paper. He shook with emotion. It was from Jeanne, his nurse.

Chapter 32

The letter was short, friendly and to the point. Jeanne Dexter was now back in Canada, having a well-earned rest after completing all her overseas duties.

She was on leave for two weeks and staying with an elderly aunt. George remembered how stunned she had been the evening she had learnt of her husband's death. He was a fighter pilot and had gone down in a raid over Germany, about the same time that George had been invalided into hospital at Arras. He was so preoccupied with his own plight and spent a remorseful three days drifting in and out of a pain-crazed nightmare.

When he had opened his eyes and realised he was still alive, she had been there! Cleaning and tending to him and all the others, he had been struck by her complete honesty and kindness. Each time he asked about his leg she had given him a truthful answer every time, for which he was grateful.

As he responded to treatment he became aware that she was not only a very conscientious nurse, but also interested in everything and everyone around her. She was there when he had those sweating fits and the nightmares... always there to calm and soothe away the pain. She laughed at his despondency and ridiculed him unmercifully into fighting back. Afterwards he knew why she hadn't let him drift into a state of helplessness.

It was exactly a week after their introductions over the new swabbings that he missed her morning call. The others in the prefabricated ward realised it too. Amid laughs and jokes about 'whose bedpan she was emptying last night' he found himself more than a little sad that she had not reported that morning for duty.

It was almost midday before she did finally show up, along with the senior surgeon. George's eyes tried to seek her out, and he became quite frantic when she almost swept through the ward in a most unseeing manner. She looked more than pale... her eyes were puffy and red, as though she had been crying. The ready smile that she always had for everyone was now replaced by a distant look, almost as if she was in a dream.

He knew without asking that there was something very wrong for her to be in that state. He wondered when he would have the chance to have a few words with her. He felt he needed to know what was wrong!

That night he was caught up in a heavy sweating nightmare, shouting and delirious. When he came to his senses he realised that she was standing next to him. He could feel her nearness without opening his eyes and he put out his arm to touch her. She caught his hand with hers and lifted it up to take his pulse. Her smile seemed to calm the fear in his pain racked body. His eyes never left her, eyes that were bright with the fever that assailed his whole being.

He tried to murmur through the waves of heat, but she put her finger to her lips and shushed him as though she were talking to an infant. His mind ran riot, visions kept floating in front of him. he saw her face as she leaned forward and wiped his forehead, such a wonderful smile. Then he saw it was Vera who was looking at him... she was talking to him but he couldn't hear what she was saying, her face dissolving into nothing. Suddenly he saw Marjie, then Vera again. He wanted them both to go away... he wanted Jeanne. Oh God, what on earth was he dreaming? He knew it was so wrong; there were faces and voices all jangled up together! Then nothing... except the pinprick he felt at the top of his arm.

The sun shone brightly the next morning and the doctor made his inspection briefly. Jeanne was there beside him, smiling as if a mask was fixed on her face. George watched her patiently until they reached his bed. 'How are we today Baxter... all right? Shall have to try and get you up pretty soon, or we'll have bother with that knee!' He carried on to the next bed while writing notes on his pad.

George tried to catch her eyes as she followed close behind the doctor. He knew it was more than his life was worth to make conversation with her while she was doing rounds.

Once the doctor had finished and left, she made her way back to the men who needed dressings changed. He caught hold of her as she skimmed past his side, almost knocking the dressings off the trolley.

'Jeanne what's wrong? What's happened? Please, tell me. You never know, I might be able to help. He kept a tight grip on her hand, which was trembling. He pleaded, 'Come on Jeanne ... nothing's that bad is it?'

As she looked down at him her eyes portrayed nothing but despair and sadness. She moistened her lips then whispered softly... 'Two planes went missing late on Monday... they never returned to base. They were shot down... Simon was with them...' She pulled herself free, and ran from the ward out of sight.

'Jesus Christ!' he muttered, '...poor girl.' He was astounded at the news, yet at the same time he wanted more than anything else to wrap his arms around her, and whisper words of comfort, as he would to a child. He would do anything to help heal the ache she must feel deep down inside.

The more George drifted in his fantasy world revolving around Jeanne, the more he knew his feelings were getting stronger for her – her wide honest smile, hazel eyes, and those fair curls that could not be controlled under her nurse's cap. He saw her face the moment he closed his eyes and slept, till he opened them again the following morning. He felt torn with guilt as he tried to shut out the memory of Vera. Oh, of course he loved Vera, but he knew that he loved Jeanne in a different kind of way. The two women were so totally opposite.

It was true that she was just as friendly with all the other wounded boys in the ward. He also knew the old cliché that patients always fall for their nurses… or vice versa. But Jeanne was different, she was a friend, a lovely friend, and he was completely mesmerised by her, and with her.

Over the next week his eyes followed her around, not missing a single move that she made. He felt physically ill when she was missing from her ward duties. In his heart he knew that he should know better, he had Vera waiting for him back home in London. And the family… Marjie and Terry, what on earth would they think of their old man if they knew what he was thinking and thirsting after!

The following week he was allowed up, and told to walk to gain strength in his weak and helpless muscles. He listened to the doctor, while his eyes never left Jeanne for one instant.

He knew that his shattered knee was almost dead, and each step would be painfully slow. But it would take time the doc had said, 'Don't attempt too much Baxter... try to push yourself a little more each day. Don't give up, remember that!' George stared after the doctor as he thrust his hands deep into his white coat pockets and strode off out of the ward.

Don't give up, that's a good one to remember. He laughed cynically, he knew that he wanted to walk again, but once that happened, he would not be staying here for long. He would be put on the first troop ship home again.

Jeanne returned to help him to his feet, and as he made a couple of painful steps, he faltered and almost fell onto his seat. She laughed unexpectedly, 'He means it you know... don't give up.' He looked up at her, groaning inwardly. How could he tell her that he didn't want to go back... to leave the hospital. How?

Just three days later, he received news that he was being put on the next Red Cross boat to leave. He was also told of Vera's hospitalisation. The officer in charge gave him brief details, and signed for his compassionate leave.

Dazed and shocked by the news, George saluted the officer and hobbled from the small room. Once outside he made for the small area at the back, where a snatched smoke could be enjoyed under the shade of the tall trees.

He rummaged through his top pocket and found a broken dog-end, which he instantly lit up. Placing his crutch against the wall he leaned against it and tried to unravel his confused mind. Although stunned to hear the news about Vera, he was awash with guilt at not wanting to leave Jeanne... God knows when he would ever see her again. He knew he should be elated at the chance to go back home again, and to support poor Vera in her worrying time. Not knowing the real truth of Vera's illness, or how serious it really was, he tried to push it to the back of his mind, and shrug it off. Of course Vera couldn't be really ill, not really... she was, and always had been, as fit as a fiddle. A drained man, his loyalties were divided, his feelings torn between his wife, and his newfound love.

It was quite late that evening when Jeanne came on duty, and with downcast eyes, he held her hands as he mumbled how sorry he was to be leaving them all. 'It's for the best George. It's true, I do think a lot of you... but that's as far as it will, and can, go. This is wartime and feelings are very much on the surface all the time. But I'll never, ever forget you.' She smiled at him, and he knew that she was talking sense. He was a married man with a family, he had obligations. But she was a widow now... what would she do? Who would look after her?

Reaching into his jacket, he found a scrap of paper and a stub of pencil, and hurriedly scrawled something across it before holding it towards her, almost willing her to take it from his shaking hand. 'Here Jeanne, it's my address in London. All I ask is that you let me know that you're safe ... after I leave here, and when you return to Canada... please!' She took it slowly and placed it in her tunic pocket.

Inwardly he felt pleased, gaining a crumb of comfort from knowing that he might get one brief letter from her, as a reminder of their existence together.

The following Tuesday George was ready to board the Red Cross, leaving the tiny hospital to travel to the border, where he would join the other wounded on their final trip back home.

He looked so despondent that Jeanne felt she must say something suitable... a bit of a boost to send him on his way. She smiled and hugged him to her briefly, as she did to each of the boys in turn. 'Take care boys... safe trip... goodbye!' Then they were all in the truck, and without further ado it was off, roaring down the dirt track towards Dunkirk. She waved again and again, calling softly, 'Goodbye… goodbye.' Her eyes were smarting, after her 36-hour shift and these final goodbyes, she felt exhausted and numb. But still, she stood her ground until the truck disappeared from view.

Behind the flap George strained his eyes until she was out of sight. The memory of that sunny smile would live with him for a long time to come, and he alone knew who she had blown that kiss to. The memory would take him across the icy sea and finally, home. He had to get through the next forty-eight hours first… after that it was all up to him. Christ, what a bloody life this had turned out to be. What a bloody war they had going on for them.

Chapter 33

The situation between George and his daughter remained uneasy for several days after Vera's funeral. Marjie only spoke to him briefly and then it was through young Cynthia. She knew how hurt and angry he was feeling, but didn't know the best way to deal with the situation. Of course, she was sorry now for the way she had behaved, and the way it must have looked to him and the others. If only Ma was here she would know how to cope with these sorts of things. Suddenly, without warning, stood by the sink filled with dirty crocks, she burst into tears... it had all been too much. She sobbed deep and long as she stood swirling the hot water absentmindedly with her hands. All the hurt and anguish of the past weeks came to the surface... she really felt that her need for love and compassion was so far away from her, and would always be.

Withdrawing her hands from the water she thrust her knuckles up to her face and pressed them under her tear-filled eyes. The more she thought about the past events, the more she cried. Oh, she wanted Alec to come back home; she wanted him to be with her. She wanted her Ma back again... never wanted her to die like she did. And more than anything, she wanted to be at peace with her dad. They, who used to be so close together, were now at daggers drawn.

As George let himself in at the street door, the newspaper in his hand, he heard the noise from the scullery. At first he thought it was young Cyn, then he realised that it was Marjie.

He stood in the doorway and stared at the bowed shape of the girl sobbing her heart out over the sink. His anger gave way to a rush of feeling as he looked at her. Poor kid, she must have had it pretty hard really, her husband had been away for nearly three and a half years now, his lovely Marjie. Now she had to come to terms with her mother's death, and had no-one to comfort her. He walked silently towards her, his mind in turmoil. As he put his hands on her shoulders, she jumped and turned round, the look on her face like a frightened rabbit. He stared into her face and she stood immobilised, wondering what he would do next. Fear flashed through her mind that he would strike her across the face.

Then his look softened, 'Marjie. Marjie my pet...' Throwing her arms round his shoulders, she sobbed, 'Oh Dad...' With deep gulping sobs she clung to him, crying how sorry she was, as she did when she had run to him as a child with a scraped knee, all those many summers ago.

The pair of them stayed together until Marjie had calmed down. George reached up and smoothed her hair back from her wet cheeks and smiled at her gently. For all her silly faults and irresponsible ways, she was still his daughter and part of the family, and he hadn't much family left now, just the two kids, and the young'n.

'Dad, I promise I'll never do anything like that ever again, I just want Al to come home. I'm sorry for everything, really sorry. Can't we be friends like we used to? Please ... can we try?' George nodded and gave her a quick cuddle to prove his point. He mustn't be too hard on the kid – after all, none of us were perfect. As he sat at the table waiting for her to make a cup of tea, the pressure of Jeanne's letter in his inside pocket seemed to burn right through to his very skin, a reminder that he was not as open and above board as he would have everyone think.

All's fair in love and war, he had told himself. Marjie smiled as she placed the tea in front of him, it was the first time she had smiled or felt so relaxed for such a long time. They sat looking at each other, sipping their tea in silence, both of them knowing there was no need for words or further explanations.

Sudden shouting at the back door and the excited voices of Gran and Janie caused them both to look up in concern. 'What's the matter with you two then?'

'It's over... it's bloody well all over! It was on the wireless just now... come on, put yours on, quickly.' Gran rushed over to the sideboard and switched on the set as fast as she could. 'Come on! Come on!' Gran tutted impatiently as the set warmed up. The voices came through in the distance, as Gran twiddled with the knobs. 'Oh, come on can't you!' Suddenly the voice of the prime minister could be heard speaking in his slow deliberate way. Everyone stopped to hear what he said, but no more mention was made of an armistice.

'Are you sure that's what he said?' George enquired. 'Of course I'm sure! I ain't daft! Keep it on... it might be repeated.'

Suddenly there was a thumping on the street door. In rushed Helen with her friends. 'Did you hear it on the news!' she exclaimed excitedly. 'It's all over... the war is OVER!'

It seemed hard to believe that what had gone on for so long, had really come to an end. Yet there it was for the whole world to know and hear... the world war was over between England and Germany.

There was so much excited chatter between the five of them, as the sudden reality of peace dawned. Marjie knew that it would only be a matter of time before her Alec would be home, and she closed her eyes in anticipation of their life together. Janie trembled with the thought of starting a new life in America with her Frankie... and the realisation that it would mean leaving most of her friends and family behind. George smiled in anticipation that, God willing, there might be a chance of a little friendship with his Jeanne. Helen laughed out loud as she realised she would have all the things that she had been missing for so long. Like new clothes and scent, and face powder, and all those wonderful things she had heard the others so often talk about. Only Gran remained quietly thoughtful, smiling to herself, what was to become of her, once Janie had gone?

Janie took such a long time getting herself ready to go out, even Gran had to call up the stairs to find out if she was going to be much longer. Poor Janie had spent the afternoon at her friend Carol's house, in the outback of Highbury Fields. The intention was for Carol to give Janie a 'Toni' hair perm. She had gone like a lamb to slaughter, expecting the end product to resemble a cross between Rita Hayworth and Betty Grable. Of Course, Carol was in no way an experienced hair stylist, and unfortunately for Janie, she returned home later that afternoon with a scarf tied tightly around her hair, and a very red face. Gran gave Janie a quizzical look as she raced indoors and started preparing the tea. Why had Janie taken off her shoes and coat, but left on the headscarf?

'Let's see your hair Janie... did it take alright?' Janie blushed and carried on with what she was doing, still not removing the headscarf. 'Well, let's have a look at it then gel.' So saying, Gran reached forward and pulled the scarf back, then gasped at Janie's hair. 'Oh... is it meant to be all frizzy like that Janie?'

Poor Janie suddenly burst into tears and tore out into the scullery, where she filled the large enamel bowl with water and immersed her head in it. She shook it free of water and brushed it through, but still it looked no better, just a mass of frizz. Janie's face looked as red as a strawberry. 'Oh Gran, what am I going to do? What will Frankie say when he sees me!'

'There's not a lot he bloody well can say is there? Whatever made you have it done for? You have such lovely hair Janie!'

Poor Janie cried and Gran tutted, brushing harder and harder until it became even more frizzy. 'One thing's for sure. It will have to grow out... in time!'

'Oh Gran, I can't go around like this... it will take months!' As Janie brushed savagely at the mop of tight springing curls, she mumbled between gritted teeth, 'Never again... never, ever, again!'

Much later that evening, Janie, Marjie and Gran were all going for a drink at the 'Orange Tree' in Euston Road. It was to be a bit of a celebration and the women were rejoicing the end of the war and Gran's birthday. And for Janie it was the first anniversary of her and Frankie going out together. It was 'The Orange Tree' where they had their first date.

Janie was all nostalgic as they alighted from the No. 73 bus opposite the tavern. It was a warm evening and quite pleasant to stroll about. Janie wondered how long it would be before she would hear about going to America. However much she tried to push it to the back of her mind, it always came back to remind her that it could be at any time now. She wanted to have Frankie back more than anything else in the world, but she knew that when it happened, he would be sent back not long after. And God knows how soon after that, she would follow him.

The barman recognised Janie and smiled, 'Hi Janie, how are you keeping? Who's the good looking dame at your side?' He knew of course, but Gran thought it was wonderful and smiled in appreciation. 'Go on... you know who I am, and for your cheek I'll have a milk stout on the house... what you having girls?' They all laughed and made their way to a table at the back, where Gran insisted they sit, so that she could watch the world go round.

Quite a few people came into the bar, but none that Janie recognised from her old working days. Then suddenly her mind clicked and she thought she must be dreaming, for there at the end of the bar, who had just come in, and was looking all around for someone?

'Frankie, Frankie!' Janie almost knocked the table over in her rush to reach him. He turned and a smile lit up his whole face. His arms went around her and he swept her off her feet and into the air.

'How...? Where...?' Questions were fired at him from all angles as they all demanded to know how he came to be there. He laughed, and then seeing how they were fit to burst with excitement if he didn't explain himself, he placed his hat down in the midst of the glasses, moistened his lips and drank the first glass of beer that came to hand.

He smiled across at Gran, 'I'll get you a replacement darlin'.'

'Not before you tell me why you're here, and for how long,' gasped Janie, planting a kiss on his cheek as she hugged him. 'Well it's like this, I had the chance of a 36-hour pass, and I had to make up my mind whether or not I wanted it. It was a yes or no situation, so I said 'yes', bearing in mind I had to get down to London under my own steam. Anyway, a guy that was leaving just after me, offered me a lift in his truck... so here I am.'

Janie still looked puzzled. 'But how did you know where we were?' He laughed, 'Oh yeah, when I did get back to Islington, and beat the hell out of the door, Helen came rushing down the stairs on her way out and told me that you'd all gone to Euston. Of course I knew where you would be heading, and I wasn't far wrong was I? I left my kit in the hallway, grabbed a cab... and here I am.'

Janie flushed with pride and happiness. She pressed herself close to him. 'So you haven't got to return back to base until tomorrow evening... that's not too bad is it?'

It was here that Frankie's face clouded over a little and he took a deep breath. 'That's where the hard bit comes in, Janie darling. When I get back to base... we're flying back to the States!'

'Oh no Frankie! No, no!' Janie started to cry softly, then seeing that people all around were staring at her, she buried her head in his chest.

'What a bleedin' shame,' mumbled Gran. 'Just when Janie thought she had it all wrapped up as well. Shame!' Throwing back her head and trying to laugh it off she called, 'Drink up folks, I'll buy the next round! Your turn next Frankie, so don't forget to come back.' The edge was taken off the evening. However much Frankie tried to make light of the situation, Janie still felt very upset.

They had several drinks and Gran started her own little sing-song over in the corner, singing loud and defiant as if the parting of tomorrow just didn't exist. Amid the false gaiety, the evening wore on, and all too soon it was time for them to be making a move back home.

Frankie managed to find a taxi for them. As it drew close to the kerb the four of them clambered in silently, the quiet mood that hung over them like a heavy cloak in winter. The only fragment of conversation was between Gran and Marjie, intercepted now and then with a polite grunt from Frank.

At the gate Marjie bade them all goodnight, then Gran led the way indoors. Janie knew she shouldn't be like this, all sad and deflated, but she'd struggled on her own long enough, and now she wanted her man beside her, more than anything else in the world.

Gran left them on their own and mooched upstairs, carefully carrying another glass of stout. 'See you in the morning ducks. G'night Frankie.'

Frank walked round the table to where Janie stood staring into space... she looked so sad. Putting his arms around her, he pulled her close, and looked her straight in the eyes. 'It won't be for long honey... once I've done the preliminary jobs, I'll see about getting you out there with me. I'll fight tooth and nail so we can be together... you know that don't you? Please have faith in me darling. Time will soon go... really.'

Janie nodded. It was true he was doing everything possible for them both, and it was only a matter of time now, she knew that in her heart... deep down inside. She looked up at him, her eyes scanning his worried face, then she softened and smiled. 'Don't let's worry about tomorrow... we still have tonight!'

Chapter 34

In the weeks following Frank's return to base, Janie wrestled with one problem after another. There was one big worry she just couldn't come to terms with. She needed to get all the family together to discuss what was going to happen to Gran, when Janie eventually had to leave.

She mulled the problem over and over in her mind, trying to sort out the best way of dealing with the situation, hoping that in a matter of time young Helen would be able to join her and Frankie. That is of course, if Terry didn't want her to do otherwise. She knew how presumptuous young people could be, and although she had nothing against Terry, she was not happy with the thought of the two of them settling down too early. Well, it was stupid... they were too young. After worrying about it for several days, she resigned herself to sit and wait... although knowing how the government worked, she could still be here at the end of a month... or even six months!

It came as a bit of a surprise one evening when Cassie came home from St Mary's and made an announcement that all but suited them all. Janie hadn't realised just how grown up Cassie was now, and how much authority and control she had in her own little way. She was quite tall for her age, and she had a manner that was very much in command of any situation, whatever it was.

After waiting for Helen to arrive home from work and join them, they had a late tea. Helen was surprised at the family gathering, only listening half-heartedly to the conversation. She had her own problems, hers and Terry's, she really didn't want to be a part of any more family trivia. Janie looked at Helen chatting at the table, every part of her obsessed with Terry, and knew instinctively that it would only be a matter of time before the two of them got seriously involved. She sighed deeply. What a box of tricks to sort out... and all she wanted was to be with her husband.

The meal finished, the four women sat around the table, each waiting for the other to make the first move. Gran stirred her tea round and round in an endless fashion, then she looked up at Janie, gave a grunt, and started to voice her opinion. 'Well, I can't see what there is to worry about? It's not as if we can't be left on our own ... it's not as if we're babies and need looking after is it!'

Cassie looked at her thoughtfully before stating her plan of action. 'Well Gran, you might have a point there, but I've thought of a way things could work out for the best for the three of us. I've applied for a transfer to a hospital near here. I've passed my exams to date, and so for the next four years, I could stay at home and not have to go into digs. In that way we could keep the old routine going as before. Helen could help you as well Gran, with the running of things. It would mean Mum wouldn't be worrying herself sick about leaving you all on your own. Now... what do you think of that for a good idea?'

Janie kept purposely quiet in order to let the idea sink in, and so that Gran or Helen could have a say in the situation. She knew that Helen might not think it a good idea – she was so full of Terry and the plans they had made. Looking after the house with Gran in it was probably not included in their plan of action!

But surprisingly, it was Gran who was the most dogmatic and up in arms. She kept protesting that she was not a child, and did not need to be 'looked after'. Quick as a flash Janie turned the conversation round. 'No, no Gran. It isn't that you need looking after by Helen... quite the reverse in fact. Cassie means that YOU can give an eye to Helen, and what she's up to... after all, she is only seventeen isn't she!' Janie winked knowingly at Cassie, who smiled back.

'Hmm... I suppose it will be alright. But I don't want you to think of me as a liability Janie...' mumbled Gran grudgingly.

Janie smiled her thanks across at Cassie. At least she could go to America with a clear conscience. She could leave knowing that she was making the right decision for both her family, and her husband. Later that evening as Cassie prepared to get back to the hospital, Janie watched her as she stood in front of the mirror over the mantle- piece, smoothing and styling her hair into its neat pageboy style. Cassie was not a pretty girl like Helen, but the character that showed in the firm profile, and the caring way she had with people, more than made up for 'prettiness'... in every way.

After scrutinising herself in the mirror, making sure that not a hair was out of place, and buttoning up her coat, Cassie turned and confronted her mother. 'Mum, I hope that everything goes the way it should for you. You deserve a bit more out of life than you've had so far. Please don't worry about anything here, Helen and I will look after Gran, we're not children you know... not anymore!'

It was that remark that brought home to Janie how the years were rolling by... none of them were getting any younger. As

215

they stood there, it seemed as if their roles in life were reversed. Janie all excited at the thought of starting a new life; and Cassie all matter of fact and in control of everything, knowing what life had dictated to her, and what was expected of her. She was her father's daughter through and through.

With a sob Janie went and threw her arms around her. The two women hugged each other, then Cassie pulled herself away, gave a slight cough, and without any more ado strode along the passage and opened the street door, stopping only to give a brief smile. 'See you soon Mum... keep well.'

Janie listened to the heavy shoes clonk down the path, until the sound was lost in the myriad of street noise. She closed the door... her mind was clearer and she felt lighter than she had for ages. It was only a matter of time now, she told herself.

But that night, Janie tossed and turned in her bed for a long time. All the plans set down by Cassie had seemed so straightforward and matter of fact. It was still heart-breaking to think that because of her and her new life, the old family was about to split apart. It worried her... knowing that Norm would never have wished it to be like this. At last sleep finally caught up with her, and she drifted in and out of dreams, until finally the bright sunlight bursting through the thin curtains brought her to her senses.

It was hearing Gran moving about downstairs that persuaded her to get up early. In spite of feeling so tired, she knew that she had to make an effort. 'Hello Gran... did you sleep alright?' Janie proceeded to fill the large kettle so she could get herself washed. Gran was strangely quiet, and looked so serious that panic began to shoot across Janie's mind. Perhaps it wasn't going to be as easy as she thought. Oh God, what a damn problem it all seemed to be!

Gran pushed a cup of tea across the table towards Janie, and sat down with her own. 'Janie, we have things to talk about.'

Janie looked surprised. Oh, not this morning, she thought to herself – she was already in for a headache as it was. Smiling wanly at Gran, she started on her tea. 'What's the matter Gran? What's worrying you dear?'

Gran put down her cup and wiped her mouth with the back of her hand. 'It's young Helen… have you spoken to her lately about her and that young Terry? Hmm, I thought you hadn't. Well, only last week she was telling me as how she and young Terry want to get married. Yes, I thought that would shake you… it did me too at the time. Well, they've had it planned for ages, and were only waiting for Helen to reach eighteen. However, seeing as how you are going off to America shortly, she wants to get it over and done early, before you go. Terry hasn't got much more of his course left to do now, a matter of about eight months. So, you see what's in both their minds.'

Janie sat staring at Gran. She couldn't believe her ears… her Helen getting married! She wasn't even eighteen till Christmas! No, no she was too young … it wasn't the answer. She fidgeted with the edge of her dressing gown, waiting for Gran to continue.

'So, what do you think of that Janie? Now you can see what I've got to consider once you've gone to America. Oh yes…' Gran added, '…and they want to set up home here, with me, to start off with.'

Janie couldn't believe what she was hearing. Why hadn't Gran told her all this before? Why hadn't Helen said anything about it last night? Come to think of it… she had been very quiet and subdued.

'Oh Gran, how can I let them get married? She's so young, not yet eighteen! How...' Gran cut her short, 'Now Janie, she is no younger that you or I were when we got married. Remember? And as for Terry... well, you couldn't wish for a better son-in-law in the whole of Islington. They've been going around with each other since they were kids, and he's got his head screwed on right, I'll say that for him. So you see Janie, you have nothing to worry about. But if I were you, I'd sit down and have a good long chat to Helen about things ... she's a young woman now, not a kiddie.'

'But why didn't she come and tell me all of this herself Gran? What is she frightened of?' Janie asked. 'She thought you might try and talk them out of it... like you have me. She was planning to get wed in the New Year, but I know she would love you to see them both tie the knot sooner, being as you're going away yerself.'

'Oh Gran, what a fool I've made of myself. I don't know what to say for the best. How can I face Helen when she comes down? Oh Gran, why didn't I open my eyes before and see what was in front of my face? One thing's for sure ... the first opportunity I have of talking to Terry, I shall have to find out what his plans are for the future.' She laughed for the first time, 'It isn't a bad thing getting wed, is it Gran?'

At Helen's request, Terry came home for the weekend, and the pair of them sat down in the front room with Janie, Gran and George to discuss the future wedding plans. Janie suddenly viewed her daughter in a very different fashion. Gone was the little girl. Here instead was a very pretty and capable young woman, so very much in love with her Terry. It took Janie back quite a number of years to when she and Norm had faced her parents in the best parlour. Norm had a doubtful job to base getting married on... but with their hearts full of love, who cared!

Terry, who now towered over the two women, promised that they wouldn't give Janie any cause for complaint, and he joked around with Gran as he always did. But then they all got down to sorting out times and dates for the big day. It was going to be the second Saturday in August... that is if the minister could manage it. They wanted to be married at the church on the corner of Balls Pond Road. It was there that Vera had been laid to rest, and Terry said it would make her seem near to them all. George was agreeable, and with that settled, said they would all go on the following day to see the minister in question. After all, it was only about six weeks away.

Janie felt so happy for the two of them. She would do her very utmost to secure their happiness before she left for America.

It was later on that next Sunday afternoon, when the door burst open and a very pink faced Helen came rushing in. Gran and Janie looked up in surprise. 'It's all arranged Mum... it's all settled for the ninth of August.' She tore through the living room and raced upstairs, and came rushing back down pulling on her jacket as she did so. Her long wavy hair coiled around her face and neck, as she laughingly struggled into her best shoes. 'Won't be long Mum... we're going to the park. For a walk...' she added. They heard the front door slam behind her.

Gran looked up from her library book and smiled. 'Ain't love grand...'

Chapter 35

During that summer of '45, the weeks leading up to the wedding sped quickly by, and with each passing day Janie kept one silent prayer close to her heart – that her notification grant to go to America should not arrive before Helen's wedding. Deep down in her heart she ached to be able join him, but her daughter's wedding was a joy that she couldn't miss.

Not a week passed when she didn't receive a letter from Frank, so full of love for her, and longing for them to be together. As she read the words it seemed as if he was standing in front of her, the feeling was so real. She read each letter countless times, over and over again, before placing them in the small dressing table drawer. During the long lonely nights, the letters were like a balm to ease her frustrations, and she clung to them as her only means of solace.

Suddenly the news hit the headlines: 'Victory over Japan'. Such wonderful news, that Janie, Gran and Helen all decided to go up the West End to celebrate. Gran looked pensive and thoughtful. 'Do you think we should ask Marjie to come along? Although it would be a bit too crowded to take the young'n.' Janie hesitated, she knew Marjie professed to have turned over a new leaf over the past months, but to take her up there, with all those servicemen, was asking a bit too much. Janie felt she couldn't be responsible for her if anything happened.

'No Gran, I don't think it would be wise.' Janie had never been deceitful in all her life, but she felt they should keep it to themselves. She needn't have worried, for an excited Marjie came rushing through the back yard waving a scrap of paper frantically in her hands. Her face was a picture of joy as she tore into the living room through the open doorway. 'He's coming home... my Alec's soon coming home!'

Amid cries of happiness Janie took the telegram from Marjie's fingers and read it out loud. 'Reporting home stop 0014 stop love you stop Alec.'

Marjie couldn't stop shaking with excitement. She was crying too, such tears of joy. Gran found a hanky inside her overall and gave it to Marjie to mop her face with. It was strange how one person's joyous news could make them all so happy.

After a while, they quietened down, and Gran made her way out to the scullery and started to fill the large kettle. 'I think we had better have a cuppa to calm us all down, don't you girls?'

Now recovered from the excitement and shock, Marjie started chattering to Janie, as excited as a young bride. 'Just think Janie... by next week, the 14th, he'll be here, home again with us. Oh Janie...' Marjie's face screwed up in anticipation of what was to come.

Janie sat frowning, turning things over in her mind. Suddenly she turned to Marjie and held out her hand in an agitated fashion. 'Here Marjie... let me see that telegram again for a minute.'

Marjie grudgingly held out the scrap of paper again for Janie's inspection. Janie's eyes scanned the typewritten words again, then she let out a whoop. 'Oh Marjie... oh you fool! This was sent early this morning from Portsmouth, and 0014 hours means that he's coming home today!'

Grabbing back the paper, Marjie, open-mouthed, read it for herself. As she did so her face lit up a thousand-fold. 'Oh

Janie! Oh Gran! It is true then... he could be home at any time. He could be travelling home now, this minute.' Without more ado she turned tail and rushed out past Gran, though the back yard and into her own home, running as if there were no tomorrow. 'Can't stop, can't stop...!' she yelled to Gran. 'ALEC'S COMING HOME TODAY.'

Gran stood in the doorway bearing aloft three cups of tea on a small tin tray, her mouth hanging open as the excited girl ran past her. 'Here, what's all the rush for? Where's she gorn?' she said to Janie. Taking the tray from her and placing it down on the table, Janie smiled. 'Well Gran, she didn't realise that Alec will be coming home today... she didn't read the telegram properly. He should be home any time... perhaps he's coming down the street even now.'

Gran looked flabbergasted that anything could happen so quickly. Shuffling along the hall, she opened the street door wide, and peered out suspiciously. 'Well, he ain't home yet, is he?'

Later that afternoon the three women left the house to go and join the celebrations going on in the West End. Gran had listened avidly to her wireless most of the day, hearing how large crowds were forming all around Buckingham Palace, hoping to see the royal family. Janie decided that they might be better to try and make for Hyde Park, for as well as the crowds, she had Gran to consider.

They got a bus quite quickly and were soon nearing Tottenham Court Road. The crowds were milling around in their thousands, so instead of getting to the end of their fare, they decided to jump off and walk along Oxford Street.

Gran had never seen so many people. Civilians, soldiers,

sailors... in fact, all creeds, from all nations, were intermingled in a happy frenzy that seemed to engulf them in its friendship. Gran had a job holding on to her hat as people waved and cheered all around her. She had no problem keeping in step with the younger two, for the simple reason they could only move along inches at a time.

A man with a chubby face and twinkling eyes suddenly leaned over and gave Gran a squeeze. As he pulled away he stuck his fingers up high in the air in a V sign, his eyebrows raised and laughing fit to bust. Gran glared back at him, trying to act all annoyed. 'Cheeky bleeder!' But she was tickled pink really, however much she complained to Janie afterwards!

After a couple of hours they had progressed no further than Oxford Circus. The crowds were coming thick and fast, and the buses were having quite a job to get along the middle of the road, there were so many revellers - all laughing, singing and dancing in the streets.

Helen looked at everything starry eyed, she had never seen or experienced anything like it before in her life. Everyone was in a jubilant mood, they were now at peace. The war was over!!

Eventually the three of them headed for a number 70 bus they saw in the distance. Gran was getting tired of being jostled, although she had really had the time of her life. She had joined hands with a group of Americans and had ended up doing a right old knees-up, encouraged by them all the way. They each kissed her in turn, all five of them, and she loved it. Her face was red and her hat was knocked sideways but she had thrown convention to the winds and really let her hair down. As she said to them all, 'Well, it is Victory night after all... come on, give us a kiss!'

Janie felt herself getting all embarrassed at Gran's behaviour. If she didn't know better she would have said that the old lady was a bit tiddly. Helen couldn't take her eyes off her Gran. She smiled and tugged at Janie's arm, nodding her head to where Gran was being danced around by the group of yanks. They were clapping and she was doing a knees-up to the best of her ability. 'Leave her be... she's enjoying herself,' Janie smiled.

When the number 70 bus got nearer, she and Helen grabbed Gran, one each side, and practically ran across the road with her until they fell into the wake of the bus, and clambered aboard in a state of near collapse. Gran sat breathing heavily, her best hat all cockeyed and her legs splayed. After resting her chin on her chest for a moment, she lifted up her face and beamed at the two of them. 'I'm glad we came Janie... I thought you'd enjoy yourself!'

Much later that evening they all went to the 'Three Crowns' where the locals were in celebratory mood. It was so crowded that with the doors permanently open, the crowds were spilling out all along the pavement. Old Bert, who kept the oil-shop down the road, had dragged the piano out to the pavement in front of the four ale bar, and was banging it for all he was worth, under the watchful eye of the publican inside.

As the women strolled along, ready to join in, Janie looked for George. They still didn't know if Alec was home or not. Spying George sitting with a group of his mates in a far corner, her heart went out to him. It must be upsetting for him being on his own, without Vera at his side. Although, by the way he was laughing his head off, he seemed to be managing pretty well.

Everyone had something, or someone to celebrate with.

Children were having fun with their families – bonfire parties were in progress in many of the side streets. Janie's thoughts drifted back over the last six years. It had seemed a very long time, a lot had happened, a lot of water had gone under the bridge. She gave a deep sigh, it was no good getting emotional... the war was over now. Peace was what they had all dreamed about, over and over. What would the future bring she wondered... for her daughters, for Gran, and for herself and Frankie.

Gran's voice broke her train of thoughts. 'Do you want a milk stout or a port and lemon, Janie?' Janie, startled, looked into the creased-up smiling face. 'Oh, a drop of stout please, Gran!' She watched as Gran pushed her way through to the counter again and shout her order. Gran could find her way to the counter faster than anyone Janie knew. Everyone knew her and gave way to her – it was easier than contradicting her.

As she waited, looking round at the faces in the crowded pub, she saw the familiar face of Alec, with Marjie at his elbow. He looked much thinner and very tanned, more adult, thought Janie to herself – but it was Alec without a doubt.

After pushing their way through the crowd, Gran and Helen returned with the drinks. Placing her glass firmly on the counter, then loosening her dress at the neck, Gran lifted her chin and in a voice that would have done credit to a Billingsgate porter, she broke into a melodious song. Helen dipped her eyes and murmured, 'Oh Gran, everyone's looking at us.' But still Gran carried on, waving her arms in unison with the music, without a care in the world. Heads turned and strangers smiled across at them, 'Go on Gel, enjoy yourself.' They laughed at her and with her.

Suddenly Gran saw Marjie, George and Alec on the far side of the saloon bar. She stopped singing and shouted across to them. They all readily waved back and pushed their way over to the corner, where they pressed themselves neatly between the counter and the mirrored wall like a human wedge.

'Hallo Alec, nice to have you back home again.' Janie leaned over and kissed him lightly on the cheek. He turned to Gran and placed an arm around her shoulders, beaming broadly and slightly the worse for wear. 'How are you, me little darlin'? What are ya drinking… port and lemon?' Gran giggled and said she thought she'd had enough for one evening. 'Nonsense gel, I'll get you another… don't you know the war's over.' Gran giggled all the more. 'Oh you are a card Alec,' she chortled, as she drained her glass in readiness.

Alec turned to Helen and placed his hand on her shoulder. His eyes swept over her from tip to toe. He was mentally devouring every inch of her, and she knew it. She flushed and looked away from his stare. A smile creased his sunburnt face and he nodded to himself. 'My… haven't we grown into a big girl now…' He carried on smiling at her, 'So, it's the big day soon isn't it?' She nodded, blushing to the tips of her ears. Alec continued to stare at her, his eyes almost disrobing her, one garment at a time. He smiled… he was enjoying himself to the very hilt.

Marjie stared at him, drumming her fingernails on the side of her glass. He must have been aware of it, but his glance never wavered from Helen. He ran his tongue around the edge of his lips slowly, then realising that the others were all watching him, he murmured, 'Well, all I can say is, lucky old Terry. Come on… give us a kiss… on account.' Without hesitation he swooped forward and grabbed hold of Helen, pressing her close to him and kissing her hard on the mouth. 'That's one for luck,' he added, as Marjie glared hard at him. He smiled and carried on drinking, knowing the awkward position he was placing everyone in.

Pretending not to have seen it all, Janie looked away, but she felt a shiver run through her. He was not to be trusted, at least not when he had downed a skinful. Perhaps Marjie knew how to control him, for being away for so long certainly hadn't quietened him down. In fact it seemed to have done quite the opposite. He ran his fingers through his hair and smiled across at Helen appealingly. 'You didn't mind did you Helen? Course not!' He gulped his drink as if to reassure himself, before draping his arm around Marjie's shoulder and kissing her neck.

Janie looked across at Helen who still looked very worried. She mouthed the words silently, but emphatically, hoping Helen would understand. 'It's the drink...' Helen nodded and smiled back, biting her lips to stop herself from shaking. Of course it was the drink, it must be! But it still didn't stop the nagging thought that kept going through her mind that she was marrying into the family. "Christ!' she told herself, 'I hope he doesn't try anything on again... now that he's home.'

Janie decided that they should take their leave. After all, it was almost midnight and Gran had indulged herself more than was good for her. The three of them said their goodbyes and Janie led the way from the crowded bar out into the street. She avoided Alec's face as she pushed Helen forward, and without looking back called, 'Cheerio' to them all. They waved and shouted back, their voices lost in the excitement and singing, that carried on well into the small hours.

The air was cool as they emerged from the heat of the crowds. They crossed the wide junction and walked slowly along the pavement, Helen in a world of her own, Gran almost asleep, and Janie lost in her own nostalgic thoughts. The old place still looked the same, despite the mounds of rubble where houses had collapsed like packs of cards, and the friendly shops that carried on regardless with all the fronts boarded up. Still, the war really was over, they were at peace... and now all they had to do was to pick up the broken pieces and start living all over again.

Janie felt herself becoming quite tearful as she reminisced, and as she thought of the wedding that would take place in a few days time, she choked back tears of happiness. Her little Helen, a child no longer... where had all those years gone?

This now was the climax of all those long fretful years, when they'd found it hard to remember when there hadn't been a war, for it had gone on so long. Now they had peace to look forward to, all their dreams and hopes had finally arrived!!

Thank God they had made it. She was thankful for Gran, who never gave up hope, for her Norm who had given everything, including his life, and for Frank... who had found her just in time.

Chapter 36

Helen stood and surveyed herself in front of the bedroom mirror. She felt hesitant and more than a little nervous. Terry had arrived home yesterday morning and the two of them had spent a few brief hours in the early evening trying to sort out the last of the arrangements before the big day itself. She knew they were doing the right thing, for she loved him with all her heart, and had done for as long as she could remember.

Her eyes misted over as she thought of her dad – he would have loved to have seen this happen... his 'babe' as he called her, getting married to the man she loved. Feeling her eyes beginning to smart with tears, she willed herself not to cry... to be seen with puffy red eyes on her wedding day would be awful!

The long white wedding dress hung resplendent on its hanger on the outside of the wardrobe. It was a vision of satin and net, and had been loaned to her by her best friend at work. Two other brides had seen it through the same ceremony, so she told herself that it must be third time lucky … that is if she had any doubts at all. Her dear friend Stella, whom she had known since they had moved to Islington, was to be her bridesmaid, and the two of them had giggled continuously for weeks during the lead up to the big day. Now that she was alone for what seemed like the first time, Helen felt nervous, but at the same time tinged with excitement.

She could hear footsteps on the stairs. It was Stella and her mum followed by Gran – they were all coming to help her get ready. Helen's face was almost devoid of make-up except for the dab of face powder to tone down her shiny cheeks. A bottle of carefully hoarded 'Californian Poppy' scent stood on the dressing table, and removing the top she placed a little on her throat and behind her ear lobes. As she stood it back on the glass top the door burst open and in trooped Stella, Gran and her mum.

She stood happily as they ooh'd and aah'd around her while getting her dressed. Stella helped to fix the headdress on top of her curls and then the three of them all stood back and admired the finished picture.

'You look lovely Helen,' murmured Gran. 'Don't she Janie... a real little smasher? Well, I never thought I'd see the day.' Gran looked all dreamy while Stella and Janie set about putting the finishing touches to their own outfits. Janie grinned to herself as the old lady sat, half smiling, in the wicker chair, obviously miles away in a world of her own.

A sudden shout came from downstairs. Derek King, who had been Norm's best mate in the fire service, was here to do the honours and give the bride away. He came striding up the stairs two at a time. 'Ladies, ladies... it's here. The car has arrived... I don't want to rush you, but...' He stopped awkwardly outside the bedroom door, not quite knowing where to put himself. Janie smiled and told him they were all ready.

Derek stood sweating profusely next to the bride in his trust, nervously stepping from one foot to the other. He smiled at her and mumbled something about not to be nervous, although it was obvious who was the one shaking like a leaf. Helen smiled at him reassuringly!

'He's all teeth and Brylcreem,' Gran muttered to Janie,

downstairs. Janie smiled. 'It's what Norm would have wanted... for his mate to do the honours... and that's all that counts.'

The wedding service was timed for three o'clock, and in spite of the warm bright afternoon, Janie found herself more than a little apprehensive. Although she was bursting with happiness for Helen, she would have given her right arm to have Frank here with them. She missed him so very much. She also worried about Gran. At night she kept herself awake for hours tossing and turning and wondering if she was doing the right thing by leaving them all, and going off to start a new life in America.

Staring distractedly at her image in the oval mirror, Janie fixed her new hat – dusty pink linen, trimmed with flowers. It made a perfect match for the navy two piece she had bought for her honeymoon. She had managed to dye a pair of gloves the same shade of pink, and the result was more than satisfying. Had she changed much over the last few months, she wondered. Would Frank see any difference in her, and did she look any older than her thirty-nine years?

Voices from downstairs brought her back to her senses as she realised that everyone was on the move. Calling 'Good luck' to Helen who was standing in the bedroom doorway, she raced down the stairs and out to the waiting car, where she found Gran and Cassie sitting smiling in the back seat.

'I thought we were going to start this wedding without you, Janie. What you been doing for gawd's sake!' grumbled Gran to herself as she fussed around with the hat she had borrowed at the last minute from Lulu, trying to get it comfortable amid a barrage of hairpins.

They filed quietly into the church and joined the rest of the relatives. Janie stood in the pew next to Cassie. Janie glanced at her and smiled fondly - the petrol blue dress and matching hat, lightened with a spray of Lily of the Valley, looked lovely on Cassie. The blue matched her eyes and the entire outfit looked smart, and complimented her lithe figure. Outwardly, she looked so calm and serene, almost as if she didn't have a nerve in the whole of her body.

Gran stood next to her, proudly wearing her best dove grey 'edge to edge' coat and the borrowed hat, which was really stylish, trimmed with osprey feathers that curled around her face. Gran had spent the entire morning asking repeatedly if she didn't look 'too done up'. Helen and Cassie, as well as Janie, had quite a job convincing her that she didn't!

As the organ started to play softly, Marjie and Cynthia, standing with Alec on the other side of the church, turned their heads in the direction of the church door. George stood awkwardly next to Rose, one of Vera's sisters, and wished with all his might that he had worn his khaki uniform instead of his demob suit. At least it fitted him better, without a doubt.

At last the service started and the bride came slowly down the aisle on Derek's arm. She looked straight at Terry and smiled.

Terry was an ambitious lad, and with his tall bearing he seemed to tower over all of them. He knew where he was going in life and he meant to get there. He looked down at Helen as he placed the ring on her finger, his face positively glowing with happiness. After the exchange of vows he smiled deeply at Helen, and she felt a shiver of excitement course through her veins. Then they turned and faced the congregation, who saw two people so much in love that it radiated from them in a warm glow.

In half an hour it was all over, and they went outside to the back of the church where a photographer tried vainly to take the wedding pictures. He was a stocky man with a red nose, wearing a check cap. Gran was fascinated by him, and said he ought to be on 'the boards'.

He kept diving back and forth under the black cloth that was draped around his camera, each time he did so, his cap kept sliding about on his head, and he would reappear waving one hand to his subject, and the other holding his hat in place.

However much they tried to look 'refined' the wedding party broke into squeals of laughter as the little man ducked under his cloth and out again. Eventually he had refilled his camera with more than enough glass plates, and seemed happy with all the shots. Grinning broadly, he touched his cap to the bride and groom, gave a wink, and then backed down the gravelled pathway, holding tight to his armful of plates wrapped up safely in his black cloth. Shouting congratulations to all and sundry, his van door slammed and he roared off down the street in a cloud of exhaust fumes.

The laughter subsided, and the women kissed the bride and gave greetings to the groom. The men all shook hands and gave each other 'the wink' – meaning they wanted to get underway with the beer, before it got too warm.

Gran wiped a tear from her eyes as she gave Terry and Helen a final kiss. She had waited so long for this day, to see one of her granddaughters wed, and she hadn't been disappointed in the least. Her hankie was quite damp with the crying she had done. Oh, it had all been a lovely wedding so far!

A sudden shower of rain sent them all hurrying back, giggling, to the cars, impatient to get back to No. 34. The front parlour was more than crowded as everybody squeezed themselves in. Derek and George were handing out drinks to everyone, and Janie ensured that the sandwiches were offered.

The white cake stood in the centre of the best damask table-cloth, all three tiers of it. Eventually Janie took away the two cardboard tiers at the top, while a woman friend helped Cassie to cut it into minute finger-sized portions.

It was a happy scene, but all too soon it had to end, for they had to leave for their honeymoon. It was an unplanned affair that hadn't materialised until the day before yesterday. Terry's Auntie Pearl owned a large house in Westgate, and she had kindly offered them a stay for as long as they wanted, and they had accepted.

George had borrowed a car from an old army friend, and was running them to the station to get the 7.30 train to Margate. When Helen had changed her dress, the pair of them struggled away from the laughing crowd and out to the waiting car. It was an old Morris Minor, covered with army camouflage and sporting a pair of army boots tied up with several tin cans, which were all strung to the back bumper of the car.

Amid the shower of confetti they ran giggling out to the street, Helen stopping only to throw her small bouquet into the air and see it caught by her friend Stella. Janie witnessed all this and felt sorry that it hadn't been Cassie to have been the lucky one. Cassie alone had deliberately backed away from the obvious throw, in favour of letting the younger girl catch it. Cassie told herself that marriage was not for her... she had a career in front of her.

Watching them from the porch, Janie watched them go, stifling a sob as Gran came up behind her and touched arm. 'Don't worry Janie. They're young... and in love... and the bleedin' war is over too.'

Janie turned and smiled at her, 'Yes I know dear... I know.' She bade goodbye to all the friends and relatives, knowing in her heart that she would most likely never set eyes on them ever again.

Janie had clung to Cassie for several moments before she felt her push herself away. 'I must get back Mum, I'm on early shift in the morning. Take care of yourself.' After kissing Janie on the cheek with a coolness that was worrying, Cassie bent down and kissed Gran the same way. 'See you soon Gran... bye for now.' Dragging the bag to her side with a toss of her head, and her usual manner of assurance, she strode off down the path, turning only to wave to the pair of them as they stood framed in the doorway.

Janie sighed deeply and reached for Gran's hand. She was all excited and happy, and yet confused. It was now that she longed for Frankie to be here with her. It was now that she couldn't wait for the moment when they would be together, as man and wife. Oh God, how much longer would they have to be apart? How long?

Feeling her shake with emotion Gran squeezed Janie's hand gently. 'Don't take on Janie... it's been a lovely wedding, hasn't it... and didn't Helen look a picture? Cassie too,' she added.

Gran walked back indoors, pleased that everyone had gone home, and that she could relieve herself of her new corsets, which had been almost strangling her. She left them on the bottom of the bed, and was now comfortable in her dressing gown. Janie locked up and wound up the large mantle clock before placing it back on the mantelpiece. She yawned. It had been a long but lovely day.

Gran fixed her hairnet in place then walked over to the cupboard for a handful of her favourite 'all-sorts' to eat in bed. 'Good night Janie love... don't get upset. Helen will be alright... you'll see.'

'Yes,' murmured Janie. '...night-night Gran.' It wasn't Helen who was on her mind. No, she wanted Frankie... here with her. Gran never saw the tears that trickled down her cheeks, or the look of longing in her eyes.

Chapter 37

During the weeks following the end of the war in Japan, and the return of the men back into civvies, Janie found herself waiting anxiously for her drafting to the USA, and to be with Frank again.

He wrote to her constantly telling her all about where, and what he was doing, but it still did nothing to stem the awful longing that she felt inside of her... to be with him, to talk with him, and to be his wife. She found herself looking enviously at Helen, who seemed to bloom with life since her marriage to Terry. Unlike Marjie and Alec, who seemed to do nothing but shout and rave at each other since Alec's return from the army. Even Gran had noticed that life was considerably less peaceful than it had been.

'I'm wondering if that young Marjie is as innocent as she looks,' Gran mumbled to Janie as the two of them sorted through the pile of ironing together. Janie looked up startled, wondering just how much Gran knew regarding Marjie and her G.I. boyfriends. 'What do you mean Gran, by innocent? What do you think she has been up to then?'

'Well, she always was a one for the boys wasn't she, and with 'im being away for all that time, well... it ain't very healthy for a young married woman is it? Perhaps she's done a bit of playing around on the side, you know? Perhaps he has found out a thing or two... perhaps...'

Looking sharply at Gran, Janie cut her short. 'Best for us not to get too involved Gran. After all, they say that adjustments have to be made by all the family once the servicemen return. It's in all the magazines and papers.' It wouldn't do for Gran to start putting two and two together. It would open up old wounds for George, as well as them, if the whole story came out.

That Saturday afternoon, Cassie was all excited as she came rushing down the pathway. Her face was alight and flushed as she turned her door key in the lock, coming face to face with Gran who was on the point of going up to Chapel market. 'Cor, where's the fire, gel? I'll have to watch I don't get knocked over in the rush, eh?'

'Sorry Gran, I didn't see you there... is Mum in? I've got some good news.'

'No, she's gone up to the Angel with young Helen ... said something about seeing an old friend of hers.'

Cassie looked disappointed; she only had the afternoon off, then she had to get back for night shift at the hospital.

Gran took off her coat, placing it over the back of the chair. 'Well, I'm going to put the kettle on and make you a cup of tea now that you're here. And you can tell me all the news Cass.'

'Don't stay in on my account Gran, please.'

'Course I'll stay in... I can go to the market for a look round any old day! Come and sit down Cass, and tell me all your news.' But Cassie seemed hesitant to talk, and they sat eyeing each other and slowly sipping their tea. Worried, Gran wondered what the news could be about.

Voices from the street door broke the uneasy silence. Helen and Janie came and Janie flung her arms around Cassie, kissing her on the cheek. 'What a lovely surprise Cass! Have you got long, or do you have to rush off soon?'

Helen grabbed a couple of cups and saucers and poured out more tea from the large brown teapot. 'Come on Cass, who's been getting the chop this week?' She avoided the sharp look that Cassie shot meaningfully across at her.

The four women sat at the table, all wondering what to say next. Janie smiled across at Cassie as she placed her teacup down. It was obvious that Cassie had something to talk about… but strange that she was clearly reluctant to discuss it in front of Gran, or even Helen.

Eventually Cassie broke the tension and with a worried look towards Gran stated, 'You remember me saying I've applied for a place in a local hospital to be nearer to home? Well, it came through, and I start at Holloway in two weeks. That means I can live at home… and also keep an eye on things.' She added hesitantly.

Her face lighting up, Janie took her hand. 'Oh Cass, that's smashing news… isn't it Gran? We shall all be together again, just like old times.' Gran shrugged her shoulders. 'Hmm, it's going to be a bit overcrowded isn't it?'

Janie bit her lip; she had been expecting this for a long time. The answer to the situation was one of two things. Either Cassie would have to share with her for the time being, or if Cassie wanted a room of her own Janie would have to give up her bedroom and sleep down in the front room.

When she put this to them Cassie pulled a face. 'Oh Mum, I couldn't let you give up your own bedroom… oh no!'

Gran, who had been weighing it all up, and knowing for whose benefit this line had been taken, suddenly puffed up her chest and announced tartly, 'If anyone is going to move out of their room, then it will be me. I'll move down to the front room, it will suit me fine. I don't want it on my conscience that I've turfed somebody out of their bed, do I?' She shot a meaningful glance at Janie as she spoke, making Janie blush, and feel even guiltier for causing so much upset. 'Oh, Gran! You don't have to you know...' Gran's answer was short... 'Hmph!'

Over the fence that evening, Gran grumbled to Marjie. 'You know Marjie, I'm beginning to feel really in the way. And they want me to be 'looked after' as if I was some kiddie.' Marjie looked thoughtful, then smiled. 'Well Gran, it doesn't have to be a problem, Cassie could always sleep in our Phyl's room. Or Helen and Terry could move over her and have Terry's old room? It would be a bit cramped but they could manage.'

Gran smiled appreciatively, 'Tell you what Marjie, I'll have a word with our Janie and see what she says.'

Suddenly, they heard the sound of Alec's voice, loud and clear, yelling out for Marjie. Flustered, she gathered the rest of the washing off the line and beat a hasty retreat indoors. 'Ta ta Gran... must go now... ta ta.'

Gran thought about Marjie's suggestion and wondered what George would have to say about it. He was a lot different now, a changed man. Since losing Vera he had taken to going out most evenings, and spent hours writing letters to some woman that he knew out in Canada. He had taken on a light warehouseman's job of work, mainly because his capabilities were more than restricted. He couldn't settle in the house, he was rarely at home, and if Gran saw him once a week, she was lucky. He never spoke of Vera or mentioned her at all, and apart from the odd remark from Marjie it would seem that she had never existed in that house at all.

Gran thought to herself that some men had a funny way of showing their feelings, and perhaps this was just his way of showing his. Perhaps it was all he was capable of now that he was a widower... strange how folk altered when they were on their own. Perhaps he needed to get married again? You never know... time will tell, she supposed.

On Sunday afternoon while Janie made scones for tea, Gran seized the opportunity to tell Janie what Marjie had suggested about Cassie having Phyl's room. 'And if she doesn't want that, then Helen and Terry could move into the Terry's old...' Janie cut her short very abruptly. 'No, Gran... No! I'm not having young Helen in that house, under the same roof as that Alec!' Janie was not at all pleased, and wouldn't hear of the plan at any cost. The mere mention of Alec seemed to set Janie's back up, for what reason Gran didn't know.

Janie thumped the dough into shape as she tried to curb her anger. She knew that Gran was looking at her as if she was mad. 'I'm sorry Gran, but I wouldn't be happy to know that Helen was next door. After all, this is her home, here. That is until they both get one of their own.'

Gran sniffed and looked the other way, knowing that Janie was talking sense really. Still, it would have eased the situation. Oh well, best to wait and see thought Gran to herself.

Janie carried on cutting small rounds of the mixture, wiping traces of flour from her forehead as she did so. 'Anyway Gran, I do know that young Terry has plans for the two of them to go to Australia as soon as possible. He has ideas of his own, wants to be a sheep farmer or something. Don't know when it will all be coming off though... still, he is adamant about going ahead.'

Gran put down her bit of knitting, 'Just think... in next to no time you might all be scattered across the bleedin' world! I don't know, the war has made everyone very restless, never thought that peacetime would be like this.'

Janie laughed softly. 'Don't blame it onto peace Gran... it's just that everyone has grown up and got plans of their own. Youngsters are more ambitious nowadays, they want so much more out of life than we ever did.'

Gran looked thoughtful, then as if to terminate the conversation between them, she reached across and turned the wireless set on, humming to herself as the music came through.

Chapter 38

As the men returned from war, the weeks drifted into months. It was a time of re-adjustment for them all. Poor Marjie and Alec seemed to be having quite a few ups and downs as he was not a man to take to civvy life easily. After his position as sergeant, he wanted to give orders to everyone, as well as his family. It caused a lot of upset between Marjie and George, who more than once told Alec to remember whose roof he lived under. Eventually Alec got himself a job on the railway, and by doing shift work he was able to keep out of his father-in-law's way.

Janie knew that George was keeping touch with a woman he'd met during the war, who lived somewhere in Canada. It was none of her business of course, as she so often told Gran, but it did make her wonder how serious it was, and if George had any ideas of going out to Canada to meet up with this ex-nurse. Time alone would tell. She knew what it was like to be left without a partner, so she wouldn't condemn George for what he might do with the rest of his life.

When Helen and Terry returned from their honeymoon on a pink cloud, Janie prepared the front bedroom for them, and she herself moved into the smallest bedroom. Her clothes, such as they were, she kept clean and pressed ready to be packed at a moment's notice, and her personal treasures didn't amount to more than she could carry in her handbag. It was all a question of time, at the drop of a hat she could receive her notification for her departure to the U.S. She tried hard not to think about it, although the longing for Frankie never eased up for a moment, night or day.

One late autumn afternoon, Helen was busy in the garden when Janie picked up the letter from the doormat. She had the back door open and heard her mother as she slammed the street door. Janie stood looking at the long envelope, her hand shaking, her emotions to the surface, and a knot in her stomach getting tighter and tighter. She stared hard at the typed address, her eyes trying to take in the formal and impersonal look of it. The address of the American Embassy was in the corner, and even before she tore open the envelope she knew what the contents would contain.

She was so wrapped up in her thoughts that she didn't hear Helen speak to her from the far end of the garden. 'Do you think I should put these spring bulbs in Mum? It would be a nice splash of colour during next spring!'

Helen stood in the doorway, her hands brown with earth, a small rusty old fork in her grip as she stared hard at her mother's face, which reflected a mixture of panic and joy, both at the same time. 'Mum... what is it? Whatever is it?' Dropping the fork and wiping her hands hastily on the old towel that hung on the back door, she rushed to Janie's side.

Janie stood shaking. 'It's come Helen... it's come! I'm too scared to open it and read it.'

'Go on Mum. This is what you've been waiting for all these long lonely weeks.' Helen guided her to a chair and pushed her down, then she sat opposite, watching her mother's face eagerly. Janie cut through the envelope and withdrew the paper slowly. She bit her bottom lip as her eyes scanned the typescript, then slowly she looked up at Helen, her voice hardly audible as she mouthed the words. 'It's next week Helen ... I'm to go next Monday.' As she spoke, she buried her face in her hands and sobbed deeply - partly from joy, partly from sorrow.

Helen threw herself into her mother's arms and hugged her excitedly. 'Oh Mum! Oh Mum!'

However joyous the news was for Janie, they both knew it was the parting from the rest of the family that was the hardest to bear. The gulf was so wide and there was no knowing when they would all meet again, or where. Helen didn't want her mother to feel sad and think about this, so she hid her own feelings as best she could.

When Gran came home from the market, Helen made sure to tell her the news before Janie had a chance to. Gran's face lit up, and she agreed with Helen, that whatever they themselves felt, they were in no way to mar the joy of Janie going to join Frankie.

By the end of the day everyone had been told of the impending departure. That evening Janie stood looking out of her bedroom window, the letter in her hand, tears forming in her eyes at the prospect of what lay ahead.

On Monday she had to make her way to Southampton, where later that evening she would board the ship that would take her to a strange new world, a new life. A life she would share with Frankie.

The girls had both insisted it was no good getting all upset and emotional. This was what they wanted, and what she had waited all those weeks for. It would only be selfish of them to be other than happy and joyful for her.

The weekend came very quickly and no reference was made

of Monday's big departure. Helen decided to finish her bulb planting, at Janie's insistence. She dug at the earth with ferocity, knowing that her mum would not be here to appreciate the colour and joy from the garden, the first bit of proper gardening since the war had started. She tried hard to obliterate the thoughts, her head bent low as she dug all the harder.

Gran made a lovely spread for Sunday tea, inviting in a few of their close friends, including her old mate Lulu. Cassie and Helen chatted together and Janie felt it was like old times. The evening was rounded off with a singsong led by Gran, with a few ripe jokes thrown in for good measure from Alec. Janie took it all in good part and sang along with them. George looked rather distant, and confided in her of his plans to visit 'a friend in Canada'. Janie wished him luck, and all too soon the goodbyes were made and the two families separated.

After seeing Lulu to the bus stop, Gran went off to bed, making no mention of tomorrow, although Janie knew that she was getting a bit nervous as the time drew near.

Cassie was making up a bed for herself in the front room, as Janie went about the business of locking up the house. It was strange, she thought – this would be the very last time she would be doing this. Even as the thought entered her head she was filled with remorse, but tried to push it away... it wasn't a part of her life any more. This would be Cassie's job now, or Terry's. She mustn't let her mind wander over these old things. It was a part of her old life... it wasn't up to her any more.

Helen came in to say goodnight, followed by Terry. He put his arm around Janie, and giving her an encouraging hug whispered, 'Don't worry about the family. I'll do all I can, with Helen's help, and of course Cassie's too.'

Then, they had all gone to bed, and she was left alone with just her thoughts. Her bag was in the hall, all labelled and packed; her papers and government instructions were safe in her handbag. All that remained now was for her to get some sleep before taking that long trip.

The chill and dampness woke, and she leapt out of bed and stared out of the window. It was just as she thought, a steady drizzle of rain accompanied by grey mists. She walked around the bedroom, trying to savour every last memory and smell that she could. The Mansion polish on the well-worn furniture, the dusty old curtains that had seen better days, the atmosphere that she had lived with for so many of her married years. Now she would leave them... for good.

She forced herself to eat the minute breakfast Cassie prepared for her, neither of them speaking very much. Then Terry came in from the back yard bearing two large buckets of coal, and she smiled as she remembered the times Norman had done the same thing! Such a long time ago. She had made up her mind over and over again that she would not be sad. She would leave them all with a smile on her face, and a happy memory to last them through the long winter.

The last minute mundane tasks completed, she stood by the window waiting. Moments later the taxi arrived and she knew that the big moment had come. Terry placed his arm around her shoulders and wished her luck, then Helen threw her arms around her, sobbing her goodbyes. Even Cassie, with her natural reserve, cried unashamedly as she held her mother to her.

Turning to Gran Janie hugged her tightly. She was too choked to speak at first, then, 'I'll be back soon... I promise. I'll come and see you. God bless you.' She wrenched herself away, not daring to look at Gran's face, and walked quickly to the front door. Terry took her suitcase out to the waiting cab then stood next to Helen, who was sobbing uncontrollably by now.

Janie gave them all a quick peck on the cheek, then turned hastily and ran to the taxi. She could see Gran standing in the porch staring out after her, with eyes dulled by age and sorrow.

The cab started to move slowly away as Janie stared out at them all, trying to imprint the last sight of them all in her memory.

As the cab picked up speed, she turned herself round to the back window, waving like a mad thing, on and on, until she could see no more. Still she searched for their faces in the grey drizzle that had swallowed them up, until giving up, she hunched herself in the corner of the seat, twisting her wedding ring to eliminate the feel of the knife that was slowly cutting her in two.

'Goodbye Gran... goodbye to all those sad and happy memories. Goodbye... till we meet again.'

Chapter 39

OCTOBER 1970

It was a bitterly cold afternoon for early autumn, and traces of frost snaked their way along the pavement that stretched in front of the parade of shops. A taxi purred slowly along the kerbside until it finally stopped opposite a small block of flats.

The excited face of a woman could be seen peering eagerly from the window at the back of the cab – a man also seemed to be craning his head forward at her side, as if to get a better view.

As the cab stopped, the door on the other side swung open, and a middle-aged man leapt out and ran round to open the other door and let his wife out.

The cabbie noted all that was happening in his rear mirror and smiled to himself. Affluence showed itself with this pair in more ways than one. The guy was dressed in what must have been a Savile Row suit, with a silk shirt and tie to match. He really did smell expensive, from his kid leather shoes to his perfectly groomed iron-grey hair. His wife was also very smart, with an immaculate pure wool dress, over which a fur stole was casually draped. Her brunette hair bobbed about her shoulders in glossy curls, and her perfume could only have come from Paris, it smelt that expensive!

Clambering out of the cab she stood clinging to her husband's arm, both just staring at the cluster of cosmopolitan shops that now formed that part of the 'Parade'.

The gent turned and smiled at the driver, 'Just hang on a few moments fella… we shan't keep you long.' They then walked along the pavement slowly, searching out something, or some place.

Acknowledging them with a nod, the cabbie left the engine running and reached for a cigarette. As he did so he thought about this fare that he had picked up from the other side of Islington. He inhaled deeply, these Americans were all alike as far as he could see, more money than sense the lot of them, touring around the world all the time, stopping off now and then, to see how the poor lived.

He drew hard on his smoke while he waited. He couldn't see what they were so interested in… just a few shops and those old houses further along. They must be mad. The woman was a good looker though… she didn't talk American either… a bit too full of her old man and his business, something to do with flying as far as he could tell. Bet they never had to go without anything, or even know the meaning of the word.

He continued to stare all around him as he sat waiting. He saw her pointing towards a distant shop; they were quite excited over something or other. Then they turned, and still chatting and smiling deeply together, they walked slowly back to the waiting cab. The cabbie flung his dog-end out of the window and coughed, glancing at the meter, which was ticking away for all it was worth. Hmm… he didn't mind at all… it was his time and their cash they were spending. With a last backwards glance, they both jumped in the back of the cab and slammed the door. 'OK cabbie… hit the road.'

Janie cuddled up close to Frankie and leaned her head against his shoulder. 'Happy, sweetheart?' He looked down at her beaming face. She nodded in answer. They had wanted to stop off and take a look at the old place. In fact, she had talked of nothing else all the way to the airport.

It had been arranged specially that the flight from the USA should be interrupted by a stopover in London. Of course, they could have done it the easy way by flying straight to Australia, but Frank knew that his lovely Janie had more than one reason to stop off in London before going on to join her married daughter and her family out in Sydney.

He reflected over his life during the last 25 years, and reckoned that he must be the luckiest man alive. This trip had come not only as a first real break in business for him, but also as a longed for treat for Janie to visit her darling Gran.

The old lady was so upset when Janie had left them all to go out to Cleveland, always promising one day to return and see her again. Then after dozens and dozens of letters, and more phone calls than she could imagine, they had met... in a joyous reunion that was awash with tears on both sides.

It was true that he had a good business in aviation. Things had gone well for him – he was more affluent now than he had ever dared to dream about. And it was Janie who had brought him all the good luck, his wonderful Janie. Oh God, he was lucky to have found her when he did, all those years ago.

Janie pulled the mink stole around her shoulders, and shivered in the east wind. She had been so excited at the thought of coming back to see the old homestead once again. What she hadn't bargained for, or even realised, was how it had all changed, had been demolished and rebuilt again. Gone was the dairy, gone was the oil shop where they queued for candles, gone were the two houses that held so many memories. That was long ago. Now, after the bombing scars had healed, there stood a block of modern apartments, and a row of completely new shops that were quite unknown to her.

At least Gran hadn't changed. In fact, she still looked the same sweet person that she was all those years ago, when Janie had tearfully left them all, on that awful wet morning on the first stage to join Frankie in the USA.

The reunion with Gran had been very traumatic. She had willed herself not to cry, all the way from the airport, but when they had found themselves outside the large house in Highbury, Janie felt herself quivering with emotion from head to foot. They were ushered into Matron's private sitting room, while she went to fetch Gran.

Janie felt every nerve in her body tingling. Then she saw her standing there in the doorway. 'Gran... oh Gran!' she cried, and breaking away from Frankie's grip she flung herself across the room and into Gran's arms. Time seemed endless as they stood locked together for almost a minute. Tears were now streaming down Janie's cheeks, and all that Gran could do was to stand and stare at her through misted eyes. 'Janie! Janie gel... Oh love!'

A tray of tea was brought in by one of the nurses, and the three of them chatted excitedly, gulping their tea as they did so. It seems the nursing home hadn't realised what had hit them years before, when Granny Howard had joined the ranks.

The home was a lovely place on the other side of Highbury. Gran had a small room which looked right out onto the gardens. If you stood on tiptoe you could just see 'The Victory' which stood on the corner of the street that ran parallel with Deans Close. There was a narrow yard that ran along the side of the house to the end of the garden, and if the side door was left open at 'Deansgate House', then it took only a minute to nip into the yard and through to the saloon bar.

Gran had put this to good use when she first arrived, although Matron had put the damper on Gran's little escapades by seeing the door was locked each tea-time. 'But it took Matron nearly six months to catch on,' Gran laughingly told Janie, as they sipped their tea.

Janie listened and felt very happy, she was pleased Gran had settled into her new home. Of course it had all been due to Cassie, who was now a SRN and loving every minute of it. She had looked after Gran for a long time, after the others had left to embark on their trip to Australia. Now Gran had found a niche of her own, being cared for and looked after in this very accommodating home for retired people. She was not lacking in friends or company either, for two elderly ladies who had been friends of the family in Essex Road, and who were now war widows, had now met up again in glorious retirement.

But the real joy came for Gran on the morning they ushered the 'new lady' into the sitting room. As Gran stared from her chair by the window to review who it was, there was no mistaking that henna'd hair, and that scent that she always did use by the gallon. Gran struggled up out of her chair and fairly raced across the sitting room, her bottom lip quivering with excitement, her arms outstretched. 'LULU! Hello me old mate! Lulu... how are you ducks?'

Lulu's face was a picture when she saw her friend standing there in front of her. The two of them fell into each other's arms, crying tears of pleasure at finding each other again after so many years.

It had pleased Janie no end when she heard from Gran in her shaky handwriting all that had transpired over the weeks. She smiled as she read the letter. So Gran had her best and faithful friend with her after all these years. It was a great comfort to know that Gran was not alone, for she did worry about her. Even though, because of the distance, she could do nothing to help matters.

The family, such as they were, were so spread out now, scattered from America to Australia. But Gran still remained in the same proximity that she had done for the last 80 or so years – her roots would never be lifted and transported to some foreign ground. She loved this area of London and would not think of living anywhere else. No, none of these new fangled climates were for her, she was a Londoner through and through.

Janie's visit with her Frankie had brought tears of pleasure to her eyes, and had wiped away all those years that were missing in Gran's life. When it was time for them to leave, she had unashamedly clung to them for dear life and willed herself not to cry. She really did love Frankie for all the joy that he had brought into their lives. He had made a good match with Janie and she glowed with love for him. Seeing this, Gran felt more than content with her lot in life. What with Helen and Terry and their four children, plus several hundred sheep out in the fertile valleys of Australia. Then Cassie, who now held a lot of responsibility at one of the top hospitals in London and who was by far one of the most devoted and caring nurses ever, as far as Gran was concerned. Yes, theirs was a good family, a family to be proud of.

All too soon it was time for them to part. Janie had been fussing around Gran, trying to obliterate the one thought that none of them wanted to be reminded off, the clock on the wall that was ticking away madly. By not looking at it, and not mentioning it, the idea was that it wasn't happening.

Then Frankie hesitatingly leaned over and whispered softly in Janie's ear, almost at once the smile froze on her face. Oh dear God, thought Janie to herself, this is it! Oh no, not yet. Where had all the time gone? How had the whole afternoon just vanished? She knew that she must do as Frankie said and say her goodbyes to Gran. She also knew that she may never see her again. The parting was unbearable... almost like a death.

She turned to Gran with a face misted by the tears that had stung the back of her eyes, until she just had to let go. Chokingly she whispered to Gran, 'I promise to come back again one day Gran. I really promise.'

Gran gave them both a final hug, her face trembling with emotion as she willed herself not to cry... at least not in front of them. Then, wrenching herself away and with her head held high, she stood to her full height, smiling at them both as they choked their last goodbyes to her.

Janie stared at her not knowing what else to say. 'Dear Gran... Oh dear Gran.' A little figure in a grey dress and soft slippers, she looked almost lost in the background. Frankie touched her arm, bringing her back to reality. She knew it was time to go.

They walked slowly to the doorway of the room and turned. Frankie grinned and gave a happy wave. Gran acknowledged it, then Janie blew a last kiss. Gran smiled as she pulled herself up, standing tall and proud, while her fingers clenched and unclenched in her folded hands.

'God bless you dears... God bless,' she murmured under her breath.

Suddenly they were gone. She could hear their footsteps echoing along the tiled hallway. In her mind's eye she could see the heavy door opening, and she waited for the thud as it closed.

From her seat next to the window, she could see them as they walked, hand in hand, down the stony driveway. She continued to stare after them long after they had disappeared from her view, until they were swallowed up in the October mists.

THE END